Decay

DDL Smith

Disclaimer

This story is a work of fiction. It is rooted in the horror of forgotten places and the silent dangers of lost things. Central to the novel is the presence of an abandoned radioactive source, known as an *orphan source.*

Orphan sources are dangerous because of the ionising radiation they emit and must always be handled with the highest care. Thankfully, they are extraordinarily rare. Modern nuclear power generation, by contrast, is one of the safest and cleanest forms of energy we have. Power plants are designed with multiple layers of safety, monitored by scientists and engineers whose work ensures they remain secure and reliable.

The tragedies of orphan sources, where radiation is left uncontrolled, do not reflect the reality of nuclear power. Do not confuse the two.

This tale exists in the shadows of rare neglect, not in the truth of the technology as a whole.

Contents

Split

The cobblestones still held last night's rain in small puddles. Water pooled between the stones slowly evaporating, lifting the scent of birch sap into the streets. A battered Volvo sat parked along the school fence, the colour dulled by years of snow slush and treks in dirt. The left wing mirror was cracked. Rust crept along the bottom edge of the door, flaking in slow curls peeling at the paintwork.

Johan leaned against the car, hands buried in his jacket pockets. His head tilted slightly forward like he was listening for something. His weight shifted now and then between feet, the right leg favoured. A pale sun sat behind the clouds, faint enough that shadows had forgotten where to fall.

He looked older than his twenty-eight years. Not dramatically. Just worn in the way people get when they stop worrying about partying with friends and have attempted to settle down. His stubble had grown soft along his jawline, patchy around the faint scar near his chin. The grey hoodie he wore had thinned at the elbows and stretched at the wrists. His fingers, marked with old work and small calluses, fidgeted with the zip of his coat. The way a child might impatiently fidget without realising.

The wind picked at him. Not harsh, but persistent. It tugged at the hem of his jeans, lifting dry grit from the road. Somewhere nearby, a bus exhaled around a corner. The town was quiet. Still too early in the year for crowds, too cool for idling. Early summer in Östersund arrived with hesitation. Lake Storsjön glimmered in the distance, wide and unmoved, likely still cold to the touch. The snow had gone, but winter hadn't quite loosened its grip.

Beneath balconies and along the shaded sides of old buildings, a few people moved homeward, their coats still zipped. Pale apartments stood clean but tired. Windows stayed shut. Nothing drifted from them. No music. Few voices. The square was empty. Festivals hadn't begun. No tourists had yet come north from the coast to ski. Even for a city tucked in the quiet centre of Sweden, it felt too still. The school term hadn't ended. Children weren't yet spilling into the streets. Johan checked the school doors again. His gaze flicked there every few seconds, always in the same rhythm. Then came the sudden thrum of voices.

Lena burst out first like a firework.

She ran as fast as she could. All elbows and knees sparked with energy not yet depleted after a day at school. Her backpack bounced behind her, a bright purple blur with one fraying strap knotted loosely with blue yarn. Stickers peeled at the corners of her backpack: space cats, sword princesses, a mushroom that had once glittered silver but now just caught the light in patches. The zip hung half open, a paper crown poking from the top like a flag in retreat.

She wore a zip-up jacket with faded unicorns across the back, sleeves too long and cuffs damp. Underneath, a cotton T-shirt, untucked from habit rather than carelessness. Her leggings were soft and worn thin at the knees, stretched slightly at the ankles. Through the fabric, two bright plasters were visible from her recent trip to the floor one lunch break last week. One orange with stars, the other shaped like a strawberry. They hugged her legs like trophies from an unknown campaign.

Her trainers were mismatched with scuffs. One looked new, the other speckled with dried mud. One lace was tied properly, the other tucked inside to stop it flapping. In her arms, her favourite rabbit teddy. White once, now greyed from years of holding. Its ears drooped unevenly. She held it tight but carefully; the way others held lunch-boxes or water bottles. Something important. Something that had to come with her everywhere.

Her hair had escaped its morning fix. Dark blonde, sun-flecked at the ends, curled in half-formed spirals that bounced as she faced through the air. It framed her face in pieces, windblown and un-tidy. A scatter of pale freckles crossed her nose and pale cheeks. Faint but noticeable, just like her mother's.

She saw her father through the crowd and lit up. A grin bloomed across her face. She shouted something he couldn't quite catch and launched herself forward, a blur of motion and rabbit limbs. He straightened, one hand already raised in a half-wave, half-sur-render.

"Hi, pappa!" She yelled, and slammed into him in a hug that nearly knocked him off balance.

"Hey, kiddo," he murmured, catching her with arms that didn't quite know what to do. They gently squeezed, then released be-fore it got awkward.

She stepped back, hands on her hips, eyes wide and gleaming. "Do we get to sleep in tents tonight? Did you pack the marshmal-lows? Can we make a fire? Are there bears? I hope there's bears!"

She fired the words at him in one breath, a spark plug in human form.

Johan smirked, shaking his head. "That's a lot of questions."

"Well?"

"Fire? Yes. Marshmallows? Of course. Bears?" Johan giggled a little at the rarity, "Let's... Hope they're busy."

Lena scrunched her nose, mockingly disappointed. "No bears? You always ruin the fun."

"Just trying to keep you alive, kiddo." He opened the back door and held it for her.

As she climbed in, still muttering about bear caves and marsh-mallow laws, he took a second to watch her settle in. His hands held the door-frame. Times like these seemed rare since the break up. She pulled her seatbelt across her chest without being asked and immediately began narrating a made-up adventure to herself.

He slid into the driver's seat and started the engine. "Your mum should be at the house by now. Her flight landed an hour ago."

"Did she bring snacks?"

"I think she brought herself. That's already a lot."

Lena giggled. "I hope she packed something chocolate."

As they pulled out of the school car park, Johan glanced in the mirror. Her reflection stared up at the sky through the window, mouth still moving as she told a story to the clouds. He let her voice fill the car, soft and chaotic. He tried not to think about how quiet it had been without her.

Only a few minutes pass until they arrive at Johan's flat. Positioned on the third floor of a pale yellow building just east of the city centre, the tiny space offered a comfortable space that was normally only occupied by Johan. Old bricks, new insulation. The stairs creaked like mice as the two ascended.

The apartment was quiet when they entered. Not the kind of quiet that feels peaceful, but the kind that feels like it's been empty too long. Johan closed the door behind them and the latch clicked sharply in the still air. The interior felt bare. Somewhat tidy. As tidy as a man might keep things where there's no one left to clean for. A dirty coffee cup sat on a low coffee table scuffed at the corners. An old stereo no longer connected to anything perched under a TV. No surface had any softness. No sign of recent joy. The living space was furnished mostly in muted greys and worn pine. A worn sofa hosting a messy folded blanket. The walls were bare except for a couple of framed prints; Maps, not art. Precise and wordless.

Lena dropped her school bag by the door and made a beeline for the kitchen.

"I'm getting something sweet," she declared, already yanking open the fridge. "We have juice, right? You always have juice."

"Top shelf," Johan called. He moved to the hallway closet, opening it with a grunt. Inside hung a slim red backpack and a box of scattered odds and ends. Spare tent pegs, long-expired batteries, a torch with a cracked lens. He sifted through the box until he found what he was looking for: a pack of half-used lithium AAs. He gave them a shake. Not ideal, but enough for the lanterns.

He glanced into the living room again, running through his mental list: *Map. Stove. Water tabs. Compass. Sleeping bags.*

Everything else was already packed in the car outside.

On the coffee table sat a printed flight itinerary.

SAS 070 – Arrival: 14:45, ARN to OSD.

Stockholm to Östersund.

She should've arrived by now. Johan lingered a moment, then turned and walked down the narrow hallway into the bedroom.

The room was dim even in the afternoon light. One curtain drawn halfway across the window, the other drooping open off its rail. Clothes were folded neatly on a chair but never put away. An unmade bed slumped in the centre, sheets twisted and shapeless from disuse. On the nightstand: a half-read paperback, an unused coaster, and a charging cable curled like a sleeping snake.

He crossed to the wardrobe. Its hinges squeaked in quiet protest as he pulled it open. Inside, a faint scent of cedar and stale air wafted out, triggering memories of neglect. He reached for the top shelf, fingers sifting past a sweater he hadn't worn in years to an old shoebox filled with papers he couldn't bear to throw away, until he touched the familiar smoothness of brown leather.

Johan carefully pulled out the journal, its cover worn soft from handling, the corners frayed from months of daily use. The leather binding had a reassuring solidity, the kind of object meant to hold important thoughts, difficult truths, and words not easily spoken aloud. He thumbed absently through the pages, the neat, careful handwriting filling lines like footprints he'd been following, step by careful step, through recovery. Some pages were densely covered, others sparse and hesitant.

He sighed quietly, slipping the journal into the side pocket of his jacket. Out of habit, he reached up to close the wardrobe door, pausing as he caught his reflection in the full-length mirror.

He saw himself clearly now, reflected in muted light. His eyes, green and tired, stared back at him. So much like Lena's eyes that strangers would always comment on it. Dark blonde hair, unkempt. Darker than it used to be, hung forward, brushing just above his eyebrows. He noticed the faint lines etched into his forehead, marks he didn't remember seeing a year ago. He brushed fingertips along his stubbled jaw, examining the shape of his face as if reacquainting himself with a stranger. His frame seemed narrower now, leaner from months of uncertain appetite and nights of interrupted sleep.

A faint noise from the kitchen, Lena's laughter, snapped him back to the present. He straightened, blinking away the self-examination. The wardrobe clicked shut, leaving his reflection behind as he turned and stepped back into the living room.

When he returned to the living room, Lena had climbed onto a kitchen stool and was balancing on tiptoe in front of the fridge, both hands wrapped around a litre carton of orange juice.

"What are you doing?" Johan queried.

"Hmm hm hmm umm hmm."

Gulp

"I found the juice!" She said, triumphantly, though her lips were still on the rim.

Johan blinked. "Lena, we have glasses."

She wiped her mouth with her sleeve, grinning. "Yeah, but this is faster."

He opened his mouth to protest, then closed it again. She was seven. If orange juice from the carton was her biggest rebellion this week, he could live with it.

Outside the front door, Freya lingered a little longer than she needed. The smell hit her first. Stale coffee, old laundry, something herbal and tired. She didn't even knock, not yet. She just stood there with her hand on the doorframe, staring at the flaking paint.

Her fingers curled once, then stilled. She had promised herself she wouldn't catalogue it all, but her mind was already assembling a list. The chipped skirting board. The faint smear on the glass. No welcome mat. No sound of music, no softness at all.

It hadn't changed. That was the worst of it.

She hadn't seen Johan since the custody switch six weeks ago. He'd looked fine enough at the handover pale, maybe, but always composed. It was the apartment she was worried about. Spaces, after all, had a way of showing the truth faster than faces did.

A kid lives here every other week. She reminded herself of that. Then frowned, because it didn't feel true. Not with how cold the hallway smelled. Not with how hollow the place looked through the thin curtains.

Her thumb drifted to the strap of her bag. She adjusted it, took a slow breath, and braced.

Before another cheeky swig from the carton was taken, a knock came at the door. Three short raps. Familiar, not urgent.

Lena squealed with delight. "Mummy!"

She jumped off the stool, skidding across the wood floor in her socks before pulling the door open with both hands. Freya stood there, framed in the evening light. She wore jeans and a light jacket. Her dark blonde hair pulled back into a no-nonsense bun. Her face looked drawn from the flight. The edges of her patience had been rubbed thin throughout the day. Still, her smile when she saw Lena was unfiltered.

"There you are," Freya said, dropping to her knees to accept the lunging hug.

Lena wrapped herself around her mother's neck. "You didn't forget!"

"I said I'd be here, didn't I?" Freya brushed a curl behind Lena's ear. "Was your day good? Did you behave for your nan and granddad?"

"We're going to fight bears and sleep on rocks," Lena grinned, beaming with excitement. "Want to see my tent-voice?"

Freya blinked. "Your what?"

"My *tent voice*," Lena replied as if it were obvious. "Come on, I'll show you!" She took a step back, then turned with her arms outstretched and whooshed past Freya, pretending to be an airplane. "SAS flight to camping departing now!" She called. "First class!"

Johan watched her vanish down the stairwell, Lena's excited footsteps echoing and fading into silence. A gentle ache tightened in his chest as she disappeared from view, a fleeting reminder of how much he'd missed these everyday moments.

Freya's nose wrinkled slightly at the smell. Faint, mildly unpleasant. Unmistakably male. Dry dust, worn cotton, the lingering trace of something herbal that might've once been soap. She didn't move past the threshold right away. Just stood there.

It hadn't changed. Same tired furniture. Same coffee table with the scratched corner from when Lena had slipped and hit it two years ago. The same map prints on the wall. Neat, quiet, impersonal. In fact, the only thing that had seemed to have changed was the absence of their family photos. No warmth. No sign of someone living here, just someone waiting to leave. She caught herself pressing her tongue against the back of her teeth; a habit she'd picked up in conference rooms when she didn't want her frustration to show.

She adjusted the strap of her bag and let her fingers trail over the frame of the doorway. Nothing to say, not yet. Not while the walls still felt like they echoed. Her eyes scanned the room briefly. Not judging, just cataloguing. Her gaze landed on the sideboard, near the window. Johan followed it instinctively. There, tucked between a compass in a leather case and a small ceramic bowl filled with coins, was a photograph in a cheap metal frame. She didn't reach for it. Didn't move toward it. Just looked.

"You still have that?" She asked, voice flat.

Johan's jaw flexed once. "Forgot it was there."

"You never forget things."

Freya didn't say the rest. That he'd always been the one to hold on longer. She wasn't sure it had ever been about her; maybe just the shape of something he'd once called home.

The frame hadn't moved since she left. Same spot, same slight angle. A quiet shrine to something unfinished. She studied the photograph like it might shift if she stared long enough. The glass had begun to fog at one edge... Moisture, maybe. Time. Her reflection hovered faintly over it, overlaying the old her: younger, freckled, squinting against the sun in borrowed sunglasses. Wind curled her hair across Johan's chest. He had one arm around her waist. His other hand wasn't visible. Probably holding Lena. They'd tried to make her laugh that day, after she screamed herself hoarse on the boat ride they'd been on.

It had been their third anniversary. Or fourth. She remembered the ferry stalling in the fjord... The way Johan had cursed under his breath, loud enough for Lena to copy him later. She remembered sleeping in a tent that barely held against the wind, the corners staked down with cutlery. She remembered waking up cold even though they were all wrapped around each other like wet laundry.

He'd taken that photo with a timer and too much optimism.

She had hated him, just a little, when he printed it. He called it a good memory. He called it proof they were happy. Said it reminded him what they were capable of. She took a half-step toward the sideboard before catching herself. Her fingers twitched once. She didn't touch the frame.

She wasn't sure who she was angrier at; him, for keeping it like it meant something, or herself, for recognising the part of her that still wanted it to. Then came the ache again, low in her chest. Something quieter. A sense that the version of them in that picture had already died before the shutter clicked. The silence between them wasn't silence at all. Just memory, waiting to be named.

"You come straight from work?" He asked instead.

A long pause. She took a step closer to the sideboard. The photo caught more light now. The glass slightly fogged at one edge, frame bent where it had been dropped once and not fixed. In the picture, they stood on a sloped outcrop of rock overlooking a deep blue inlet, somewhere in the Norwegian fjords north of

Ålesund. Behind them, the water stretched like folded glass between the cliffs, dotted with gulls.

Their tent had been just out of frame. An orange canvas pitched awkwardly against a wind that hadn't let up for three days. Freya was laughing in the photo, wind tangling her hair across her face, sunglasses crooked on the bridge of her nose. Johan had his arm around her waist, leaner then, sun on his face, smiling like someone who hadn't yet learned what it meant to watch something fall apart slowly.

They'd taken Lena with them. Only four years old at the time. She'd screamed the entire boat ride across the fjord and slept like a stone every night in the cold tent, warm between them.

Johan didn't move, but his breath caught slightly.

"It was a good trip," he said. Quietly. Maybe the walls would answer if she didn't.

"That day didn't make up for the others," she replied. "You always carry the version of us that worked. You never carry the rest."

"Maybe because the rest wasn't worth keeping."

Freya's eyes flicked toward him sharply. "I didn't just wake up and leave, you know. You disappeared, long before I packed anything."

Johan didn't answer. His fingers curled slightly at his side, the muscles in his jaw twitching like something caged and angry.

Freya exhaled, slow. "You should really clean this place. It feels like no one lives here." Then, after a brief moment... "Maybe no one does."

She turned toward the door without waiting for a reply, her boots clicking across the wooden floor. At the threshold she paused just long enough to call down after Lena/ Then she was gone, the stairwell swallowing her footsteps.

Johan stood for a moment longer. Then quietly picked up the last duffel bag. Heavier than it looked, and followed them down.

The duffel bag hit the floor of the boot with a soft thud, knocking over the rolled sleeping mats. Johan adjusted them with care, lining everything up with military neatness. Out of sight, Freya coaxed Lena into her seat in the back, helping her buckle the straps while Lena chattered about bugs, the exact ratio of snacks to dinners, and whether they'd be allowed to sleep outside *"without a roof this time."* Johan closed the boot with a solid, final-sounding *clunk*. He stood at the edge of the curb for a moment. This could be a long trip, but it was all for Lena.

They left Östersund just after five.

The town peeled away in slow gradients. From apartment blocks to clustered wood houses, then to open fields, and finally into thick forest that swallowed the road whole. The E45 road narrowed and curved gently south, flanked by walls of pine and spruce. In the back seat, Lena kicked off her shoes and pressed her face to the window, watching the trees blur into a green river.

Freya sat in the front passenger seat of the run down volo with her arms folded. Sunglasses on even though the sun was low enough now that the light came sideways, flickering through the trees as they travelled down the road.

No one spoke for a while.

Johan drove with the windows cracked just enough to let the scent of sap and distant glacier water drift in. The hum of the tyres on uneven tarmac was loud enough to disguise silence, but not enough to erase it.

"Still working part-time?" Freya asked eventually, without looking at him.

"Monday to Thursday. Ten to two. Same crew. We've got a new guy from Åre. Can't sharpen a blade to save his life."

Freya exhaled sharply. "Of course. Still the golden schedule. Town pays you to go camping."

"Not camping," Johan replied, still trying not to bite into the bitterness of Freya's words. "Logging. Some of us still work with our hands."

"I work with people," she replied. "It's harder."

He didn't respond.

Lena leaned forward between the seats, clutching her stuffed rabbit like a co-pilot.

"Do you think we'll see reindeer?"

"Maybe," Johan said.

"Do you think we'll see trolls?"

"I think trolls mostly live in tunnels," Freya replied, turning her head toward the back of the car to see Lena; shoes off, rabbit in hand with a cheeky grin.

"Oh," Lena muttered, disappointed. The cheeky grin melted off her face.

Lena leaned back into her seat with a small huff, her legs folded beneath her like she was trying to shrink herself into the shape of comfort. The seatbelt scratched against her collarbone, but she didn't complain. Her rabbit, soft in places but scratchy in others, was tucked under her chin. Nose-first into her shoulder like he was listening to her thoughts.

Outside, the forest rolled by in a blur of tree trunks and flickering light. The pines rushed past like they were running alongside the car; Maybe they wanted to keep her in the forest forever.

She tried to imagine what it would be like if trolls lived here. Not scary trolls but the nice kind with mossy beards and sleepy eyes. She pictured them waving from behind rocks, sipping tea from pinecones and grumbling gently about noisy cars. She liked when it was quiet. Not like at school, or when Mum and Dad had voices that sounded like ice. This quiet was different. Soft and green and buzzing with secrets.

She looked up at the sky. It wasn't really day anymore, but not night either. Just that bluish colour where the sun had gone to bed but forgot to switch the lights off. It had been like that for a while now. Even when they got home late from swimming lessons, the sky didn't go dark. Just stayed in that sort of in-between.

She thought about asking why the sky never got black during the summer like in movies. About where the proper night had gone, and if it would come back. But grown-ups didn't always like those kinds of questions. Sometimes they gave her too-long answers with words that looped back on themselves. Or worse... No answer at all, just a "hmm" like they hadn't heard her.

She tucked Rabbit tighter under her chin. "I'll ask dad later," she thought to herself. "Dad knows about trees and fire. He probably knows where the night went too."

Another long stretch of road passed in silence. The shadows of the trees stretched longer across the road. Somewhere far off, the sun began its slow descent behind the canopy to rest at the horizon.

Wind pushed through the trees in waves, whispering across their roof rack and through the cracked side windows. Lena sat in the back with her rabbit pressed against her cheek, one hand drawing invisible shapes in the condensation of the glass. Every so often she'd murmur something under her breath, half a song, half a spell, then go quiet again.

A small wooden sign passed in a blur. *Östnår*. Just as quickly as a few buildings came into view, they disappeared again, covered in green.

"I always forget how many towns there are out here," Freya muttered.

Johan adjusted his grip on the wheel, not responding to the comment. They drove on. The light was shifting now, softening with a golden glow. Somewhere between Svenstavik and Åsarna, the forest opened just long enough to reveal a glint of distant water and the faded red of a gas station that looked abandoned, even when it was open.

Lena leaned forward between them. "Can we stop for snacks?"

"We have snacks," Johan said.

"Not *shop* snacks," she clarified.

"No."

"Ugh."

Another village blinked past just after an hour of driving. *Åsarna*; population barely a ripple on the map. Two buildings with pitched roofs, a school maybe, a single yellow postbox. Then it was gone, swallowed by green once more. The road unfurled straight and flat for a time, flanked on both sides by thick pine and wet lowland marsh.

The radio had been on since Östersund. Johan's station, of course. Not modern pop or talk radio, but some nostalgia-heavy feed full of crackling brass sections and lazy upright bass.

It rolled on quietly: Sheldon Allman, The Five Stars, Eartha Kitt, Les Baxter. Tucked between chipper crooners and faux-exotic orchestras. The melodies were upbeat. The subject matter was not.

Freya reached forward and turned the dial, clicking the silence into the car. Johan didn't look away from the road. "Why'd you do that?' He questioned.

"It's morbid," she added, after a pause.

"It's nostalgic. *Toppen!*"

The silence felt sharper now the radio was off. Wind rushing through the windows was the only thing heard in the car.

Lena perked up again. "Mum? What do you think dad would be if he wasn't a wood chopper?"

Freya raised an eyebrow. "A tree?"

Johan gave a snort he tried to disguise as a cough.

"Maybe a bear," Lena said thoughtfully. "He's grumpy. He sleeps a lot... He likes fish."

Johan smiled in spite of himself. Freya and Johan shared a glance and a smirk. A subtle hint of tensions easing between them.

Ahead, the trees thinned as the road dipped briefly and ran parallel to a stretch of cleared land. On the far side of the field, partially obscured by a line of spruce, sat a cluster of half-cylinder shelters. Rusted and mottled like the belly of some old ship left to rot inland. Their corrugated skins were subtly bleached pale by sun and seasons, patched in places with flaking tape and boards nailed hastily decades ago. The doors were long gone. One yawned open to reveal stacked wooden crates, black with damp. Another housed the shell of an old tractor, its tyres flat and split at the rim.

"What are those?" Lena asked from the back seat, peering through the window.

"Storage huts," Freya replied without looking. "Used to be military around here."

Johan said nothing, but his eyes lingered on them in the mirror. A shape from a different time, still holding its place among the moss and nettles. The forest crept around them, reclaiming everything as the age was slowly forgotten. A crow lifted from one of the low roofs, wings heavy with flight, and vanished overhead.

Far in the distance, a dull thwop-thwop-thwop began to rise. Johan cracked the window slightly. The noise resolved into the beat of rotor blades. A yellow helicopter passed low over the treetops, skimming eastward across the valley toward the river's curve.

Freya squinted up through the windscreen. A flicker of yellow passed low over the trees, rotors humming faintly through the closed glass.

"Air ambulance," she murmured. "Probably from Frösön."

Lena twisted in her seat, wide-eyed. The helicopter banked once, then dipped beyond the ridge and vanished behind a wall of spruce.

"Maybe someone's hurt," she said, voice quiet.

Freya didn't answer right away. The hum of the engine filled the space between them.

"Maybe," she said eventually. "Or just checking in somewhere."

The road curved again, narrow and uneven, flanked by forest that crept closer with each bend.

"Turn-off's soon," Johan said under his breath, more to himself than to anyone else.

Freya straightened slightly, scanning the verge. A blue road sign slid past on the right. *Rätanbyn – 500m.* Beneath it, a weather-faded one in white, pointing east.

"You're going to miss it."

"I'm not going to miss it."

Freya's arms folded. "Like Åsarna?"

"We were already on the right road," he muttered. "How could I have missed it?"

The indicator clicked once. Then again. The Volvo turned off, tyres crunching over loose gravel. The trees pressed in almost instantly, the road narrowing to little more than a track. The village flickered past: a few cabins, an empty bus stop, a yellow postbox with its paint sun-faded to a dull yellow. It was gone in seconds.

From the back seat, Lena spoke again, starting to sound bored of the journey.

"Are we there yet?"

"Not yet," Johan replied.

Freya glanced over her shoulder. "Half an hour," she said. "Maybe longer, if your dad takes another scenic route."

Johan replied silently with a raised eyebrow. He was focused now. They drove on. The land grew softer, rolling in slow hills beneath them. Forest on every side now. The occasional glimpse of a lake or stream came and went like a mirage; water flashing crystal clear between the branches. Once, a red fox darted across the road, vanishing without a sound.

For the next half hour, the road carried them through slow bends and long, empty stretches of forest. They crossed a bridge over a broad stretch of water: The western end of Handsjön lake. The lake opened wide on either side, mirror-like and impossibly still. Lena leaned against the window, watching the sunlight ripple in glints across the water. A lone fisherman stood in a flat-bottomed boat near the far shore, so still he might've been part of the scenery.

The forest returned thick and uninterrupted. Birch gave way to spruce, then back again. Another blue sign appeared: *Strandgård-arna.* A few red cabins blinked past, half-hidden behind tufts of fir and long grass. Then the village disappeared behind them without another word.

"Next left," Freya said quietly.

"I know," Johan replied, already easing his foot onto the brake.

The turn came suddenly. A dip in the road followed by a sharp cut between two leaning trees. The road quickly turned into a narrow tarmac, then gravel, then dirt. Just a few kilometres further the forest closed in. Past one lake, and past one more.

"This should do it." Johan said, bringing the car to a stop and switching off the ignition. The trio emerged from the car and stretched their legs. The forest felt in the middle of no-where. Off the grid. Perfect for camping.

Clearing

C ar doors shut with soft thumps, sounds swallowed quickly by layers of spruce and birch. The forest absorbed everything, softening into a profound silence. Johan stood still for a moment, taking a deep breath. Crisp evening air felt cool and fresh in their lungs.

Freya stepped out slowly, circling the car to stretch. Three hours on the road after her flight had knotted her shoulders and lower back. She twisted slightly, arms rising above her head, spine clicking in places she'd learned not to ignore. Lena was already a few paces ahead, bouncing on her toes. Her rabbit pressed to her chest like a co-pilot. It had been decided to take their backpacks to find a spot to camp. They could return for tents once a suitable location had been discovered.

"Stay close, Lena," Freya called gently. "Let's not wander too far just yet."

"It's okay," Johan murmured softly, adjusting backpack straps to get more comfortable. "There's nobody out here. We've got the place to ourselves."

Freya raised an eyebrow but said nothing. She followed Johan down a shallow slope, footing uneven beneath soft-soled boots.

Moss spread thick between stones, and fallen pine needles blanketed the ground in a hush. Every step seemed swallowed before it landed.

Ahead, Lena continued to dash forward. A flash of motion and bright curls in the evening twilight, moving too fast for silence. She skidded to a stop beside a decaying trunk, long fallen and half-sunk into the forest floor. The wood had hollowed from within, eaten by time, and ringed with shelf fungus shaped like tiny fans in rows.

"It looks like a cake," she announced, not to anyone directly. Her fingers hovered near the layers, close enough to feel their texture without touching.

"Don't eat the forest," Johan warned from behind.

"Just looking!" She chirped, though her fingers drifted a little closer anyway.

Freya exhaled, slow and careful, eyes flicking over the trees. Her muscles were still unwinding from the drive.

They passed a lake on the left. A still, shallow pool tucked between tree trunks and stone. Barely wider than the clearing they'd left behind. Water like glass, glacier-clear, held a perfect copy of the canopy above.

Lena slowed, crouching beside the edge where black flies drifted lazily above patches of marsh grass. She knelt down, one knee sinking into damp moss. Water soaked through fabric almost instantly.

"There's something down there," she whispered.

Freya stepped forward, scanning the surface. "It's probably another stick."

"No," Lena said, voice quieter now. "It's... Wrapped in something."

Not frightened but just curious. That deep, still sort of curiosity children carry before adults teach them doubt and restraint. Johan stepped closer, squinting at the water's surface, but light skewed across the pool at the wrong angle. Reflections broke apart with the slightest ripple, scattering tree shapes and sky. Whatever Lena saw had already vanished beneath them.

"Come on," he said gently. "Plenty of treasures waiting for you tomorrow."

Lena lingered a moment longer. She pressed her hand to the moss beside her knee before standing. She brushed her palms along her thighs. Her leggings clung to her skin, wet and damp. As they continued along the curve of the trail, she looked back three times. Each glance shorter than the last. Near a crooked birch further along the path, something pale caught in the roots caught her eye. She veered off again, drawn to it.

When Freya rounded the bend, she found her daughter crouched low with hands resting on a bed of damp leaves. Lena was whispering.

"What are you doing?"

Lena looked up. Her smile came slowly, secretive, like she was offering something only half-remembered.

"They're bones," she said in a hush. "But nice ones. The kind from stories."

Freya's spine tightened without reason. What Lena knelt beside wasn't bones. Just smooth, pale stones tucked under leaf litter.

Cold white against the forest floor. The air felt still. Like breath held. The trees around them didn't rustle. Even Lena's voice had felt muffled.

"They're just rocks," Freya said, softly. Not to convince Lena, but herself.

"I know," Lena whispered, tracing one with a fingertip. Then let it go.

They continued a little further, feeling like they had been walking for nearly half an hour by this point. Lena had been dragging behind her parents. Tiredness had set in a little, but her delay was mostly curiosity. Constant stopping and starting as new wonders were discovered. A swarm of flies gathered ahead on the path. Lena ran directly into them, coming to a sudden stop.

"Ew," she muttered, waving a hand in front of her face. "Do black flies bite?"

"Only if you taste good," Johan replied without looking back, adjusting the straps of his pack.

"I taste like carrots," Lena announced, entirely serious.

Freya stifled a laugh as she caught up. The trail curved gently, skimming the water's edge before veering upward into deeper forest. As they climbed the gradual slope, the air seemed to shift; Cooler despite the day's lingering warmth. Pine branches swayed high above. Brushing against each other with a dry whisper. The ground was softer here, damp moss giving beneath their boots. Pale lichen plants decorated the trunks like old runes.

Lena stopped again, her gaze caught by something in the under-brush. A pair of red mushrooms, impossibly vivid, jutted from the base of a tree stump. "Are those venomous?" She asked.

"Poisonous, not Venomous. And yes, Very," Johan said. "They're called fly agaric. Classic fairy tale mushrooms."

Lena tilted her head, frowning. "So no touching?"

"No eating either."

She sighed. "Nature is full of rules."

They continued. The path narrowed until the trees pressed close on either side. Insects buzzed in chorus, but their density seemed to thin the deeper they went. Johan noted it absently but said nothing. Lena seemed too enthralled by every leaf and feather she passed. She stopped occasionally to point out twisted roots or strange patterns in bark. At one point she stood motionless beneath a crooked birch, listening.

"I can't hear birds anymore," she said softly.

Freya glanced around. "There were some back at the lake."

"But not here," Lena murmured. "Did they get lost?"

Johan smiled, but something in his gaze began to drift. He kept scanning the tree-line. They walked on without speaking. Just the sound of boots brushing pine needles and the occasional crack of brittle twigs underfoot. About five minutes later, the trees thinned a little. Johan paused, nodding ahead toward a glint through the trunks.

"Second lake's just there," he said. "Might be a good spot coming up."

Lena jogged ahead again with her rabbit in one hand. Just beyond it, the forest opened. No warning. One moment: trees and shadow. Next there was sky. Water lay flat and clear in a lake nearby, cradled by stone coated in soft green lichen. No ripples.

No birds overhead. No flies.

Lena slowed, eyes narrowed. "Where'd all the bugs go?"

Johan tilted his head, listening.

"Maybe they don't like it here," he said, quieter now. His tone had dropped, just enough for Freya to notice. No one replied. The trail narrowed more and dipped gently. Moss thickened beneath their feet, softer than carpet, rising between roots in thick cushions. Trees around them spaced out evenly, unnaturally even, like something had rearranged them long ago and they'd simply agreed to stay that way.

Lena gasped.

"There!"

She took off running again, feet whispering over moss, curls bouncing. Freya called after her, but her voice landed flat. Swallowed. Johan stepped ahead, past Freya, as the trees opened around them. A clearing. Nearly circular.

Bare earth stretched out in its centre, seemingly untouched. No moss. No roots. No grass. The ground sloped gently inward, like something heavy had once pressed down there.

Above, branches parted in a perfect gap around the clearing. To the south, past a narrow gap in the trees, water glinted faintly between trunks. The lake again. Watching. Johan stepped into the exposed space. Paused.

Heat rose through his boots. Soft like sun-warmed stone. He crouched and placed his palm against the dirt. It was warm. Not summer-warm. Not sun-warm. Something else.

"It's warm here," he said, more to the ground than anyone else.

"Geothermal vent, maybe. Perfect to keep the chill off tonight."

A pleasant, gentle heat. Freya approached slowly, her eyes scanning the clearing. She rubbed her arms absently, as if warding off a chill Johan couldn't feel. Freya didn't reply, instead looking at Lena, who was already pacing excitedly around the perimeter of the clearing. Lena knelt, pressing her hand against the ground like Johan, her rabbit dangling from her other hand. Her smile was wide, her eyes bright with wonder. She almost immediately jumped back up with excitement.

"Can this be my fort, pappa?" Lena asked, eyes wide with anticipation. "Can I put my tent right over there?"

She pointed a few metres away towards the centre of the opening. Johan nodded, a faint smile rising. "Of course, älskling. Best spot in the whole forest."

Freya didn't speak at first. She watched Johan instead, eyes narrowed but not in anger. In a way that suggested she was measuring something.

Finally, she sighed. "Alright then," she said softly, glancing back along the trail. "Let's get started while there's still proper light."

Johan turned, brushing his hands off on his jeans. "I'll go get the tents. Be right back."

He vanished into the trees without looking back. Lena spun in a slow circle, arms held out like wings. Her curls caught the sunlight pouring through the break in the canopy. Freya stepped onto the cleared soil. Her boots pressed shallow prints into the dry dust. She crouched down to touch the surface with her fingers. It really was warm. Not sun-warmed. It felt like something else.

Lena had already started building. She started collecting twigs, laying them out in a rectangle, dragging stones over to mark corners. She talked quietly to herself as she worked.

"This side's for the door. That rock's the table. Rabbit gets the corner, so he can see everything."

Freya let her eyes wander. Trees circled the clearing in perfect, unnatural symmetry. No birdsong. Not even flies. Only the faint hush of wind moving somewhere distant but not here. She sat down eventually, resting back on her hands, legs stretched out in front of her. Her spine ached from walking and from her flight. Her neck had stiffened from the long drive.

"You okay, Mum?"

Freya blinked. "Fine, älskling. Just tired."

Lena returned to her project. Her focus was absolute. The kind that children fall into when the world makes sense for once.

Minutes passed. Minutes turned to thirty. Freya found herself watching her daughter more than the trees. How precise she was, how fiercely determined. Like Johan used to be, before things bent out of shape.

A small cluster of mushrooms grew near the base of a nearby spruce. She stared at them, frowning slightly. Pale, round, spaced too neatly. Instead, she leaned back further, letting her eyes close. For a few moments, she just breathed.

"Do you think it's always been like this?"

Freya opened her eyes after being disturbed by Lena who was beside her now. Her hands were dirt-smudged, rabbit clutched under one arm.

"Like what?" Freya questioned.

"This place. All circle-y."

Freya reached for her water bottle and drank before answering.

"Probably. Forests grow strange when no one's watching."

Lena nodded, as if that made perfect sense. She ran off to continue her grand plan. Silence settled again. Deeper now. When Johan finally returned, his boots gave a soft crunch just beyond the tree line. He was carrying tents, slung awkwardly over one shoulder.

Lena ran to meet him whilst shouting "You're just in time! We've got floor-plans now."

Setting up camp was a practiced ritual for Johan. He had been camping so many times before that each movement was precise, efficient, and familiar. He began by unfurling the tents then laying them out neatly over the cleared earth. Carefully, he oriented each opening toward the warmth at the clearing's centre. Lena eagerly joined in, fetching tent stakes with determination. Her small fingers fumbled around as she pressed each one into the earth. The ground was uneven in places. Dry and stubborn. One of the stakes bent slightly as she tried to hammer it in with a nearby rock.

"Like this, pappa?" She asked, breathless, holding it at an angle that would never hold.

"Almost," Johan said, crouching beside her. He didn't correct her immediately; he just watched her try again. Only when the stake wobbled dangerously did he reach out and guide it with a gentle hand.

"Here, twist it a bit. Push straight down, then angle."

"Like this?" She said, straining.

"Perfect," Johan warmly replied, easing the stake into the earth with a slow, steady pressure. "You're a natural, kiddo."

Lena beamed with joy. Enthusiasm practically radiated from her as she sprang to her feet, racing back to the small pile of stakes and grabbing another handful. Her boots thudded softly on the bare earth, and her jacket flared behind her like a cape. She was lost in the joy of purpose.

Freya busied herself quietly, unpacking their supplies, arranging food and equipment with thoughtful care. She laid out their cooking utensils, stacking them neatly beside some camping plates and a cooler. But her eyes kept drifting. Not toward the task, but toward the orange tent as Johan lay its crumpled fabric across the ground.

It flapped once in the breeze. A flare of burnt colour, faded now. One of the zippers stuck halfway. Johan gave it a tug and muttered under his breath. Freya watched, unmoving. That tent. It had been the one they'd taken to Norway, on the trip Johan still carried in that photo she'd seen in his apartment. The wind had howled through the fjord that night, so loud it had drowned even Lena's tears. The tent hadn't held up then either. Johan had lashed it to a rock with their shoelaces just to keep it from flying off the ridge.

She hadn't thought of that trip in months. Freya blinked, focusing again on the task at hand. She unfolded a thin cutting board and placed it neatly beside a small folding knife. Lena let out a frustrated groan from nearby. One of the stakes she'd set had come loose, tipping her half-raised tent backward. She stared at it, bewildered, then gave it a kick that did nothing but cover her boots in dust.

"Need a hand?" Freya asked.

Lena hesitated, pride flaring for a second. "I had it."

Freya smiled, moving over. "I know. But tents are tricky. They're like people... They don't always hold up when you want them to."

Johan looked up at that, but said nothing. He tapped a corner of his tent flat, then turned to his own pack again. Together, Freya and Lena realigned her purple tent. Each time Lena fumbled, Freya adjusted. Each time Freya tried to help too much, Lena pulled back. But between them, the little tent finally stood firm. A bright and defiant beacon in the centre of the clearing.

"Not bad for your first build," Freya said, brushing pine needles from her knees.

"I'm gonna sleep with the flap open," Lena said proudly. "So the dragons can see I'm friendly."

Freya laughed, genuine and short. "Just don't let the mosquitoes know."

"I didn't see any," Lena said thoughtfully. "Only by the lake."

Freya paused for a bit looking around, then nodded. The clearing seemed quieter than it should be. Still. Perfect for a camping trip. She continued to unpack lanterns, checking batteries systematically; a practical counterbalance to Lena's carefree excitement.

"Think we'll need an extra blanket?" Freya asked quietly, unfolding sleeping bags and stacking them neatly ready for the tents.

Johan shook his head, glancing toward the clearing's centre again. "With that warmth, we should be fine. Seems pretty steady."

Freya nodded, though her eyes narrowed slightly, unconvinced.

Lena, oblivious to the tension beneath their words, bounced happily between them. She had already begun enforcing her plan for the "fort". She dragged her stuffed rabbit behind her like a loyal companion on a grand expedition. Animated conversations filled the air about castles and knights, her imagination filling the clearing with tales of daring escapades and magical creatures.

"Pappa, do you think dragons live in this forest?" Lena asked seriously, pausing mid-step with her eyes wide with curiosity. A cheeky grin she tried to hide emerged.

Johan smiled gently, kneeling down to her level. "Only the friendly kind. Maybe they'll visit while you're sleeping to say hello."

Lena considered this thoughtfully for a moment before releasing her grin broadly and resuming her energetic preparations, murmuring excitedly about dragon friends.

As the last tent pole clicked securely into place, Johan stepped back, wiping his hands on his jeans. He surveyed their modest camp-site with a careful eye. Lena's small purple tent stood brightly close to the middle of the clearing. Its fabric was vivid against the muted earth tones around it. Flanking the purple tent was a brand new dark blue tent for Freya, and their original orange tent for Johan. Their orange tent now seemed dull and worn from the many trips the family had been on before, not to mention the extra space for a single person now doubled as a storage area. Freya stored their extra gear neatly organized in Johan's tent. The warmth beneath their feet offered a comforting reassurance as the evening shadows deepened. Despite Freya's lingering uncertainty, Johan allowed himself a moment of quiet satisfaction.

"This is perfect," Lena announced happily, sitting cross-legged at the mouth of her vibrant tent. She hugged her rabbit tightly, her eyes bright with anticipation. "I think we should stay here forever."

Johan exchanged a glance with Freya, a fleeting shared moment of warmth bridging the gap between them. "Maybe not forever," he said softly, smiling gently at Lena. "But a few days might be nice."

Freya stretched her arms, casting a glance at the pale light above the trees. "Alright," she said. "If we want dinner before twilight, we should get started."

Johan stood with a slight groan, brushing the dirt from his hands. "You up for helping me build the fire?" He asked Lena.

She jumped to her feet immediately. "Yes! Can I do the matches?"

"Let's start with the stones," he said, already walking toward the edge of the clearing. "Matches come later. Fire's more than a spark, äskling"

Freya watched them wander off together. Johan gestured toward the tree line as he explained something in a quiet tone. Lena nodded solemnly, then darted toward the under-brush with the single-minded intensity of a child on a treasure hunt. Freya shook her head, a smile ghosting across her face despite herself, and re-turned to sorting their supplies.

Johan returned to the centre of the camp with some stones ready to start building a circular border for the start of a camp-fire. Smooth stones were placed in the slight ditch between the tents. The task was conducted in silence while Freya started getting some sausages and cans of vegetables ready. Lena returned moments with her hands clasped together holding a pile of rocks. She knelt beside him, her blue denim jacket smeared with dust and her knees dotted with new flecks of woodland.

"Like these ones?" She asked, holding up a chunk of cracked granite.

Johan shook his head slightly, tapping the ring in front of him. "Too brittle. It'll break in the heat."

She huffed and got to her feet, brushing her hands on her leggings. "I'm gonna find a good one."

"Look for something smooth," he called after her.

She was already off, darting toward the edge of the clearing, near where the forest crept back in. Freya stood at the open flap of the orange tent, arms folded, watching them both with a faint crease between her brows.

"She's determined," Johan said, without looking up.

"Always has been." Freya's voice was soft, but something in it carried a thread of distance. She turned her attention back to sorting their food ready to be cooked.

Johan placed another stone and adjusted it a few millimetres. He didn't need to, but it helped ground him in the silence. He could feel Freya's eyes on him occasionally, the way one might watch a stranger who looked vaguely familiar. Still not speaking, still not arguing. That, at least, was something.

"Got one!" Lena returned a few minutes later, triumphantly holding something above her head.

The stone was smooth and grey, shaped oddly like a river pebble but dry and clean. She handed it to Johan, who turned it over in his hand.

"It's a bit warm," he muttered.

"It was sitting in the sun," Lena said, as though that explained everything.

He gave it back. "Perfect for the ring."

She looked at it, then hugged it close instead. "Actually... I think I want to keep it."

Johan raised an eyebrow. "A rock?"

"It's not just a rock," she said seriously. "Her name is Pebble."

Freya looked over. "You named it?"

Johan gave a soft chuckle. "Alright. No burning Pebble then."

With the fire pit finally built after a few more trips of Lena dropping off rocks, Johan set down the last of the stones with quiet satisfaction. The ring was a little crooked, a little improvised, but solid. He glanced toward the trees, where Lena was crouched near a fallen pine, tugging at something between the bark and root.

"What've you got there?" He asked.

She looked up, triumphant. Her fingers were sticky and shining with amber-gold. "Sap!" She declared. "It's sticky! On a stick!"

Johan crossed to her side, crouched beside her, and took a pinch between thumb and forefinger. "That's good resin," he said. "Good for fire."

"Like dragon glue?" She asked, eyes wide.

"Exactly," he smiled, and gave a little laugh. "Dragons used it to breathe fire. Or so I've heard."

Lena beamed as he guided her hands toward a small scrap of bark, pressing the resin into it like a secret ingredient. She followed him back to the ring of stones, her steps light despite the growing dimness. The resin made her fingers glisten in the firelight, and she waved them like magic. Johan built the bundle carefully; dry twigs beneath, split kindling above, the resin-soaked bark tucked near the centre like a heart. When he struck the match, it flared to life not with the reluctant sputter of damp wood but a quick, eager hiss. The flame licked the resin, caught the curl of birch bark, and bloomed in a low orange sigh.

A soft hiss followed by a clean *whump* of flame lit the space with a warm orange glow. Lena clapped quietly, still cradling Pebble.

Freya joined them then, her expression unreadable but her movements relaxed. She passed out paper plates, careful to keep her fingers away from the flame. Dinner was simple: pre-marinated sausages wrapped in foil, vegetables skewered on thin sticks and a couple of slices of bread. However, the loaf of bread had been squashed slightly during travel.

"Don't forget, I'm roasting marshmallows after," Lena said, holding up the bag with both hands as though presenting treasure.

Freya smiled faintly. "You'll need to eat something real first."

"I am!" She declared, already biting into a piece of bread, ripping the bread with her teeth while giggling. Johan flipped the sausages on top of the metal grill above the fire, then passed a stick to Lena. "Hold this over the heat. Not in the flame. Let it toast."

Lena watched it intently, tongue poking out in concentration. Freya sat opposite Johan, legs crossed, rubbing her palms together as if to shake off the last of the day's travel. "You always did like your little projects," she said, nodding at the stone ring.

Johan shrugged. "Fire deserves some respect."

Freya's mouth twitched, just slightly. "You were always more romantic about it than I was."

"I'm not romantic," he said, handing her a foil packet. "Just thorough."

"For some people, that's the same thing."

They ate with minimal talk, but not in silence. The fire crackled steadily. Warmth from the earth and fire leached through their shoes, comforting the family with its warm glow. The last of the foil packets were set aside. Lena stood up sharply with her marshmallow bag held like a sacred offering. Her face was already sticky with dinner, but her energy had only sharpened.

"Can I do the first one?" She asked, not waiting for permission as she tore the plastic open and held up a squishy white marshmallow between thumb and forefinger.

Johan passed her a clean stick. "If you can hold it still."

"I'm *very* still," she said, already jabbing the marshmallow onto the end with more force than necessary. Freya pulled her chair a little closer to the fire and took the bag, plucking one out for herself and another for Johan without asking. The flames curled a lazy, golden and low, casting long flickers across the trees and tents around them. The evening had deepened into a hush that settled like mist. Lena crouched near the fire with brow furrowed in intense concentration. "Not *in* the fire, right?"

"Just above it," Johan said. "Let the heat do the work."

She adjusted her grip slightly, tongue poking out of the side of her mouth in concentration. The stick trembled in her small hands. Freya leaned back, watching the flames rather than her daughter.

"You're very serious about marshmallows."

"She gets it from you," Johan said.

Freya smirked faintly. "You think I taught her that?"

"Structure. Precision. High marshmallow standards."

Lena's marshmallow caught a flame anyway, blooming orange before she yelped and blew at it like her life depended on it. Johan plucked it from her hands and gave it a few quick puffs before peeling the crisped layer free.

"I like it like that," Lena said, grabbing it back with glee and popping it in her mouth.

"Of course you do," Freya said, passing Johan another. "Another round?"

They sat like that for a while, letting the rhythm of it pull them into something softer than conversation. Marshmallow by marshmallow, they built a small moment of peace. A kind of quiet that only appears when no one tries to fill it. The fire crackled and popped gently as the stars began to shine high above their heads. Eventually, Lena sagged sideways towards Freya, her eyes still watching the fire. Watching the fire dance slowly, wearily, a heavy blink of a child fighting sleep.

"I think that's our cue," Freya said, brushing her fingers through Lena's curls.

Johan gave a nod, standing and brushing his hands against his trousers. "Want help with the zip?"

"I've got it." Freya rose slowly, cradling Lena's hand in hers. A slight coldness returned in her voice, a nice flame-lit evening coming to a close back to reality. "Come on, little ember. Time to turn in."

Lena grumbled something sleepy but followed, her bunny and the still-clutched Pebble making the journey with her. They stepped into the purple tent, Freya holding the flap open as Lena crawled inside and flopped onto her sleeping bag with dramatic flair. She adjusted her stuffed rabbit beside her pillow and tucked Pebble carefully under the edge of her sleeping bag like a companion.

Freya knelt beside her, smoothing the sleeping bag and brushing a curl from Lena's forehead. "Comfortable?"

Lena nodded, but her eyes were still bright. "Mum... Can you tell me a story?"

Freya hesitated. "What kind of story?"

"Grandma told me about the Vittra once. The ones who live underground. Do you know about them?"

Freya blinked, surprised. "Mormor told you about the Vittra? That's an old one..."

Freya glanced once toward the soft orange light of the fire still flickering outside, then settled in beside her daughter, lowering her voice to a gentle whisper.

"Long ago, long before roads or radio towers, there was the Vittra. They lived beneath the forests and fields, not far from the roots of trees or the veins of stone. They were not like us. They had their own paths, hidden ones, the kind only wild things remember. Narrow trails beneath the moss, tunnels through the bedrock, invisible unless you listened very, very closely.

The Vittra don't like to be disturbed. That's why, when people used to live on farms, they'd always whisper 'Se upp!' Before pouring hot water outside, or throwing out scraps, or even going to the toilet in the woods. It was a warning. Not for people, but for the Vittra. So they could move away from the danger. So they wouldn't be burned, or bothered, or trampled by mistake.

Because if you forget to warn them... They might not forget you.

They don't hurt out of cruelty. They just... Remember. And sometimes, when they've been wronged, they'll bring sickness. Not fevers and sneezes, but a slow kind. A weariness that won't go away. A strange feeling, like the world is watching, like your dreams are no longer your own.

But if you're kind to them. If you respect their places and don't make too much noise in their woods, they leave you be. Sometimes they even help. There are stories of farmers who left out cream or porridge at night, and their animals never grew sick. Or children who got lost in the forest and heard voices in the wind showing them the way home.

But they only help those who remember. So if you ever hear something whisper beneath your feet, or feel the warmth of the ground when there's no sun... Don't be afraid. Just say 'Look out.' And mean it."

Freya looked down at Lena who was now fast asleep. She gave a loving smile and she exited the tent, zipping the tent gently behind her. The fire had sunk into a bed of softly glowing embers. Johan sat at the edge of the circle, shoulders hunched, watching the quiet flicker of flame play against the base of the trees. High above, the sky hadn't darkened so much as faded; a pale indigo veil that refused to give way to night. The treetops didn't vanish into shadow as they might further south; instead, they hovered in silhouette. Crisp against a sky that glowed on with the stubborn light of Scandinavian summer.

Johan stared up for a moment, squinting. "She's asleep?"

"Yep."

Freya pulled the chair closer and sat down again, rubbing her palms together like the warmth had suddenly faded. Johan lingered a few moments more, then bent down to grab something from his backpack. The worn, leather-bound book with its spine softened from use. Freya glanced at it, then away. Johan didn't offer an explanation. He slipped away from the firelight, walking slowly toward the edge of the clearing, the book held at his side.

The earth was still warm underfoot, that strange ambient heat that seemed to rise from the soil itself. He moved just beyond the trees, where the ground dipped slightly, and walked to the edge of the lake they'd passed earlier. The water lay flat and silver, unbroken. No wind. No movement. Just the breathless hush of the hour between days.

He sat at the bank and opened the book. The page glowed faintly in the twilight. The sky is still deep blue and unyielding. This far north the stars don't appear, not for months. Just a quiet that refused to darken. He raised the pen. Held it still. Then began to write.

Lena seems happy. Freya too I think. Things feel tough, but I'm coping.

He paused. Listened to the fire crackle faintly in the distance. No other sound could be heard. No wind. No owls. No under-brush rustling. Just quiet. Heavy and complete.

He closed the book, running his thumb along the spine. Then stood, brushed the soil from his jeans, and walked back to the fire. By the time Johan stepped back into the fading light of the campfire, Freya had already receded into her tent, zip close. He decided to do the same. It at least seemed to have been a successful day.

Inhabit

" Daddy! Pebble grew eyes!" Johan was greeted suddenly by Lena. He rubbed his eyes, trying to wake up against the high pitched excitement, to discover Lena in his tent holding the rock she found the evening before in his face. He pushed the rock away a little to focus his eyes. Lena and Freya had been up for a while before he was awoken with some art supplies that had been packed. Googly eyes were stuck to the rock unevenly with a little smile shakily drawn on in a marker pen.

"Aren't her eyes great, pappa?" Lena screeched before heading straight out the tent again towards her mother.

Johan slowly awoke, rubbing the sleep from his eyes. The sun had risen hours ago, although it was only half seven. Pale light filtered through the canopy in long strips, cutting lines across the inside of his tent. He sat for a moment, listening. Birds chirped faintly, far in the distance. No mosquitoes were seen. No bites anywhere from the night. Giggling and the occasional squeak was heard from Lena and Freya already sorting out breakfast. The zipper stuck halfway before sliding down with a reluctant hiss. He stepped out, the chill of morning air hitting his face with a soft sting. His boots were damp from the ground. The fire pit still smouldered faintly, and Johan crouched to stir the embers with a stick. Heat clung to the stones longer than it should've.

He joined the two out in their mini camp site.

Freya smiled in greeting but didn't say anything to Johan. Her hair was loose at the front, a curl caught in the crook of her collar. She was stirring something in a cup with the edge of a spoon that clinked in uneven rhythm. The cooler sat half-open near her feet, condensation already gathering on its sides.

"We're having marshmallow cereal," Lena announced. "But not *real* marshmallows. The squishy fake kind. So it still counts as breakfast!"

"You only eat the colourful bits," Freya said lightly, half to Johan. "She leaves the rest for the ants."

"They need breakfast too," Lena chirped, then yawned. Sudden and a bit too long.

Johan blinked at her, just a little too slow. "Did you sleep okay?"

She nodded, but the motion dragged. "I think Pebble talked in the night," she murmured. "She doesn't like cold feet."

Johan exchanged a look with Freya, but neither commented. Not then.

For breakfast: cereal and milk they were waiting to retrieve from the cooler in Johan's storage tent. Three camping chairs sat around the unlit fire from the evening before. Though the fire was out, the wood still felt warm in the cold early sun. Johan touched one log and frowned slightly but said nothing.

The three sat around talking for a while, chatting about what they wanted to get up to today. Lena wanted to build a tower from pinecones. Freya had her eye on the trail that looped around the second lake. Johan didn't join in the conversation as much as the rest. He stirred his cup absent-mindedly, the plastic spoon knocking once, then again, like a metronome out of rhythm.

"I want to see a dragon today!" Lena exclaimed, waving her arms up in the air; nearly knocking her cereal bowl flying.

"Maybe not a dragon, dear... Perhaps a reindeer?" Freya said with a sweet smile.

"Toppen!"

Only a few minutes passed until they had all finished their cereal. Johan didn't seem so interested just yet in a hike and wildlife spotting. He, much to Freya's discontent, decided to stay behind. Sulking.

"Can Pebble come along, mummy?"

"Sure, älskling."

Pebble was placed in Lena's front pocket of her blue jeans as she began to run, excited to get going.

"Remember your comfy shoes, Lena. They'll be a lot of walking." Johan reminded as he began clearing away the plastic breakfast bowls. Lena ran back enthusiastically, darting like an arrow head first into her tent. She emerged a few moments later in her brilliantly polished white sneakers. Tugging at Freya in protest of leaving immediately. Johan started walking off towards the lake with the breakfast bowls to rinse them out. He didn't say anything to anyone as he left, leaving Lena and Freya to head in the opposite direction into the wilderness.

Lena trotted along ahead, happily skipping and jumping around with morning excitement. Freya walked behind, still trying to wake up; missing her usual routine of coffee in a warm house. Her footsteps were light and erratic. Little darting sprints followed by sudden pauses to investigate whatever new leaf or rock caught her attention. The morning air still held a chill, but the sun was climbing now. Dust motes danced in the beams like drifting pollen. The forest smelled damp and alive; moss and wet bark, with a thread of something sweeter, like berries somewhere just out of reach.

Freya walked behind, slower, her boots soft in the moss. Birds started chirping close again, a sound that seemed absent from their camp. A pair of Willow Warblers whistled somewhere to her left, while high above, the haunting cry of a lone thrush echoed once through the branches and was gone.

They continued north for another five minutes. The path was half-formed at best; just a meandering split in the under-brush where deer trails had worn the foliage down over time. Fallen twigs cracked gently underfoot, and Lena's shoes were already dirtied around the edges. She didn't care.

"Ooh! The bugs are back!"

She crouched suddenly, balancing on the balls of her feet, eyes fixed to a patch of green where a bright dot of red trembled in the breeze.

"There seemed to be no bugs at camp," she said, eyes wide. "Maybe they all live *here* instead."

Freya peered over her daughter's shoulder.

A ladybird; small and glossy, with three black dots spread like ink blots on its back, clung to the edge of a delicate leaf. The red of it looked impossibly vibrant against the desaturated greens of the forest floor.

"Mummy, look! A ladybird!"

Freya smiled. "She's pretty."

"She's a *princess*," Lena corrected.

They paused there for a while, watching the tiny creature edge its way up the trembling leaf stem. Then the wind shifted, and the ladybird flew off. A flicker of red vanishing between the trees.

They walked on.

By midday, hunger stirred. Lena was the first to say so, one hand resting on her stomach, eyes scanning the path ahead for promise. The sun had climbed high now, threading pale beams through the birch canopy. Ahead, terrain dipped gently into a shallow fold. A natural pause in the trail. A fallen trunk stretched across one side like a forgotten bench, bark half-peeled, pale wood showing through in dry, splintered ribbons. Noticing the rumbling of Lena's stomach, Freya decided it was time to have some lunch. They perched themselves upon a fallen log.

Freya dropped her rucksack with a quiet grunt, rolled her shoulders, then leaned over to open the zip. From inside came a small snap-lock tub, sandwiches neatly stacked in wax paper. The bread still held its shape. Freya handed one to Lena: thick-cut ham and creamy cheese. Lena smiled faintly, crossed her legs at the base of the log, unwrapping her lunch with quiet care.

Freya took her own out: rye bread layered with pickled cucumber and a smear of butter. That familiar tang lifted briefly into the air. Lena gave her the same look she always did of amused disapproval.

"You're so weird," she muttered, just loud enough to count.

Freya only shrugged. Soon after came the crisps.

'Shop snacks,' Lena called them. A term she'd invented after realising Freya never kept anything that crinkled at home. Dill in a green bag, her mother's pick. Sour cream and onion in blue. Lena's favourite.

The packets opened with sharp crinkles that cracked briefly through the silence, scattering a squirrel up the nearest tree in a flurry of claws and tail.

Freya chewed slowly, her eyes drifting between bites to watch her daughter. Lena stopped eating her sandwich after about half-way. It now rested against her knee, waiting without any chewing rhythm. A couple more bits. Then back down. One more then she stopped entirely. Her gaze wandered off into the woods like she was trying to remember something just out of reach. The fingers holding her sandwich slackened a little more each time, until finally it rested in her lap.

Freya swallowed and leaned slightly forward. "Eat up, darling. Still a walk back ahead of us."

"I know…" Lena replied, but her voice sounded uncertain, unfocused. Freya glanced at her more carefully now. Her posture was different. Shoulders were slightly hunched. The bounce had gone from her spine. There was a flush to her cheeks that hadn't been there earlier, though the breeze was cool and steady. She wasn't complaining, not outwardly, but her eyes kept drifting into the distance.

"You sure you're okay?" Freya asked gently.

Lena blinked, slowly turning her eyes back. "Yeah, I just…" She paused for a short while, still staring ahead. "I think I'm full already."

The sandwich had only been half-eaten. Yet, Freya didn't push. She handed over a water bottle instead and watched as Lena took a small sip, then set it down beside her without much care. A beetle clambered up the edge of the log between them and was promptly flicked away by Lena. No usual giggle or comment about bug names.

"Why didn't dad join us?"

"Probably sulking, sweetie."

***

Back at camp, Johan sat alone, his brown leather notebook cradled between both hands. It pressed against his chest like something important, though no words had yet taken root inside it. After a while, he opened to a clean page and began to write, the pen moving with an effort that didn't quite match the stillness around him.

It's been difficult today. I didn't want to go hiking with Freya and Lena. Too much reconnecting all at once. Being around her again after everything; it sticks in the air.

He paused, staring at the words like they'd come from somewhere else. A breath caught in his throat. He closed the book more firmly than necessary, the sound sharp in the quiet. *This is stupid*: those words flooded Johan's thoughts.

He hadn't touched lunch. Couldn't stomach it. Something about food felt wrong lately. Not repulsive exactly, but just his stomach didn't seem to like it. His appetite hadn't come back since breakfast.

He sat with the book resting on his lap, eyes half-lidded. A patch of sun now reached further toward the centre as the day had passed on. The fire pit remained untouched but still warm from the morning smouldering. He had started to feel more tired as the day dragged on

Johan reached out to adjust a corner of the blanket left by the tent. Folded it back into place without thought. Then he lay down slowly, arms behind his head, letting the weight of his body settle into the earth.

Sun warmth gathered across his chest. Above, wind blew through the trees in slow motions. The sound reminded him of something. Waves against a jetty, maybe.

He let his eyes close. Just for a minute. Sleep came the way it does when exhaustion is too proud to admit itself. Like a trickle through a cracked pane. The last thing he remembered was the scent of old pine sap.

***

A couple of kilometres north, and heading back, Freya and Lena continued their hike. It was getting later in the day, so Freya had decided to circle round for a slow walk back to camp. The ground rose into soft ridges, broken by stretches of shallow bog where reeds stood tall and motionless like tired sentries. Freya picked a careful path along the drier edges, boot prints filling with brown water behind her. Lena trotted behind, not quite skipping anymore, her earlier exuberance dulled by the weight in her limbs. She had picked up a stick somewhere and now dragged it gently across the undergrowth, humming something tuneless under her breath.

Even the insects seemed fewer here than earlier. The occasional black fly, a spider-web stretched silver between twigs. The afternoon had tipped quietly into late day.

In the distance, Lena spotted a reindeer and called out in excitement.

"Look! Look! It's got a big nose like Grandpa's!"

The reindeer didn't move. It stood rigid at the far edge of the clearing, half-sunk behind a rise of mossy stone, its shape mottled in the dappled light. For a moment, Freya thought it might be a stump. Then it blinked. Once. Slow.

As they walked closer, the reindeer didn't flinch or bolt. It simply stood, staring at the two humans in the distance. Its antlers tilted slightly, one longer than the other.

"It's not scared," Lena whispered, delighted. "Maybe it wants to come with us."

They moved carefully around the thicket, but still the animal didn't budge. The reindeer remained still, but not alert. A few more steps and Freya could see it clearly now. Legs trembled under its weight, thin limbs quivering with each breath. Drool hung in a long, unbroken thread from the slack of its mouth, glistening where it caught the light.

Its fur should've been sleek by now, but patches had slipped free across its haunches, exposing raw, pink skin beneath. Like something had burnt away the coat instead of shedding it. A slow, rhythmic shudder passed through its chest. Not quite breathing but more like trembling from within. Its antlers listed slightly to one side, uneven and dulled. But it was the eyes that held her. Mottled black and dull. Lena, however, continued prancing toward the animal.

"Lena, stop," Freya said, arm gently blocking her daughter's path.

Lena slowed reluctantly, only a few metres ahead. "But... He's not doing anything."

"Exactly. That's not how reindeer act. Let's walk around, sweetie."

She tried to keep her voice even. The last thing she wanted was fear settling into Lena like it had settled into her own chest.

"I think that deer might be feeling a little unwell."

"Me too, Mummy. Reindeer and me can be sick together!" Lena declared cheerfully. "I shall name them Antler!"

Freya let out a silent sigh, one hand tightening briefly on her daughter's shoulder before letting go. The forest felt closer now. Too close. Like it had been holding its breath. Behind them, the reindeer swayed slightly before dropping its head low toward the moss, as if the weight of its skull had grown too much. They kept walking, back toward the camp. Freya didn't look back. Lena did.

Back at camp, Johan was at the water's edge.

He stood ankle-deep in the marshy shallows, jeans rolled to the knee, a line cast far out where the lake fell darker. He didn't move much. Just the subtle shift of wrist and shoulder, the occasional quiet reel. It was patience he wore like a second skin. The air was damp here. Carried the scent of water-weed and wet bark. The surface of the lake shimmered in long ribbons of orange, tugged gently by a breeze that never made it past the tree-line. Every so often a ripple broke the stillness. A slow, wide arc under the surface. Trout.

His second cast landed closer to the rocks, near where the moss dipped into shadow. Moments passed. A flick. Then tension. The rod bowed with a taut certainty, and Johan's stance shifted. Focused and quiet. The line danced once, then again. With slow, steady hands, he pulled.

The fish broke the surface in a flash of silver. Another Trout. A Good size too! Its sides shimmered like wet slate, speckled and glinting in the low sun. Johan knelt, fingers working the line free. The fish kicked once against his hand, still fighting. Then he brought it to the shore.

By the time Freya and Lena returned from the forest, the sun had begun to retreat towards the horizon. Lena was dragging her feet now, each step slower than the last, though her cheeks were pink from the wind and her hands still clutched Pebble like a talisman. Freya looked tired too. Not just in her body, but in the kind of way people looked when they'd walked too far with thoughts they weren't ready to say aloud.

Lena paused when she saw Johan, her eyes catching on the fish glinting on a flat stone by the fire-pit.

"Pappa caught a fish!" She said, voice still light, but not as loud as it had been earlier.

Johan raised a hand in lazy greeting, his other already reaching for the tin knife in his pocket. Freya knelt by Lena and started unlacing her boots without a word. Johan glanced over.

"Saw a sick reindeer" Freya greeted Johan, not with a *hello*, just with an informative statement. "Maybe rabies or something. Throughout the wildlife in this area was fine."

He nodded, not paying much attention. "I'll gut this quickly, we'll have dinner soon."

Johan crouched low, the trout firm beneath his left palm, tin knife slicing with quiet expertise just below the gills. Blood slicked the stone beneath it in a neat, practiced line. Lena watched from a few feet away, transfixed but silent. Freya sat on the edge of one of the foam mats, rubbing her calves absent-mindedly as she kept one eye on her daughter.

"You sure she should be watching that?" She asked softly, nodding toward the scene.

Lena answered before Johan could. "It's not gross. It's just nature."

Johan grunted, flicking the innards neatly into a paper bag beside him. "You used to say that too," he muttered to Freya. Freya didn't answer. She was watching the tree line, frowning faintly.

Lena edged a little closer, squatting beside the gutted fish. "Does it hurt them?" She asked.

"Not now," Johan said simply. "But when it was caught? Probably a bit. But that's the way things go out here."

She considered this deeply with her brow creased. "I guess that's fair," she said, then looked back toward the lake.

The water had taken on a deeper tone, no longer orange but steel-grey, brushed with low sky and broken reflections. Freya followed her gaze. "No ducks," she murmured absently. Lena didn't seem to notice. She was staring into the reeds now, squinting.

"There's something moving in there," Lena interrupted. She stood and tiptoed toward the shallow inlet where thick weeds swayed near the edge of the shore. She crouched low again, peering in. "It's just... It's a fish, I think. But it's not swimming right."

Freya walked over to join her daughter. There, caught in the tangled reeds, was a small fish. Perhaps ten centimetres long. Its back was arched unnaturally, the scales on one side dull and flaking. It didn't swim so much as twitch, its tail making feeble kicks in the muck. Its gills pulsed sluggishly, open and close, open and close.

"Should we help it?" Lena asked. "It looks like it's stuck."

Freya watched it for a long moment, then exhaled. "No, sweetheart. I think it's... Already too late for that one."

Lena was quiet. "Do you think it's sick, like the reindeer?"

Freya didn't answer at first. Then: "Maybe."

Johan stood now, wiping his blade clean with a folded rag. He glanced toward them but didn't speak. His eyes lingered on the half-sunken fish for just a moment longer than necessary.

"Time to eat," he said finally, voice low.

Lena turned, skipping a step back toward the fire. "I want the crispy skin bit."

The fire in the middle of camp was lit once more with fresh firewood gathered right at the edge of the forest. Trout was placed on the grill rack to cook, releasing steam and a smell that reminded Johan of rivers far older than him. Smoke curled again into the air. The wind carried it sideways into the trees.

Dinner cooked slowly. They didn't speak much. The hush of the forest crept in; wind between branches, the low groan of trees that had stood through longer winters than any of them. When the fish was ready, Johan served it across the plates, dividing it into uneven but fair portions. Freya's fingers brushed his as he passed her a plate. She didn't look at him.

They ate seated in a loose triangle around the fire. Lena was eating noticeably slower than usual. She picked at the edges, careful, lips parted as if expecting to say something but deciding against it. Johan chewed in silence, eyes on the flames.

"Tastes like smoke," Lena said finally, not quite complaining.

Johan glanced up. "That's the point."

"Does smoke have a point?"

"Makes things warmer. Drier. Keeps bugs away."

"There aren't any bugs," she murmured, and pushed her fork gently against a piece of fish. "Maybe the smoke already worked."

Freya looked at her, then down at her plate. "Try to eat a little more, sweetie."

Lena didn't answer. Her legs were tucked under the camping chair now, twisted tight. Pebble lay by her foot, face-down in the dirt.

Johan tried a smile. "You named a rock but won't name your dinner?"

"Fish are harder to talk to," she said, voice quiet again. "They don't have eyelids."

A branch cracked somewhere beyond the clearing. Not loud, but real. Freya's head turned sharply toward the trees, fork frozen mid-air. Nothing followed. Just wind again. Just trees.

"Probably a moose," Johan said, but softer this time. Like even he didn't believe it.

Lena shifted in her seat. Her elbow knocked into her cup. Water sloshed, then stilled. She didn't apologise. Halfway through her meal, Lena paused. Her fork hovered above the trout, then slowly lowered. Her eyes drifted out past the fire-pit, toward the trees.

"Mamma?" She said softly. "I don't want the rest."

Freya turned to her. "What's wrong?"

"I just feel... Funny." Her voice trembled slightly, and her hand drifted to her stomach.

Freya set down her plate instantly. "What kind of funny?"

"Floaty. And heavy at the same time. My head feels bad."

Then, suddenly, Lena scrambled upright and staggered two steps away before doubling over. The sound was awful. Wet and helpless, vomit hit the earth in a thin splash. She heaved again, knees sinking into the dirt, her hands pressed into the pine needles for balance. Freya was beside her in seconds, holding her by the shoulders, brushing her hair away from her face as Lena sobbed softly.

Johan sat frozen, then approached slowly, guilt rising like heat from his chest.

"She barely ate," he muttered. "That shouldn't've..."

Freya looked up, sharp. "Don't."

"What?"

"You always do this, like she didn't just vomit her lunch up."

"I'm saying maybe it's not the fish."

"Oh, I'm sure the forest did it," Freya hissed. "Maybe the wind. Or maybe it was undercooked."

"I've cooked trout since I was fifteen..."

"She's *seven*, Johan. Maybe next time you focus less on perfect fire angles and more on making sure your kid isn't poisoned."

He flinched at the word. Poisoned.

"It was cooked," he said again, quieter. "I checked it. It flaked."

Lena whimpered softly, her forehead resting against Freya's collarbone.

Freya's eyes stayed on Johan, sharp as flint. "Then something else is wrong."

Johan didn't answer. The fire snapped in front of them. Lena continued to lay next to her mother. Her hands caught Freya's eyes. The palms had begun turning red, like a rash. A concerned look swept Freya's face as she contemplated what might've caused the rash. Freya guided Lena to the tent, one arm steadying her daughter's weight. Pebble was waiting near the entrance, lying sideways in the dirt. Johan watched them go, then turned back to the fish.

His own plate lay half-full where he'd left it. The fire smoked upward into the growing twilight. Far across the lake, something moved. A ripple, maybe. Or just the wind again. The air had turned colder without warning. Johan glanced down at his plate once more, then nudged it into the flames.

Freya eased Lena down onto the sleeping mat inside the tent, careful not to jostle her too much. Lena whimpered again but didn't protest. Her limbs felt heavy, uncoordinated. The lazy sprawl of someone half-asleep. Freya adjusted the sleeping bag around her daughter's small frame, tucking it up just beneath her arms. She reached for the lamp hanging from the tent's roof beam and flicked it on.

A soft glow filled the space. Warm. Amber. Gentle.

Freya knelt beside her, brushing hair from Lena's flushed forehead. Her breathing was shallow. The redness on her hands had darkened, spreading up the wrist in mottled patches. Not inflamed, not hot to the touch, but angry-looking all the same.

"Does it itch, honey?" Freya asked, lowering her voice.

Lena nodded faintly, eyelids drooping. "It's like ants... But inside."

Freya's jaw tightened. Her mind worked fast. Could it be sun exposure? An allergic reaction, perhaps? Maybe it was something in the fish after all. Pebble lay sideways near the tent flap, its single remaining googly eye staring up at nothing. Freya reached down and set it gently beside Lena's pillow, brushing off a smear of dirt.

"I'll be back in a minute, love. Just stay still. Don't scratch, okay?"

Lena nodded again without opening her eyes.

"Mummy, why does Pebble hum when the sun goes away?"

A concerned look appeared on Freya's face as her daughter lay with her eyes still closed. She shrugs it off and steps out into the twilight. Johan was still by the fire, sitting low on one of the folding chairs with his elbows on his knees. He didn't look up as she passed.

"I'm going to the car. There's cream in the glove box. Might help with the rash."

He gave a small nod. "Keys?"

She caught them mid-air as he tossed them. The forest felt different now. The kind of quiet that felt less like stillness and more like waiting. Branches moved high above yet there was no breeze against her skin. Only the fire behind her crackled.

The car was parked a little way off from the day before. Her boots snapped twigs under her feet. Moss pulled at her heels. When she reached the car, she opened the driver's door with a squeak, easing herself in behind the wheel.

The glovebox appeared stuck. After a sharp tug, it gave way. She fished around inside: an old receipt, some loose paracetamol, a crumpled bag of wet wipes, a half-used tube of hand cream. *There.* She held it up to check the label, just in case, and reached for the light above the mirror.

Click.

The light flickered, blinked once, then cut out.

She frowned. Pressed it again.

Click.

A dim glow. Then it flickered again. A faint electric hiss. Then nothing.

She tried the passenger side.

Same thing. A short-lived pulse of amber, then dark.

"Seriously?"

She sat back in the seat and stared at the dashboard, half-expecting the car to groan or cough next. Nothing. Just silence. She gave the cream a shake and slammed the glovebox shut harder than necessary. Back at the fire, Johan had stood again. He turned when he heard her approach.

"What's wrong?"

"Your car lights are screwed," Freya muttered, stepping back into the firelight. "Both sides flicker then die. Isn't it about time you got them looked at?"

Johan rubbed a hand over his jaw. "They were fine last month."

"Well, they're not now."

She paused, eyes lingering on the closed zip of the purple tent. "Something's wrong with her," Freya said, voice low. "That rash... It's not just a skin thing. She's burning up."

Johan didn't answer. The fire crackled. A wet pop from a trout bone split the quiet.

Freya turned the tube of cream over in her hand again, her thumb tracing the label, then vanished back inside with Lena.

Johan stayed where he was. His body heavy in the camping chair, spine aching like he'd carried more than weight that day. He rubbed at his temple. Slow, rhythmic circles. A headache pulsing behind his eyes like a dull heartbeat.

Could've been dehydration. Could've been nothing. But it was there.

The firelight hissed and flared as another log split in half. The light curled softly across the dirt, but it didn't push back the sky. It didn't need to. Even now, past midnight, the twilight lingered. A soft grey, like smoke on glass. No stars. No full darkness. Just a constant hush of almost-night.

The clearing held its breath. It was quieter now. Not silent, not really... But still in that slow, pressing way that made him feel like he'd stepped too far into something sacred. Johan rubbed the heel of his hand into his forehead. The ache wasn't sharp, but it pulsed behind his eyes in a way that made the world blur around the edges. He'd blamed the glare off the lake. Maybe fishing. But now it sat with a kind of permanence. He picked up the journal from beside his sleeping bag but didn't open it. The leather felt cool in his hand, edges softened from years of being moved but rarely read. He turned it over once, then again. There were things he could write. Things he probably should. About Lena, mostly. About how she'd seemed more tired than usual. About her cheeks, pink at first, then flushed. And the way Freya had looked at him like he should've noticed earlier.

Instead, he looked up.

Twilight had barely shifted. The sky held its blue-grey breath above the treetops, refusing to darken completely. It was a strange thing, this endless dusk. You never really saw the night, not properly. It made him feel like time had stopped. Like they'd driven out of the world into a forever twilight limbo.

His eyes tracked the silhouette of their tents. Three shapes, low and harmless against the weight of the trees. Freya's was still. Lena shifted once, faintly, as if a leg had kicked in sleep. A child's dream of running. Or falling.

Johan exhaled, slow and long. The warmth from the soil hadn't faded. If anything, it had deepened, soaking into his boots and pressed into his spine. There was comfort in it, but also something else. Something more difficult to name.

He opened the journal. He didn't write too much.

> *Felt off today. Lena too. Fish tasted like metal. Probably just lake water. Still... Need to watch her. And Freya. And myself.*

He closed it gently, slipping it back beside the bedroll. His head throbbed again, a little sharper now. He stood finally, stretching slowly. Then ducked into the orange tent. The zip closed with a soft rasp, swallowed by the stillness. The ground stayed warm, even through the floor. And the sky outside never darkened.

Echoes

The fire stirred reluctantly back to life, coaxed from ash and ember as the family emerged into morning. Johan crouched low beside it, one knee in the soil, feeding splinters of pine into the coals with the same silent precision he'd once used to patch broken furniture. A ribbon of smoke coiled upward, twisting briefly in the unmoving air before vanishing into the pale dome above.

Dawn had returned without flourish. It had been barely noticeable through the long lasting twilight. The sky hung blank and flat, a faded parchment hue tinged faintly pewter, as though some ancient god had scraped the sun just beneath the horizon and left it there, waiting.

Freya sat quietly in her folding chair, knees drawn up, tying her hair back with a stretched band she'd worn thin from years of habit. Her sleeves were bunched above her elbows, and though the chill didn't quite reach her skin, it clung to her thoughts like fog. She watched Johan without speaking as he settled a kettle into the cradle of stones. That strange warmth still pulsed from the ground; neither comforting nor alarming now, just there. Constant. Lena sat close, her denim jacket bunched at the wrists, slightly too long for her. Pebble held securely in her lap. She drew lazy circles in the loose dirt with a stick, watching as each one collapsed back into nothing.

"Coffee?" Johan's voice broke gently through.

Freya nodded, reaching for a chipped enamel mug. Roasted grounds hit their nose before the steam. An earthy, bitter, grounding scent. Perfect for waking up for a long day. It anchored her. Reminded her she still had a body, still had breath, even as everything around her felt like it had begun to come undone.

"I don't like coffee," Lena muttered, not looking up. Her voice was rough-edged from sleep, more whisper than speech.

Freya smiled, soft but tired. "You're still on the juice tier."

Johan lifted the kettle and balanced the last of the coffee between two cups. Then, without ceremony, he flicked the dregs toward the trees beyond Lena's tent.

"Pappa!" Lena shot upright. "You didn't say akta! You have to warn them first!"

Johan blinked, caught between confusion and amusement. "What?"

"The Vittra," Lena said solemnly. "Mormor said if you throw hot water without warning them, they get mad. You can burn them. Then they remember you."

Freya looked at Johan over the rim of her cup, one brow raised. She stared while clasping her cup with both hands as the steam drifted upward.

Lena nodded seriously, brushing loose soil from Pebble's scratched eye. "They don't forgive easily. They make you sick. Or lost."

"I'll shout next time," Johan offered, hand over heart. "Loud as I can."

Lena considered this, then gave a distinct nod before sitting back down. Her weight curled inward, spine folded around her rabbit and her rock, as if gravity had grown heavier overnight. Stillness returned. Not peaceful. No rustle of paws or brush in the undergrowth. The air sat unnaturally still, every breath tasting faintly of stale outdoor air. Freya sipped from her mug, listening without realising she was listening to nothing. No buzz of flies, no distant chirr. Just the soft crackle of fire.

Johan stood slowly and stretched, one hand pressed into his back. He didn't speak, just wandered toward the path that led to the lake, feet dragging a little more than usual. He felt smaller than he had previously. Lena yawned and curled tighter into herself, arms wrapped around Pebble and rabbit both. Her eyelids drooped. Freya watched her from behind the steam of her coffee.

Freya frowned. "You tired already?"

Lena nodded, eyes unfocused. "A little."

Freya reached over and pressed a hand to her forehead. Still warm. Maybe warmer.

"Go lie down for a bit more," she said gently. "We'll plan something fun when you're rested."

Lena didn't argue. She rose without complaint, her small frame folding inward around Pebble, still clasped to her chest like a sacred relic. Wordlessly, she padded toward the tent, slow and uneven, as though guided less by intention and more by instinct. Freya watched her go, eyes tracking the slight sway of the purple canvas as it closed behind her.

Left alone in the quiet, she exhaled deeply through her nose and reached for her phone. Signal at just one bar. Flickering. Mocking. She opened the camera app, then lifted it toward the fire and pressed the shutter. A crisp click. Then nothing. When the image appeared, her stomach twisted.

Static.

Not a digital smudge or lens flare. A true, granular wash of interference. Grainy and grey, like the fractured lines of a damaged VHS. She stared at it, frowning. The device was practically new at only two months old. Top of the line, chosen precisely because she needed something reliable for client calls and late-night syncs with Stockholm. It wasn't the kind of phone that glitched. She took another. This time of the trees. A slow pan and click. Another image, again, that strange distortion. Not across the whole frame, but isolated to the lower half. A murky ripple of interference, smeared just above the forest floor.

Her frown deepened. She turned the lens down, snapped a third. This time, her boot pressed into the spongy moss near the fire-pit. When the photo appeared, the same warped band of grey shimmered along the bottom edge. Faint. Almost ignorable. But undeniable.

She pinched to zoom. The static swam beneath her foot like some subterranean current, as though the distortion wasn't coming from the device. Something old. Analogue. She adjusted her grip, cleaned the lens with the edge of her shirt. Then tried again. Click. Static.

Always at the bottom. Always brushing the earth like a ghost trying to rise.

A shiver passed through her. Her thumb hovered over the screen, hesitating. Then moved. She swiped up her messages and tapped on the thread with Alva. Her fingers began to type.

Alva, Lena's still running a temp. Has a rash on her hands. Food poisoning maybe? Just a bit worried.

She stared at the blinking cursor for a moment, then added:

We're in the woods. Signal's spotty. Just wanted to check if this sounds normal.

She hit send. It didn't. A red exclamation mark bloomed beside the message like a wound. She tapped it. The signal bar flickered between one and nothing. She turned the phone slightly, then raised it toward the sky. It didn't help.

Alva had been Freya's closest friend since gymnasiet. Those final two years of secondary school when everything felt raw, and far too permanent. They'd shared a battered locker lined with fading stickers, survived a spectacularly failed chemistry practical.

Even after their lives had veered apart: Freya into structured sentences and boardroom lighting, Alva into blood pressure cuffs and emergency kits, they'd never truly drifted. There was a softness in that kind of history. A worn-in closeness that distance didn't erase.

Alva didn't just work at any other hospital, one of what would be many in the cities. She anchored the kind of healthcare that mattered for half the villages most maps forgot. Her base was Östersund Hospital, the only major facility for hundreds of kilometres, yet her reach extended like a spider-web through the forests and uplands. She was always in motion. One week a trauma nurse, the next a lifeline in small village clinics.

Freya had once joked, over late-night texts and too many glasses of wine, that Alva was fast becoming a mountain paramedic, despite the fact neither of them had ever managed to stay upright on skis.

Now, Freya stood, sat in the clearing, arm raised, phone tilted toward the faintest sliver of sky. One bar. Then none. Her thumb hovered uselessly over the retry button. Still nothing. She copied the text, opened a different app. She tried to send it through a social feed instead. The spinning icon rotated once, then froze mid-turn before collapsing into silence.

"Come on," she whispered.

She tapped the screen again. Once. Twice. The signal flickered briefly. Then died altogether.

A sigh escaped her. She pressed a thumb to the inner corner of her eye, kneading gently. She hadn't realised how much her head throbbed. A dull, persistent ache, as if the bones of her skull were trying to hum. She placed her phone back into her pocket.

Johan had returned. He crouched low beside the fire pit, stirring the damp remains of the morning's ashes with a half-charred stick. Its smoke had thinned to a pale wisp, barely worth chasing. When he glanced up, something in his face looked older. Drawn tight. The lines at the corners of his mouth etched deeper than they had been that morning.

"Are you feeling alright?" She asked, watching him closely.

Johan blinked. "Yeah. Just thinking. Fire's nearly out again."

Freya paused, then said, "I tried to message Alva. The photo didn't go through. But even without it, the text won't send."

He shrugged, brushing ash from his palms. "We knew the signal was patchy."

She didn't reply. Instead, she pulled her phone back out and opened the gallery. She flipped back to the photo she'd just taken and paused. She swiped to the next image. Johan and Lena near the tents, from last night. Another band, this one broader. She hadn't noticed this last night.

"What?" Johan asked, looking up from the smouldering fire.

"Look at these." She held out the screen. "Lines. Across the photos. I thought it was glare, but it's all of them. Even ones from yesterday."

He frowned, taking the phone and tilting it. "Weird. Probably the lens."

"It's not the lens." She sounded more clipped than she meant to. "It's interference."

He passed it back. "So? The phone's glitchy."

"It wasn't before."

She said nothing else. Johan stood slowly, brushing his hands off again. "Let's go for a walk. Get some fresh air. Might do her good."

Lena stirred inside her tent, rubbing at her eyes like someone still half-dreaming. The canvas above her rustled faintly. She blinked once, then again. Almost as if the space around her didn't quite match the one she'd fallen asleep in. Freya helped her into a jacket, buttoning the top slowly as Lena mumbled about bunnies and something with wings. Pebble remained clutched to her chest. Nearby, Johan packed bread and cheese into a cloth bundle, sliding a Thermos in beside it.

They headed north, following a path that curved past the second lake and into thickening pines. Sunlight filtered through thin cloud cover, but warmth didn't follow. The air felt dense. Dry and cold. Lena walked a few paces behind, dragging her feet. Pebble stuffed in her pocket like a sleeping pet. Freya trailed further still. Her gaze moved from branches to soil to sky, each step slower than the last. Up ahead, a sudden splash of colour. Lena plucked a yellow flower and held it high.

"Mamma, look! Like the ones near the river."

Johan reached for it, sniffed. "Doesn't smell like much."

"You don't have to smell it," she said solemnly. "It's just supposed to be nice."

Freya almost smiled. Then Johan stumbled. Just a hitch in his step. His hand went to his stomach, and his face tightened.

"You alright?" Freya turned just enough to witness his stumble.

He nodded, laughing once without humour. "Breakfast didn't sit right."

Freya said nothing, but her eyes stayed on him a moment longer. Lena had already wandered ahead, muttering softly to trees. Freya checked her phone once again. The message finally had been sent. No reply, but something about it felt like progress. They reached a break in the pines. Water stretched ahead. Still, reflective, almost too still. Clouded light slid across its surface like oil. No birds. No ripples across the lake. Just quiet.

"Here?" Lena asked, already kicking off her shoes, one landing beside Johan's foot with a soft thud.

"Perfect," he said.

Freya set down the blanket with a grunt, brushing dry pine needles from the flattened space between the birches. She looked up to see Johan in the lake already. Wading through the water, jeans rolled above his knees. Laughs from Lena as she chased him like a duckling.

"Wait up!" She called, splashing ankle-deep into the water. "I want to ride the waves!"

"There are no waves," Johan called back, "just ripples. You'll have to pretend."

Freya sat on the edge of the blanket, watching them. The lake, icy-cold despite the warmth of the air, seemed to steal their breath with every movement. Johan dipped under once, then re-emerged with a gasp and a shaking of his hair like a wet dog. Lena squealed, wiping droplets from her nose. Her curly hair became straight the wetter it got.

"You look like you've been hit by lightning," she told him through giggles.

"Feel like it too," he said, teeth chattering faintly. "That water could wake the dead."

Freya smiled; a real, heart-warming one. Brief, and unguarded. "You'll frighten her."

Lena beamed, unphazed. She climbed onto Johan's back. He staggered slightly under her weight, play-acting exhaustion, ready to throw her into the water. But when he lifted her off again, his expression faltered.

A hand came briefly to his stomach. He rubbed it, then passed the moment off with a forced exhale. Johan waded back to shore and helped Lena to the towel, wrapping her tightly. Her limbs moved slower now. Her shoulders sagged into his as he held her. She was flushed in a way that didn't match the coolness of the lake.

"I'm okay," she said, blinking. Her speech was fine, just... Softer. She laid her head on a rolled sweater Freya had placed beside the bag and closed her eyes without being told. Freya glanced at her. Lena's hand still held the corner of the towel, but without tension.

The sort of stillness that made Freya hesitate. She busied herself with the food instead, quietly ripping a flatbread in half, then re-arranging the slices of apple that no one seemed eager to eat. She told herself it was just a long day. Too much sun. Not enough sleep. Freya pulled out a comb to start arranging Lena's hair. There was no opposition.

"She usually fights me on this," Freya said, quietly. "Says the brush has too many opinions."

Lena shifted slightly, a crease forming between her brows as she curled further inward. She exhaled, slow and long. A determined sigh. Too long to be accidental.

"Maybe the swim wore her out," Johan said.

"Maybe." Freya's voice had changed. She seemed less certain now.

Johan settled beside her, towel draped across his shoulders. He didn't shiver. Freya opened a small container of flatbread and soft cheese. Apple slices sat beside them, their edges browning in the sun. She took a bite, barely tasting it. Johan hadn't touched his. Neither had Lena yet.

"You're not eating?"

He waved her off. "I will. Just not hungry yet."

"Uh-huh."

Their eyes met. Brief and cautious. Johan looked away first. He leaned forward, gently brushed a bead of water from Lena's temple. Freya reached for her phone once again. Not deliberately. Just out of habit. Thumb slid to the camera before she'd even formed the thought. She tilted the lens toward them. Johan crouched beside Lena, who was curled loosely in her towel, eyes half-lidded. Peaceful. Her finger hovered. Click.

The preview blinked once, then froze. Seconds passed. The screen pulsed, and came back. The image appeared slightly out of focus. As if the lens had hesitated to correct itself. But not distorted. Not like the others. Freya frowned, took another. This time, the lake. She scrolled back. Earlier images shimmered with interference. Bands of grey, static brushed across the base like fingerprints. But here? Just blur. Nothing else.

She opened the message thread with Alva. The photo from earlier still sat in purgatory. She tapped resend. A spinning wheel. One bar. Then, green. Sent. Freya stared at the screen, unmoving. Then powered it off and placed it face-down in her lap. Her fingertips pressed lightly to her brow. A low ache had bloomed behind her eyes: dull, persistent, like pressure before a storm.

Johan finally picked up a slice of apple and chewed it slowly. "Still think there was something in the fish?" He said without looking at her.

Freya didn't answer. The sun was high now. The lake no longer shimmered; it just sat. Unmoving. Soundless.

By late afternoon, the air felt sluggish. As though the forest itself had begun to exhale in slow defeat. No insect hum threaded the silence now, only the groan of old trunks adjusting under a tepid breeze.

The camp lay barely a kilometre from where their wandering had ended, yet it felt far removed. Quiet and still, awaiting their return.

Lena had drifted in and out of sleep all afternoon. Each time she woke, her movements grew slower, her words fewer. Freya's worry accumulated like sediment; Johan, meanwhile, dismissed it with a half-hearted shrug. He'd vomited not long after lunch, but claimed it was nothing. Heat. Water. Fatigue. Upon returning to camp, Freya crouched beside Lena's tent and frowned. The centre pole leaned precariously, fabric sagging like a soggy canvas abandoned in a downpour. Beneath it, the earth had slumped inward. Not quite a hole, but enough to make the structure buckle. Something beneath had betrayed its ground.

"Lena, did you move your peg?"

"No," came the reply, small and distracted. She sat nearby on a log, cross-legged, Pebble limp in her lap. "It just started tipping."

Freya lowered her hand to the soil and pressed. It yielded immediately; soft, crumbly, strangely warm. Its texture felt wrong. Not compacted forest loam, not even dried mud. Something looser. Powdered. Like charcoal mixed with dust.

"Johan?"

He emerged from behind the orange tent, sleeves streaked with dirt, sweat lining his temples.

"Come feel this."

He knelt beside her and ran his palm across the same patch. A flicker of uncertainty crossed his expression, then vanished beneath a shrug.

"Probably bad drainage. Foxes or voles tunnels. Or the last storm probably loosened it."

Freya didn't look up. "Doesn't feel like burrows."

She pushed deeper. The ground surrendered too easily. It wasn't wet. More like decomposed matter; agitated and flaky. Warmer than it should be. No recent rain. No moisture. Still, it clung.

"Could be root rot," Johan offered after some thought. "Sometimes trees die underground. Leaves the ground spongy."

Freya stood in silence. She wiped her hands on her trousers, then hesitated. A smear of soil streaked her palm. Not damp nor grainy. It smeared like paste. Darker than expected. Greasier, almost. Johan crouched again, shifting his weight onto one knee. The ground dipped beneath him with an audible crunch. Enough to feel it in his shin.

Freya stared at the spot where his boot had sunk. "That's not burrowing."

"No," Johan admitted. "That's something else." He stared for a while longer before giving way, "Alright," he sighed. "We'll move it."

Lena was still sitting on the log with her legs drawn up. Her arms wrapped around her knees. Her eyes tracked her parents investigating, but said nothing.

"Hey, helper," Johan called gently. "Want to pick a new spot with me?"

Lena nodded once but didn't get up immediately. When she did, she walked slower than usual. Together they picked a patch a few metres over. Flatter, firmer ground, closer to the fire-pit. Johan hammered the stakes again with a small mallet. The tent canvas flopped heavily as they reassembled it.

"This ground's better," he said.

Freya didn't answer. Her eyes were fixed on Lena who had sat down mid-task and seemed content to watch the sky instead of help.

"Is she okay?" Johan asked.

Freya gave a slight nod, although she wasn't convinced herself. Lena had stood up once her tent was newly pegged. Her face had gone pale, revealing her freckles more than usual. "Lena?" The girl wobbled, then lurched forward and vomited onto the dry moss. Freya caught her before she fell. "Okay. Hey, hey, shh," Freya said quickly, holding her steady. "I'm okay," Lena whispered, weakly. "I'm dizzy." Freya knelt with her, brushing the hair from her face. Lena's skin felt warm and clammy. "Let's get you changed." Inside the tent, Freya peeled the shirt from her daughter's side. Her breath caught. A faint rash, mottled and red, curled along Lena's ribs. Angry-looking, spreading. She didn't wait. Pulled out her phone, turned the camera on. Another photo, It looked fine until it saved. Then, once again, horizontal grey static blurred the lower half yet again. Freya cursed softly and typed: *"Rash, nausea. No fever earlier. Ideas?"* She hit send. The signal circle spun, flickered, vanished. Then reappeared. A green tick. Sent. No signal once more. At least this time it was sent. However, relief was short-lived. The reply blinked in: *"Could be an allergic reaction. Keep an eye."*

Beyond the nylon flap, Johan moved in silence, stacking dry pine logs ready for the evening. Each motion performed with slow, deliberate rhythm.

He glanced toward the newly re-pitched purple tent. Freya slipped outside without a word, letting the fabric fall shut behind her.

The air had cooled since midday. Not sharply, but in increments. A subtle thinning. The camp had grown dimmer as evening set upon them. The fire whispered over kindling, its glow licking low across bark and moss. Warmth bled from the ground beneath the pot, where stew simmered: tomatoes and lentils, familiar yet bland. Its scent clung like a comfort still to soothe. Johan crouched nearby, forearms resting on knees, a bottle of water between his fingers. Damp glistened along his face, incongruous in the cooling air. He hadn't spoken since they'd reset Lena's tent. He hadn't eaten much throughout the day either.

Freya stirred the pot. She could feel tension stretching thin behind her ribs. A tautness that had grown steadily throughout the afternoon. The soil beneath Lena's bedding had felt unstable, feeble, hollowed from within. And now the rash, spreading in delicate red fingers along her child's side like poisoned ivy.

She ladled two bowls without comment, passing one across the flame. Johan accepted, gave a nod that didn't reach his eyes. He stared into it, unmoving.

"She's worse," Freya said softly, eyes on the flames. "Alva saw the new photo. It's creeping across her ribs now."

No answer. Johan took a sip from his bottle then set it down.

"She said she might be allergic. Or viral." A pause. "But if Lena throws up again. If she spikes..."

Freya stopped. Let the words hang. A low breath escaped Johan; weary and resentful. Too far from help. Too far from clean answers. He didn't need to say it aloud. Freya wiped her palms against her trousers, suddenly aware of her hands trembling.

"We'll go if it gets worse tonight. I'm not waiting."

Still nothing. She looked up properly this time. She saw exhaustion etched beneath Johan's cheekbones. Fear sitting behind his silence, tightly sealed beneath stubbornness. He hadn't stopped trying to hold this place together. Yet something in him was fraying, thread by thread. Johan finally met her gaze. Something unspoken passed between them. He looked away first.

Words hovered behind his lips but didn't form. A flash of resentment. A hint of shame. Freya broke the silence.

"This place isn't helping. You know that."

He didn't reply, only shifted where he sat. His bowl remained untouched. From the tent, a rustle. Fabric scraped against nylon. A sleepy voice called out, muffled and small.

Freya rose quickly, brushing soot from her knees. "It's alright, älskling. Go back to sleep."

A sigh. A murmur. Silence returned. Johan stood slower. Less certain. He lingered by the fire before steadying himself, then turned towards the forest.

He turned to grab his journal and made his way out of sight. Trees swallowed his silhouette. Twilight settled like a veil. That strange northern dusk that never gave way to night. The sky remained pale, almost translucent. A washed-out canvas holding too much quiet. Johan dropped onto a mossy boulder, knees wide, elbows balanced across them. Earth pulsed faint heat beneath his boots, unnatural and steady.

He closed his eyes. Tried to count each inhale. Each exhale. Something inside his chest remained clenched. Tension. His breath came shallow. His pulse felt fast. Maybe he was just anxious. He pulled the journal from his coat pocket and flipped it open to a blank page.

> *Lena's rash is worse. Freya's scared. I don't blame her. I feel off too. Like my insides are running too hot. I keep telling myself it's nothing. That I'm just tired. But some thing feels stronger while I feel weaker.*

> *I should want to leave. But I don't. Lena's been laughing. Smiling. She never gets to do that with me anymore. These moments feel like something I don't want to lose. Even if it hurts.*

He stopped writing. The pen tip hovered for a moment, then dropped back into the spine. He closed the book gently, fingers lingering on the leather cover.

From somewhere deep in the woods, an owl called once. Then silence again. He sat a little longer. Then, slowly, he stood and walked back toward the thinning firelight. He kept trying not to think about how much his head ached. The lake never looked dark. The sky above it held the dim glow of a day refusing to end. Johan stood at the water's edge again, arms loose at his sides, Pebble's subtle warmth still clinging to his palm from earlier in the day. He'd set it down near Lena's tent without much thought, but his fingertips remembered it. That strange, unnatural warmth.

The lake was flat as glass. A motionless plane disturbed only by the faint rings of insects skimming the surface and the occasional soft clatter of reeds shifting in the breeze. But there wasn't much wind tonight.

There it was again. A weird sound. A thin, dragging whisper. A high-pitched fizz. Almost electric. Like radio static caught on the edge of hearing. Faint, intermittent, just enough to make his skin prickle.

He turned slowly, half-expecting to see a loose wire or phone left on. But there was nothing. Just the clearing behind him. Three tents crouched quietly in the ambient glow. The fire was low now. Freya sat nearby, arms wrapped around her knees. A flicker of movement overhead caught his eye. Johan looked up.

A bird circled high above; gulls perhaps. It faltered once mid-flight, its wing dipping unevenly. The movement wasn't right. A stutter in its arc. It adjusted after a moment and glided away beyond the tree-line. Johan kept staring long after it vanished.

The static was gone. Or maybe it had never been there at all. He made his way back to camp, boots crunching softly over the thin layer of pine needles. Freya looked up, her face tight with worry, the lines at the corners of her eyes deeper than he remembered.

"She woke up," she said softly, nodding toward Lena's tent.

Lena sat on a folded blanket near the fire-pit, the dim glow of firewood reflecting off her cheeks. She had a half-eaten rice cake in one hand and the Thermos cup in the other. Her eyes were glassy, ringed with dark shadows, but she offered a smile when she saw him.

"I was hungry," she said sleepily.

Freya stood and walked over, crouching beside her. "Eat slow. How's your stomach?"

Lena shrugged, nibbling another bite. Then she grimaced and spat it into her hand.

"It tastes weird."

Freya frowned. "What do you mean?"

"Like... Metal," Lena said. "Like chewing a spoon."

Freya took the soup from Lena and set it down near the fire. "We'll try something else tomorrow," she said soothingly, brushing a stray curl from Lena's forehead. "Let's just get some sleep, sweetheart."

Lena didn't protest. Her body moved like memory rather than will. Small limbs folding inward, eyes already unfocused. She allowed herself to be guided back toward her tent, fingers limp in Freya's hand. Pebble remained by the fire-pit, half-buried beneath pine ash and shadow. Forgotten. She settled herself back in her tent in silence.

Johan sat hunched near the flames, coaxing kindling into embers that no longer needed tending. His face remained downcast, eyes fixed on the gentle collapse of bark against firewood. He didn't speak. Didn't even look up. Freya lingered until she heard the soft rustle of sleeping fabric, the tell-tale breath of a child fading into a shallow rhythm. Then she returned. Slower this time. Each step deliberate. Silence had become habitual, like blinking.

Her phone glowed briefly in her hand. Still no further response other than to 'keep an eye'. Stillness stretched across camp like soaked wool: Heavy, muffling and suffocating. Nothing moved beyond their fire. Johan shifted slightly, one palm rising to press into his temple. Fingers dug into his scalp, knuckles white. He winced but made no sound. Freya remained seated, gaze turned outward, unfocused. There were no words left to say. Not tonight.

When she finally rose, her knees crackled. Canvas brushed against her shoulder as she entered her tent, the motion silent, solemn. No goodnight. No final glance. Johan stayed where he was. The fire crackled continuously. Ground heat pulsed through worn soles, rising in slow waves along his spine. It no longer soothed. It pulsed. He stared into the flames, not with thought, but vacancy. His journal was placed, zipped inside his pack, untouched.

Eventually, he crawled into the orange tent, joints stiff, hands unsteady. His jacket stuck to his back with cold sweat. He lay flat, arms to his sides like something embalmed. Shaking fingers twitched long after his eyes closed. Sleep didn't arrive. It crept.

Somewhere past midnight, Freya jolted upright. A wave of nausea tore through her centre with sudden violence. She scrambled at the zipper, fingers fumbling, throat already closing. She barely made it beyond the flap before collapsing to her knees. The retching came hard. Guttural. Wet. Acid stung her tongue as bile splattered across pine needles and moss. Her hand braced against the tent floor, nails scraping fabric as her body convulsed again and again.

When it passed, she remained kneeling. A palm in the dirt, one arm draped across her stomach like a failed shield. Her breath came in uneven gasps, face damp, hair sticking to skin. She wiped her mouth on her sleeve and spat twice, but the taste wouldn't leave. Metallic. Rusted iron. Her lips tingled. She pressed cool fingers to her forehead. Skin felt strange. It became slick and swollen. Slightly numb, like it had detached from muscle. A soft breeze stirred leaves above, but the tents nearby stayed still. Lena's breathing, faint but steady, drifted through the fabric. Johan snored in the deeper tent, jagged and harsh; not a sound she missed.

Freya looked down. The patch of soil where she'd vomited shimmered faintly in the firelight. Something darker caught her eye, streaked the edges.

Not only bile.

Not just sickness.

Blood.

And beneath it, a blackened dust. Like ash. She leaned back, spine thudding lightly against a tree root. She didn't reach for her phone this time. There was no diagnosis needed for her to know this was serious.

Noticed

The morning came like it had forgotten how to be bright. A storm had gathered during the night making the sky darker than it had been in weeks.

Pale light stretched across the tops of the trees, neither golden or bold. Just dark grey and reluctant; as if the sun had risen out of duty, late for work. Freya was already up. She crouched beside the camp-fire, coaxing flame from last night. Shoulders hunched against the heavy rain. The air didn't feel fresh anymore. Not crisp nor alpine. It clung. Damp and metallic. A faint, earthy bitterness she couldn't place.

She added a dry pine-cone, watched it flare, and rubbed her hands together. Behind her, the tents lay still. The forest had no voice except the falling of rain. She stood slowly, stretching the tension from her spine, her eyes taking in the scenery. She tried to focus on practicalities: water to boil for coffee, food to prepare for breakfast, yet her eyes kept drifting to Lena's tent. The flap was half-zipped. A pale arm dangled limply out, fingers twitching once, then lay still. Inside, Lena was curled in on herself, her rabbit clutched to her chest like a lifeline. Her cheeks glistened with sweat, strands of hair stuck to her forehead. Freya reached out into the tent to place her hand on her daughter's forehead.

Clammy. Cool. Too cool.

Then Lena stirred with a soft grunt. Her whole body jerked. Freya barely had time to shift before yellow bile spilled from her lips, soaking the top edge of her sleeping bag.

"Oh, älsking" Freya whispered, catching her, turning her gently to one side. The smell was sharp and sour. She grabbed the edge of a blanket and wiped her daughter's mouth, then her chin. Lena blinked slowly, unfocused, lips slack.

Behind her, Johan's tent unzipped with a rustle. He stepped out barefoot, rubbing at his face. His short hair sticking up in all directions. He looked like he'd aged five years overnight. His skin was pale in the dull light, jaw rough with three-day stubble. He took a step forward and stopped mid-motion.

"Lena?"

"She vomited," Freya said.

Johan hesitated. "Maybe it's... Dinner didn't sit right. She was eating fast. Remember?"

"She's cold to the touch, Johan." Freya's voice had no room for theory. "She's sweating. And the rash," she pulled back Lena's sleeve, "it's spreading again."

Johan crouched beside them slowly. He didn't speak. Freya could see tension sweep over him. His gaze flicked over their daughter, and he reached out for Lena's forehead.

"We need to leave," Freya continued sharply.

Johan didn't answer right away. Instead, he stood again. Slow and stiff. He looked around, finding a reason to evade the statement.

"Oh, it's just a bit of food poisoning. Ingen ko på isen. What's for breakfast?"

Freya glared at Johan. "No cow on the ice?" She repeated, snapping. "She's vomiting!"

Soon after, Lena awoke from her slumber. She slowly stretched as she saw her mother stood by the tent flap. Freya glanced over, concerned. "How are you feeling today, sweetie?"

Lena jumped up full of energy. "I feel great mum, what's for breakfast?" The response was unexpected. Johan looked over while standing over the fire. He smiled. Freya was also taken back, he hesitated before asking what cereals Lena would like. Of course, the answer was chocolate ones.

Johan seemed to feel a little better too; less groggy than the night before. They all sat down at the edge of their tents to have breakfast together. The rain was still heavy, so the tent cover gave a relief from soaked hair. They all started chatting about what they wanted to do during the day as the rain was slowly easing off. Suggestions of hiking, fishing or sitting around the fire playing board games. All sounded fascinating to Lena.

Although Freya was happy to see some of Lena's energy reappear, concern still hung in the air. The rash was still across Lena's ribs. The area still felt off. No mosquitoes had bitten them in the three days. No flies. No animals near the camp.

Johan had scraped the pans clean with a curl of birch bark by the time rain faded to mist. Above them, clouds sagged like damp wool: swollen, grey, undecided. The forest breathed in waves now, exhaling scents of soaked bark, bitter leaf rot, and a trace of metal beneath it all.

Freya lingered near camp's edge, phone lifted skyward toward a thinning strip of east where reception sometimes blinked to life. Raindrops streaked the screen. A single bar. Then none. She waited. Shifted her stance. Still nothing.

By the fire-pit, Lena arranged small stones with deliberate care, muttering quietly to herself. Freya watched while not interfering. Each pebble placed with precision, each crooked one corrected. Something reverent in her rhythm. Purposeful. Almost a ritual. She hadn't seen that focus in days. But Lena's mouth hung open slightly, breath shallow. Shadows clung beneath both eyes.

Freya lifted the phone again, aiming toward trees where Johan had gone for wood. He was barely visible. Hunched, arms full of logs for firewood. Lena crouched nearby, tongue out in fierce concentration. Freya took the picture.

A pause.

Then static.

That static persisted.

Thin grey bands streaked across the image like radio interference on an old television. She noticed and tried again. This time of the trees. Another banded distortion. She stared at the second photo, thumb hovering.

She flicked open the messaging app. Tapped Alva's name.

Still in the woods. Rash is spreading again. Lena seems better now... But... This static?

"There should be enough wood for tonight," he said, letting the load fall with a soft thud beside the tarp.

Freya didn't answer straight away. Instead, she stepped toward him, arm extended, phone unlocked.

"Look at this. Something's wrong with the images."

Johan squinted at the screen. More static lines cut faintly across the frame. Horizontal, greyish, like old tape distortion. "Could be moisture," he muttered. "Lens fogged up maybe."

"It's not the lens," Freya said, voice sharper than she intended. "It's in the data. Same glitch. Same pattern. Two photos, different subjects, same interference."

He passed the phone back with a frown. "We're miles from a tower. Signal's probably messing with it."

Freya pressed her tongue to the back of her teeth, fighting the urge to argue. Something about this photo, the silence, the weight in the air. It all ached with wrongness. Johan opened his mouth again, but another voice cut cleanly through.

"Can we go to the lake?" Lena asked.

They turned. She stood a few paces away, cheeks flushed pink, eyes bright again with a strange eagerness. Rain had stopped, though droplets still fell from branches above like the trees hadn't realised yet.

Freya blinked. The sudden spark in Lena's voice jarred her. "You're up for a walk?"

Lena nodded earnestly. "I feel strong again. I can carry the snacks!"

Freya met Johan's eyes, reading the same mix of relief but doubt. A small hike might do them good. If nothing else, it gave her more time to observe. More time to watch the quiet things. She grabbed a small bag and dropped in some food and three water bottles.

"Alright," Freya announced, "let's walk."

The path out of the camp was familiar by now. A gentle descent toward the larger lake they'd passed on their first day. Water still dripped from the canopy in slow rhythm, landing with hollow plinks. Branches bowed under the weight of rain that had now mostly ceased. They passed one birch whose bark had peeled back in strips like old paint, exposing a sun-bleached wooden flesh beneath.

Johan and Lena walked ahead, her hand clutched in his. He seemed slower now. But he didn't mention it. Lena handed him a pine-cone at one point, declaring it was *dragon bait*. He thanked her and tucked it into his pocket. Freya hung back just enough to let them have the moment. Halfway to the water, Lena began to slow. Her breath came shorter. Her steps hesitated. She stopped completely and stared at her hand.

"What's wrong?" Freya asked.

Lena shook her head. "Just dizzy for a second."

Her speech was fine. Her balance returned quickly. But something behind her eyes looked distant. Faded. They reached the lake-shore in silence. The water was almost motionless. Soft rings of ripples touched the banks but didn't disturb the reeds. The sky had begun to split a little above the. Blue strips emerged, breaking the grey clouds.

They sat on a fallen log, shared berries and a sandwich each. Johan wasn't hungry. He picked at a piece of bread and let it fall from his hands when he thought Freya wasn't watching. Lena curled into Freya's side, wrapped in her jacket. Her fingers were colder than they should have been. Freya kissed her temple and held her close. Lena ate quickly and was ready to continue the hike. Yet,

Freya noticed Lena was pale again. Not in the sickly way of the morning.

"Stay close," Freya murmured, watching the unevenness of her step.

The forest pressed close around them, dense with the weight of unspoken things. Branches laced above like the rafters of some forgotten hall, their leaves trembling in a hush that wasn't quite wind. The ground was thick with old growth: flattened ghosts of last year's ferns, the crisp lace of birch catkins underfoot. Somewhere overhead, something creaked. The sound of the woods shifting in their bones. A single feather drifted down between the trunks, white against green. Lena reached for it, caught it mid-fall, and then stilled entirely with her gaze distant.

"Wait," she said while dragging behind her parents. She held still.

Freya stopped too. "What is it, sweetie?"

Lena's face had gone rigid. She touched her upper lip with the back of her hand. When she pulled it away. There was blood. A thin red line drawn from her nostril to the curve of her chin. Johan turned at the same time Freya stepped forward, already pulling a tissue from her coat pocket. She crouched low, cupped the girl's cheeks gently.

"It doesn't even hurt," Lena said, voice flat.

"I know, Just hold still." Freya dabbed carefully, trying not to show the way her pulse had started thundering in her ears. The bleeding wasn't heavy, but it wasn't stopping either. A slow, steady seep. Her fingers trembled just once before she steadied herself.

Johan hovered nearby, hands in his pockets.

"I'll carry her," he said softly.

"No," Freya snapped, sharper than she intended. Then softer, correcting herself. "Not yet. Let's sit first."

They eased Lena down onto a low rock beside the trail. Freya wrapped her coat around her daughter's shoulders, then brushed her hair gently from her face. The blood had stopped almost as quickly as it began.

"Maybe a burst vessel," Johan offered. "She was breathing hard. Hikes like this could do it." Freya didn't answer.

Instead, she took out her phone again and opened the camera. She pulled Lena's shirt up slightly, exposing her side. The rash was visible again. Raised now, inflamed, stretched like red moss across pale skin.

She took a photo. Two, then three. This time, the images were clear. No static. No distortion. Just sickness, documented cleanly. Freya stared at the photos for a beat too long.

"We need to get back," Johan said.

"Yeah," she murmured, still looking at the screen.

She sent one of the images to Alva with no caption. Just the photo. The message sent. Freya let the phone fall into her lap, resting her hand over it like it might grow hot. Lena shifted against her shoulder. Freya reached over and placed a hand on her daughter's forehead. Still no fever. But her skin was warm in a way that wasn't quite right. Her breath came slow now, her eyes unfocused.

They started walking again once Lena said she felt steady enough. Her steps were slower now, but purposeful, as though she didn't want to show how tired she really was.

Johan offered to carry her, but she shook her head, chin lifted.

For a while, the forest path was gentle. Their boots crushed the soft carpet of last year's ferns and faded blueberry stems. The rain had left everything smelling clean and faintly green. Lena was the first to break the silence. She began to sing.

Rida, rida ranka, hästen heter Blanka,

Ride, ride the rocker, the horse is named Blanka

Far han red till skogen svart, aldrig kom han åter snart.

Father rode into the darkened wood, and he did not return too soon.

Just a few lines, softly, not quite under her breath. The melody was minor, slow. Words rolled together in a rhythm too smooth for something just made up. It wasn't tuneless either. It had weight and shape. The kind of song learned long ago.

Freya glanced at Johan. He was watching their daughter too with an eyebrow raised.

"Do you know that one?" Freya asked quietly.

Johan shook his head. "No. You?"

"I don't think so." She frowned. "Maybe my mum? Or at school?"

Lena kept singing, oblivious. It felt like the kind of lullaby whispered during fever nights and early winters, when a memory gets passed down without asking.

Freya pulled her jacket tighter. "I don't remember anyone singing that to her."

"She could've picked it up anywhere," Johan said, but his voice lacked conviction.

They let her go on. Neither interrupted.

Sussa, sussa lilla vän, mamma vakar än.

Hush now, hush now little friend, mama still keeps watch.

Solen sjunker bakom fjäll, månen rider silverställd.

The sun sinks behind the mountain's crown, the moon rides out on a silver saddle.

Freya walked closer now, her hand brushing lightly along Lena's back as they walked back to camp. The lullaby ended on a descending note, as if whoever had taught it hadn't finished the last line.

The trees began to thin.

Vindar viskar under gran, vättar smyger över plan.

Winds whisper beneath the fir, the wight creeps across the glade.

Om du somnar, håll dig still, drömmen vet vart den vill.

If you sleep, be very still, dreams will go where they will.

By the time they stepped through the tree-line, the sky was still pale again with a layer of clouds. The clearing was as they'd left it. The tents squatted in their places like they'd been waiting. The fire ring hadn't shifted. Even the stones around it looked cleaner than they should have after rain. Freya paused near the centre of the clearing. Lena had already wandered back to her blanket. Johan stood still beside the orange tent, arms crossed, eyes unfocused. Freya's backpack thudded softly as she dropped it beside the tent. She moved quickly, wordlessly, hands shaking as she rolled up sleeping mats, folding with the precision of someone trying not to scream. Johan sat by the fire-pit, elbows resting on his knees, staring into the shallow ash where the flames had long since died.

She didn't look at him. "We're not waiting another night."

Johan didn't answer.

"She threw up blood this morning," Freya said, her voice sharp now "She's too tired to walk. She didn't eat lunch. Her nose is bleeding."

"She's resting now," Johan murmured.

"She's deteriorating," Freya snapped. "And so are you."

That made him look up. His face was slack, eyes underscored with the kind of grey that didn't come from lack of sleep. His skin looked paler than it had yesterday. Less *alive* somehow.

"I'm fine."

"You're sweating. You've had a headache for a day and a half. You threw up yesterday. You think I didn't notice?" She shoved a sleeping bag into its bag. "We can't play house anymore, Johan. This isn't a game."

He stood slowly, not with any purpose. "Panicking won't fix this. She needs calm. Rest. Not a chaotic hike back through the forest in this weather."

"She needs a doctor."

"Oh, Dra åt skogen!."

Freya froze, turned toward him. "How dare you tell me to go to the forest! What even is your plan? Sit around and hope she stops bleeding?"

Johan flinched at that. Then turned his gaze down, fists clenching. "We can try the road again tomorrow. Maybe it was just the cold. It happens."

"You always do this." Freya's voice cracked. "You pretend everything's fine until it's so broken it can't be fixed."

He snapped, voice suddenly too loud. "Because I *don't get to break down. That's your job.*"

Freya recoiled slightly. Johan swallowed, hands dropping to his sides. "One of us has to stay calm."

There was silence.

The rain had started again. Not a downpour, but a steady whisper threading through the trees. Lena's tent rustled. A faint sound. Fabric brushing against itself. Then the zipper jolted, just slightly. A small face appeared in the gap. Pale. Watching. Johan saw her first. His shoulders sank. Freya turned and followed his gaze. Her expression folded inwards. Lena didn't say anything. Just blinked. Then retreated. The tent zipped shut again.

Johan turned away. He walked toward the tree line with stiff, jerking steps. Branches caught at his coat, but he didn't stop.

Didn't look back. Freya stood in the clearing alone. The clearing settled into silence. Rain traced soft lines through the trees, hushing everything else. Freya didn't move at first. She stood where Johan had left her with her arms folded. Her gaze fixed on nothing. Time passed in that slow, forested way. Minutes, maybe more. Just enough for the stillness to stretch.

Twilight had started to cling like mist, low and silver, softening every edge. Johan returned an hour later with damp boots and slower footsteps. His face looked drawn, like he'd walked the weight off his shoulders. By this time, the rain had subsided. Just a short shower, a staple of a Swedish summer.

Freya was kneeling beside the fire, feeding it thin branches while the ground still lay damp. She didn't stand when she saw him. Just nodded. The air between them was no longer sharp. Lena sat a little to the side, bundled in her blanket, knees pulled to her chest. Her rabbit sat beside her, and Pebble rested like a treasured relic in her lap. A small pencil moved across a scrap of paper; she was drawing something, lines faint and lopsided. When Johan stepped into the clearing, she looked up.

"Hi, pappa," she said, her voice light but a little hoarse.

He smiled. "That's your castle?"

She held it up, squinting one eye as if judging her own work. The paper was smudged with soft graphite, lines etched deep where she'd pressed harder. Trees crowded the edges in sharp, vertical strokes. In the centre: a rough patch of darkness, scribbled deep enough to crease the paper. Two pale circles hovered in the black, eyes or lights, it wasn't clear.

"No," she said. "It's the fire. But big. And something watching it."

Johan's brow twitched. "Watching it?"

She nodded, brushing her curls from her eyes. "Yeah, but it's nice. Like a shadow that stays near you when you're sleeping."

Freya stood, brushing her hands on her jeans. "You've been gone a while."

"Yeah, I walked a bit," Johan said. "Past the lake. Thought I saw ducks." He sat near the fire with a soft grunt, stretching his legs out in front of him. "Turned out to be a rock and a plastic bag."

Freya didn't laugh, but a smile tugged briefly at the corner of her mouth. She passed him a tin with rehydrated stew and half a cracker. Johan sniffed it. "Ah. Military gourmet."

"Don't complain. I didn't add the powdered egg."

"Luxury." He took a bite. Lena shifted slightly, setting her drawing aside. She reached for a cracker and nibbled at it, not quite finishing a bite. Still, she didn't look sick. Not like before. A faint flush had returned to her cheeks. She blinked a little slower, but her eyes weren't dull. They tracked the fire. She hummed under her breath; something tuneless this time.

Johan watched her for a while, his spoon stirring aimlessly. "She's better," he said softly. "Look at her."

Freya didn't look away from the flame. "Maybe."

"Maybe it was something simple. Something passing."

Freya's hands tightened around her tin. "And the car? The phones? The photo glitches?"

"Maybe just bad luck."

She didn't reply.

Johan let out a breath, long and shallow. "She hasn't bled since earlier. No vomiting. Rash looks lighter. I mean... It's possible, isn't it? That she's turned a corner?"

Freya wanted to believe it. She wanted it so badly her throat tightened with the weight of it. Lena took another sip of water and yawned into her sleeve, small shoulders curling forward like a creature burrowing.

After dinner, Lena pushed herself to her feet with a soft grunt and wandered towards her tent. Her limbs moved loosely, as if strung together by thread, each step unsure but determined. The tent flap shifted in the breeze as she climbed inside, pausing halfway. She glanced back once, not quite at Freya, not quite at anything, then disappeared into the canvas gloom.

Inside came the quiet shuffle of her getting ready. The unzipping of a bag. The clumsy tug of fabric. A faint grumble as she struggled with her pyjama top. Then the soft thud of her small frame curling down onto the mat. No complaints. No laughter. Just the gentle rustle of tired flesh against synthetic fabric.

Outside, the fire had fallen to ember-glow. A low, red breath pulsing in the dark. Twilight lingered overhead, refusing to give way to night. Freya crouched by the tent opening, a folded jumper in her hands. She didn't remember packing this one. It smelled faintly of laundry powder and old wool. A thread hung loose from the hem.

She leaned forward and peered inside.

Lena lay on her side, turned away, facing the forest beyond the canvas wall. Her curls fanned across the pillow, sweat-darkened and tangled. The air in the tent resembled pine, plastic, and warm skin. Freya stayed where she was, quiet and still.

"I brought you this," she whispered, setting the jumper beside her daughter. "In case you get cold."

Lena didn't respond at first. Her eyes remained open, steady. Watching the greenish-grey shadows ripple across the tent wall.

"Do you think ghosts are real?" She asked, voice low and level.

Freya blinked. The question sat oddly in the air, like a wind that shouldn't exist. She shifted her weight slightly, dropping to her knees, and reached across to rest her hand on Lena's forehead. Still flushed. Still too warm.

"Why do you ask?"

There was a pause.

"There was a girl," Lena murmured, gaze unmoving. "Last night. I think she was here."

Freya's breath caught. Her hand, still resting against Lena's brow, twitched slightly.

"Sweetheart..."

"She had red shoes," Lena continued, dreamy and flat, as though describing something inevitable. "She didn't say much. But she cried. Really quietly. Like when you're not supposed to make noise. Like the kind of crying that hurts your chest."

Freya kept her hand in place, thumb gently brushing a damp strand from Lena's temple. "Did she talk to you?"

Lena nodded. Barely more than a movement. "She said she used to live by the lake. She said the water got too cold."

Freya's chest tightened. Something about the words sat wrong.

They sounded like pieces of a story, fractured and rearranged. Child-logic. Dream-language. And yet, there was weight to it. Red shoes. Cold lake-water.

A shape of something old stirred in her mind. A memory without a name. A story told once, half-laughed at, then buried in sleep and adult logic. It clawed at the edge of recall, stubborn, unwelcome.

"She said no one ever saw her," Lena whispered. "Even when she screamed. Not even her mummy. She said her mummy let her go under. She said she screamed and kicked and clawed at the sky... But the sky didn't move."

Freya froze listening.

"She said she sank," Lena added. "Because no one was holding her anymore."

The tent was suddenly too quiet. No breeze or bugs. Just the soft rustle of canvas and Freya's breath; shallow and sharp. Her eyes adjusted slowly to the dim light inside. Lena's features were soft, relaxed

"She came into the tent last night," Lena said after a pause. "I didn't hear her come in. But when I opened my eyes... She was there."

Freya gently reached out, pulling the sleeping bag up a little higher on her daughter's chest. "Did she... Say anything else?"

Lena nodded again, slower this time. "She said she wasn't mad. Not at me. Just that it hurts when people look at her. That's why her eyes are bright. She doesn't like being seen."

Freya blinked, startled. "Bright?"

"They glowed," Lena murmured. "Like fire. She was all shadows except her eyes. But she wasn't scary."

Freya said nothing. Just leaned closer, brushing damp curls off Lena's forehead. Her pulse thudded in her throat.

"She only stayed a little while," Lena said. "Then she was gone again. She said she goes where people forget."

A silence settled then, thick as the soil beneath them. Freya pressed a kiss to her daughter's forehead, more to anchor herself than anything else. Lena rolled onto her side, Pebble tucked under her chin, already halfway to sleep. Outside, the camp-fire hissed in the damp air. Inside the tent, Freya stayed there a moment longer, watching her. Johan stood near the fire, unmoving. He'd overheard enough to have growing concerns.

"She's been sick," Freya said again, her voice more to herself than him.

Johan's gaze didn't shift. "That's not a Vittra story."

Freya gave a short hum of agreement. Silence settled again. Clouds hadn't shifted all evening. Forest stillness held. Thick and watchful. The fire had burned low. Johan sat with knees drawn up, journal balanced on one thigh, pen loose in hand. Ember-light made the ink glisten like blood that hadn't dried.

> *She smiled today. Maybe it's enough. Maybe I don't need anything more than that.*

He paused, scratching the edge of his hairline with the pen's tip. Something felt loose. He looked down. A clump of blonde strands clung to his fingers. His breath caught, just for a second. He wiped them on his jeans like dirt and kept writing.

Freya still watches everything like it's a test. I used to love that about her. That she never let the world just happen. I used to want her to look at me like that. Now I just want her to stop.

The words didn't make him feel better. But they anchored something. A page in time. A held breath. His thoughts of being grounded felt interrupted. A hum beneath the earth had returned. Faint, low, like standing near a high-voltage cable. It buzzed in the base of his skull. In his jaw. Johan set the pen down and pressed his palms into the dirt. Warm. Constant.

Freya had taken a seat opposite Johan whilst he was writing. Lena's voice lingered in Freya's head. The words hadn't faded. If anything, they'd grown louder since she'd crept from the tent. Not just the story of the girl with red shoes, but the way Lena had said it. Without fear. Like the shadow in her tent had been as natural as rainfall.

"She said no one heard her scream."

Not a Vittra, not a creature from the woods. A child. Drowned. Forgotten. Left to linger beneath the surface of still water. A Myling? The word sat unspoken between them. Freya didn't want to say it aloud. It didn't feel like a name; it felt like a warning. A secret meant to stay quiet.

Johan didn't ask about what he overheard from the tent. His eyes were distant, fixed on the edge of the fire-pit where the embers bled slowly into the dirt. There was something about his posture. The slow curl of his spine. The way his hands clenched and unclenched suggested he wasn't entirely here either.

Freya sighed. The warmth of the fire wasn't reaching her anymore. Lena had described the girl in her tent like she was someone remembered. Not imagined. The way children sometimes remember things adults never told them. Freya wanted to change the subject rambling in her head.

"You always liked nearly getting us killed" Freya breaking the silence across to Johan.

Johan arched his eyebrow. "Is that a metaphor?"

"You know what I mean," she said, half-smiling. "Camping in winter. Wild hikes. Making fires on top of warm dirt like it's just luck." She looked over at him. "Remember the trip to Sarek?"

He snorted. "When you fell through the ice and blamed me for melting it?"

"It was *your* idea to test how deep the snow was... With your leg."

He chuckled, shaking his head. "We nearly froze that night."

"You snored in the tent so loud you must've scared the only elk away twenty kilometres."

Johan smiled despite himself. "Good times."

They stayed like that for a while, fire snapping gently beside them. Freya tilted her head, studying the shadows that danced across Johan's face. Her voice softened.

"She's strong, you know. Like you."

He didn't answer, but she saw the movement in his throat, a swallow too slow to pass unnoticed. Sparks twisted up into the blue. Freya shifted across the fire, attempting to warm herself against the dying embers. Her knee brushed his. Then her fingers came to rest near his, not quite touching, just close enough to feel the warmth radiate across skin.

Their hands sat like unanswered questions.

Smoke clung to the silence between them. Johan glanced sideways. Their eyes met. Held. Neither looked away. She leaned in. Not far. Just enough for breath to mingle. Cold gave way to proximity. A strand of hair slipped across her cheek, lit faintly at the edges by firelight. A few years ago, this would've been reflex. Familiarity in motion. Muscle memory.

Johan didn't move closer. He didn't back away. A tremor flickered in his hand. Faint. Almost imagined. She didn't pull back. Didn't speak. Her expression held unreadable. When the quiet returned, it felt sharper. Hungrier. Eventually, her hand dropped into her lap. Still, she said nothing. Johan was the one who looked away.

"You've always been a coward," she muttered.

"I've always been tired," he replied.

They didn't speak again. Freya rose first, brushing ash from her palms. "Get some sleep," she murmured, turning toward her tent. "You'll need it."

Johan lingered. Then reached for the journal. He closed it slowly, smudging the last line without realising.

It was time for some rest.

Consume

The sky hadn't yet decided if it was morning. That thin blue-grey that clung to everything; neither dusk nor daylight. Just that stretched-out cold Scandinavian stillness. It wrapped the clearing in quiet and left the trees looking like paper cut-outs, unmoving and sharp.

Johan sat cross-legged beside the fire-pit. A half-burnt log crackled faintly under the ash. He hadn't stoked it. He hadn't touched it at all. The warmth still clung to the ground though, like a second skin. His journal lay open on his knee, the corner of the page fluttering occasionally in the breeze. Ink bled slightly where the tip had paused too long. His handwriting was neat by force of habit, a carpenter's steadiness, but it was sloping now. Hesitant.

> *Day... Five? Doesn't feel like it. Time slips differently out here. Light never really leaves. Maybe that's why I can't sleep. Maybe it's not the light. I keep seeing something by the tree-line. Still. Watching. I know what withdrawals*
> *feel   like. This isn't that.*

> *He stopped. The silence was too complete. It didn't feel hollow like a city at 3am; it was thick. Close.*

His pen tapped once on the page.

I used to wake up hearing birds. Now I wake up because I don't.

Another line scratched. Then scratched out.

Freya was right. The air tastes wrong. It sticks to your mouth.

A rustle. Not behind. Not ahead. Off to the side. In the trees where needles hung heavy and the trunks pressed too close. Johan turned his head slowly. Nothing.

The hairs on his arms rose. He stared into the green-topped distance, pen frozen mid-air. Thinking back before the nausea, before the copper sting on his tongue. He started a new sentence but faltered halfway through. His pen hovered, uncertain. The wind started to consume the forest. It carried the scent of pine and wet stone. Something else, too. Metallic. Sour.

The journal closed with a soft thud. Johan laid it beside him, fingers trembling faintly. He rubbed his temple with the edge of his thumb.

Freya awoke with a soft cough, dry and sharp against the back of her throat. The inside of the tent was bathed in that dull diffusion. Sunlight filtered through layers of nylon, giving everything a washed-out look. She blinked once, then again, before pushing herself upright.

Her phone sat just where she'd left it. The screen lit under her thumb: 3% battery. No signal. She reached for the small power bank from the rucksack at her feet, fingertips clumsy with cold. The cable clicked in place. Nothing. No charge. The indicator light blinked once, then died completely.

She frowned, checking the connection again, but it was no use.

The pack was dead. She sighed through her nose and pulled at the zip. The teeth parted with a soft rasp, noticing Johan sat by the fire.

"The battery pack's flat," she called, her voice low and still rough from sleep.

"Yours too?" Johan's voice came from somewhere nearby. She saw him rise to his feet, one hand raised halfway in response. He turned without speaking further and began walking the narrow path toward the car, shoulders hunched slightly.

Freya watched as the trees swallowed him. She lingered, sat at the edge of the tent flap. One hand rested on the canvas listening to the forest. Still no birds. Nor hum of insects.

Johan's boots tracked quietly through soaked earth from yesterday's showers. Moss softly crunched beneath each tired step. The further he moved from the clearing, the cooler the air felt. Less suffocating. A breeze moved here, low to the ground, sliding over ferns and slick bark. It smelt faintly of resin, not like industry.

The Volvo sat crouched at the end of the trail, still streaked with dried mud from the drive in. A scatter of pine needles had begun to gather in the corners of the windscreen, and moisture clung to the door handles, beading in slow droplets that never quite fell. The car looked untouched. Undisturbed, like for its owner to return. Johan opened the driver's side door and slid in. The seat was damp with humidity, the fabric clinging cold through his jeans. Familiar, though.

Key in ignition.

Key turned.

A slow crank. The dash lights flickered once. Then nothing. Just a flat, final click. Johan sighed, and tried again.

Once.

Twice.

The car was dead.

He leaned back against the seat. The key hung there, useless. No lights. No engine roar. The silence in the car was stale. Stale as the trapped air and the faint smell of damp fabric. He sat still. Listening. The only sound was his own breath, slow and deliberate. After a moment, he leaned forward and opened the glovebox. Paper rattled like dry leaves. Crumpled receipts, an old multi-tool, maps with edges softened from years of folding. He pawed through them without purpose, knowing nothing in there would help. No power pack could be found either. He got out, and swung open the back door.

The rear seat was heaped with leftover gear. Sleeping mats, a tangled fishing line, one of Lena's jumpers crumpled in the corner. Beneath it, wedged against the foot-well, was a duffel bag he didn't remember packing. Grey canvas. Stiff Zip.

Inside: Freya's things. A spare hoodie, matching socks bundled together, one of his old t-shirts she still wore for sleep. They smelled faintly of her. Detergent and something flower-like. Beneath them all, cocooned in another sweater, something hard clinked against his knuckles.

He reached in and pulled out a bottle. An amber bottle. An all too familiar shape.

The label was frayed, gold foil dulled to a tired brass sheen. A brand he recognised instantly: cheap Irish. The kind that pretended warmth but burned all the way down. The cap sat slightly askew, the seal of the nearly-flat bottle was already cracked. He didn't open it. Just held the bottle in both hands, turning it slowly. Its weight gave a soft slosh.

Even sealed, the scent was rising. Not strong, just a trace, enough to stir something. Old oak. Vanilla. A sweetness that stuck to the back of the throat.

He sat with it for a while. Let the moment draw out. This wasn't a choice. Not yet. The woods stood behind him. Silent. The camp tucked somewhere between trunks and cold earth. Freya would be waiting. Or she wouldn't.

He twisted the cap, just far enough to feel the thread catch. Then stopped. The bottle didn't return to the duffel. He turned it again, thumb brushing the torn edge of the label. A promise in foil and glass, one he'd broken before.

He should've shoved it under the mats. Left it in the boot. Tossed it into the lake without a second thought. Instead, his grip tightened. The glass weighed heavy in his palm. Like it wanted to be held.

Just in case, he thought.

Just... In case.

He slipped it inside his coat, where the lining still smelled faintly of forest smoke and sweat. It rested against his ribs like a secret. Not yet a sin. Not yet a crime. Just something he hadn't done. He sighed, sharp and quiet. A battery pack waited in the duffel. A green light blinking steadily, oblivious. He held it for a moment longer than needed, then flicked it on.

The car door shut with a hollow sound. A tone that didn't quite echo. When he stepped back onto the path, the light had shifted again; flatter, duller. The air held a different weight now. The kind that stuck to your skin like damp wool.

He started his trek back to the camp-site. For the whole half hour or so, he kept thinking of the glass bottle pressing against his ribs. When he arrived, Johan sat on the edge of his sleeping mat at the mouth of his tent. His elbows pressed to his knees. His boots were muddy, the laces stiff with dried grit. A patch of ash clung to the side where he'd kicked out the fire too fast earlier. His hands were still. For once.

His coat lay to rest next to him. The bottle sat beside his thigh, hidden beneath the fold of his coat like a secret whispered to the dirt. He didn't touch it. Not yet. He looked around the clearing.

Freya stood near the tents, frowning at her phone with the screen dim. Her battery now completely dead. She tapped it once. She shook her head. Johan reached into his coat, holding out the battery pack he had just collected from the car. The green light blinked steadily. Still holding charge. He didn't say anything, just kept his hand extended toward her. She took it without thanks, her fingers brushing his in passing.

"Going to try the ridge again," she said, already turning. "Might catch a bar this time."

She walked off without waiting for a reply, phone in one hand, cable trailing like a tether. Johan watched until the trees swallowed her shape. And then, only then, did he move. He reached inside his coat. The cap gave a soft pop. Nothing dramatic. Just a dull twist of something already half-open. He didn't hesitate this time. He just raised it, tipped a shallow swig into his mouth. No toast. No breath held.

It burned. Burned more than he remembered.

The swallow chased itself down his throat and lodged somewhere low. Not warm. Not comforting. Just heat, narrow and sharp, tracing a path to his core. Like swallowing a nail and feeling it stay lodged in your throat. His hands remained steady, but something beneath his ribs drew in. He screwed the cap back on. Quick and quiet. Wiped his mouth with the edge of his thumb, then slid the bottle under the sleeping mat. Out of sight.

He rose, slowly, and wandered toward the fire-pit. The ring of stones looked smaller than he remembered. They had sunk deeper into the dirt, as if the ground had tried to swallow them. Johan nudged one with his boot. A cloud of cold soot lifted, then settled across the toe of his boot like dust on old furniture. The fire hadn't been lit since breakfast. He turned and walked back to his tent.

The mat gave way under him. A faint clink from underneath. The bottle pressed through the fabric. Still there. He pulled it free again. Held it in his hands without ceremony. The glass had lost its chill. It now felt like part of him. He twisted the cap and took a second swig.

More this time.

It didn't catch in his throat. It didn't claw at his chest. The second always went down easier. His breath leaked between his teeth in a slow sigh. He tipped the bottle in the light, watching the amber pool slide against the inside of the bottle. The label peeled further at the corner, soft with wear. He caught it with his thumb and rubbed at it absently.

He waited. For guilt, maybe. Or some invisible line to appear. It didn't. He drank again.

At the edge of the clearing, Lena's humming had returned. Not the lullaby this time. Something wordless, broken into fragments. She wandered in small arcs between the tents, rabbit in tow, dragging one limp arm behind her like a prop in a forgotten play. Her feet made no sound against the moss.

She crouched near a patch of lichen, whispered to something unseen, then stood again and drifted toward the trees. Not far. Just enough to make Johan's eyes track her. He didn't call out. Didn't rise. She wasn't running around. That was something.

He drank again. The third swallow didn't even register. It slipped into him like a breath. He screwed the cap back on and slid the bottle under the mat again. Stored like a tool. Something you might need. Something that belonged.

Then he lay back. Arms loose. Head tilted slightly. The warmth from the ground bled up through the mat and soaked into his spine. He let it hold him.

Time frayed a little.

The rustle of branches cut across the clearing. He blinked up.

Freya had returned with her phone in hand. Her thumb tapping at the screen as if brute persistence could summon a reply. The battery pack blinked dimly in her other hand. Her hair was wind-tangled. She scanned the camp like someone re-entering a room they hadn't meant to leave. Lena gave a vague wave and kept humming. Still pacing, still drifting. Still somewhere else.

Freya's gaze settled on Johan. Still seated. Still distant.

"We need to get the fire going again," she said eventually, voice flat.

He shrugged. "Later."

"No," she said, crouching to unzip a pack. "Lunches and dinners won't cook themselves"

Freya pulled out Lena's flask then unscrewed the cap. She sniffed it. Then frowned.

"It's warm," she muttered. "This water needs to be changed." She turned. "Were you even watching her?"

Johan's head tilted. "She didn't go far."

"She's sick, Johan. You need to *keep track* of her!"

His jaw tightened, but he kept his voice level. "She's stable. Better than yesterday."

Freya stood shaking her head.

That landed true. The bottle pressed into him beneath the mat, warm now from his body. Yet still familiar and comforting. He didn't reach for it again, not yet. But his mind constantly thought about it. A breeze sighed through the treetops. Freya's silhouette moved between tents, slower now, her shoulders stiff with something unspoken.

Lena wandered a lazy loop around the clearing, dragging her rabbit through the thin moss like a plough. She paused near a clump of ferns and crouched, whispering something inaudible. Maybe to herself, maybe not. When she stood again, she held a stick like a ladle.

"I'll stir," she said, stepping closer to Freya's side. "I used to do this with mormor."

Freya had just started making lunch while Johan sat idle admiring the empty sky. Freya glanced down at her, surprised but soft. She passed Lena a spoon. "Stir gently."

Together they hovered near the pot, the scent of lukewarm stew curling upward. Lena hummed under her breath, she'd always be humming unknown tunes lately. Her hair clung to her forehead, damp with sweat despite the chill. Freya didn't mention it, though concern showed on her face.

Johan watched them from a few feet away, elbows on knees, hands clasped loosely. The scene should've looked ordinary. A girl cooking with her mother. But it didn't. Something about the posture, the pace, the lack of insects. Even Johan, now tipsy, felt more concerned about their surroundings.

Eventually, Freya portioned out the food, handing Johan his with a nod. No words. No eye contact. They ate in silence, sat around the now half-hearted fire, chewing their lunch slowly without conviction. Lena picked at a slice of dry bread, pulling it into little pieces to feed the ants that never came. She'd been quiet all morning, until now.

"She said she used to live by the lake," Lena said suddenly, mouth full of bread. "The girl. My new friend."

Freya looked up. "The one with the red shoes?"

Lena nodded. "She said that people used to come here, but not anymore. They stopped listening. That's why she's still here."

Johan tried to meet Freya's eyes, but she was watching Lena too closely.

"She told me her name, but I can't remember it now," Lena continued, leaning her head sideways against her bunny. "She said her mum put her under the water because she wouldn't stop crying."

Freya's breath caught, but she didn't speak.

Johan stood up without a word, brushing crumbs from his jeans, and crossed to the tent. He crouched inside for a moment, unzipped a side pocket in his bag, and pulled out the leather-bound journal. He returned to the fire, flipping the book open on his knee, pen already in hand.

Lena wandered off again after just a few bites of her stew. Freya watched her go, hugging the bunny under one arm and humming faintly under her breath. The song had no melody. Just breath and rhythm.

Johan's pen dragged across the page, his handwriting slower now, more deliberate. He paused. Let the tip rest against the paper as if the next word refused to come. The edge of the journal curled in the breeze, a ripple against still fingers.

Freya shifted closer, just enough to see the tension in his shoulders: how he was hunched, how his breath didn't rise evenly. The air between them was laced with something sour. Familiar in a way she wished it wasn't. She caught it then. That scent.

"You've been drinking," she said. Quietly. No accusation in her tone, just a cold kind of knowing.

His head jerked up. But it wasn't denial. Freya didn't continue to answer right away. Her eyes narrowed, studying the way his pupils looked darker. His movements were too careful.

"You smell like it," she said. "And you're quieter than usual."

He closed the journal with more force than necessary. The sound was soft, but final. "It wasn't much," he muttered. "Just a little. This morning."

She watched him for a moment longer, gaze steady. Then let out a slow breath. Not quite a sigh. "So you brought it back here. Carried it in. And hid it."

Johan's jaw flexed. "It was in your bag."

"And you kept it," she bickered back.

His voice, when it came again, was softer. "I didn't mean to drink it."

"But you did."

"I stayed, Freya."

"I know."

Her hands opened slightly at her sides, then closed again. She stepped forward. Not confrontational. Something gentler. Quieter.

"You still have it?"

He hesitated.

Then, wordlessly, reached beneath the sleeping mat. He drew out the bottle with both hands. Its pale gold liquid, half-full. The glass glinted like something buried and unearthed. He held it out to her without meeting her eyes.

Freya grabbed it with no words. She turned toward the trees. Unscrewed the cap, then poured it away. The sound was almost nothing. Just a soft glug as amber liquid met moss. The soil drank fast. The scent rose briefly, bitter yet sweet, then vanished into the forest floor like it had never been.

She held the empty bottle a moment longer, thumb brushing the rim. Then let it hang at her side. Johan hadn't moved. She handed the empty bottle back. "You can keep the bottle if you want. Something to look at."

Johan didn't respond. Just watched the empty curve of it catch the grey light. Hollow. Just like him, some days. Freya sat down again. Not close. But not far.

"I swear, Johan, sometimes I think you're a dane." She muttered, breaking the tension that had clung in the air from the confrontation.

Johan only replied with a slight smirk. He picked up the pen again. He scratched out the last thing he'd written and started a new line. She saw that his hands were still shaking. But he didn't stop writing. After a couple more lines, Johan needed air. He told Freya he'd fetch more firewood. She gave an acknowledging smile but remained silent.

Johan slipped past the tents without a word, boots silent on the damp bed of pine. The light had gone strange; a flat grey that seeped through the trees rather than falling from above. He didn't glance back. Whatever waited behind was quieter than what lay ahead.

The undergrowth thickened quickly. Low ferns curled toward his knees, snagging at the fabric of his trousers. Birch trunks leaned like question marks with their bark peeling in strips the colour of old paper. The air had a weight to it here. He didn't bother with firewood yet. Deeper into the forest he went, like something leading him unconsciously.

A raven called once across the ridge. A single mechanical caw that didn't echo. Then nothing. At the edge of a shallow dip, the trees began to part. A natural grove, ringed in pale birch. The trunks rose like bones, peeled clean and bare, untouched by moss.

And then, between the trees, someone stood. Still. Deliberate.

The figure lingered. Slender, unmoving, carved from shadow and stillness. Mid-turn, perhaps. Her face was obscured by the tilt of her head and the weight of long hair. Tangled and dark, the colour of wet moss, trailing past her waist. No breeze disturbed it. No motion at all. She looked like she'd been there a long time, waiting in the same position.

What might have been a dress clung to her. Threaded like lichen, or bark softened by rot. The shade was wrong for this place. Birch-grey, but heavy. Stained with age. Fused to her rather than worn.

Johan blinked. Once. Then again.

Where she stood, the forest seemed altered. The birch trees nearest her had darkened along their trunks, bark blistered in places, mottled with a quiet decay that hadn't been there before. As if her presence hadn't just occupied space but it had infected it. The shadows around her clung with purpose, the ground beneath her feet sunken slightly. She didn't move. Didn't breathe either. She just was. Present and eternal.

It was as though the forest had grown around her, or she had been waiting there long enough that the trees decided to make room. Johan's heart beat louder than his footsteps. His breath turned shallow, cold in the back of his throat. Then came the sound.

A harp.

It didn't feel like music... Not something played. Yet, it was present. Everywhere. The suggestion of strings being drawn through the soil. Soft crescendos echoed through the forest in waves too even to be wind. The sound vibrated behind his teeth. Behind his eyes. It crawled up through the soles of his boots like something searching his body.

He swayed, just slightly. The weight of his body no longer sitting quite right. The air felt denser, as though he'd stepped behind glass without knowing it. Like the forest wasn't a place anymore, but a stage set behind thin plastic. His fingertips tingled. A rising hum in his chest mimicked the resonance of the sound, like a tuning fork struck somewhere behind his heart. The edges of things: bark, leaves, the dark curve of the figure ahead. It all seemed rimmed with a faint brightness, like after staring at a candle too long.

Johan blinked again. Once. Twice.

The figure hadn't moved, but something about her shape had moved. Her head now slightly more turned. The drape of her moss-dark hair changed, thinner at the ends, like river-weed left to dry. He took one step forward. The world leaned with him, and the weight in his chest didn't shift back. Her head turned just enough to catch the barest angle of movement. No face. Or not that he could see.

She stepped backward, folding into the birches, vanishing with a motion so fluid it almost looked like falling. No sound of retreat. No crunch of moss. Just the trees, shivering slightly like someone had exhaled through them.

Johan stood frozen, throat tight, the weight of the forest pressing close. The damp stuck to his skin like sap. Something in him said *leave*. But something else, old and irrational, pulled him forward. He stepped once. Another pace. His boots sank slightly into the moss, its softness deceptive. Then again. Still nothing. The trail was gone. A flicker. To the right this time. A pale shoulder vanishing behind a birch. He moved without thinking.

"Wait..."

His voice sounded wrong in the stillness. Too loud. Like it had been dropped in water and echoed back in a different shape. He pushed through the undergrowth. Branches whispered against his coat, snagged at his sleeves. The earth was slicker here, the moss giving underfoot like wet velvet.

There! Ahead again. The silhouette. Slender and drifting. Her feet never quite met the forest floor. Just far enough to be uncertain. Johan picked up pace. His legs didn't feel like his own anymore. Heavy in the wrong places. Light in others. Running without knowing why.

She turned a little more this time. Just a tilt. Enough for him to catch the glint of something where a face should've been. The suggestion of wet stone for eyes. A body without a spine. A glimpse of a tail.

He stumbled forward. A low branch clawed at his temple. He didn't stop. The trees thickened. Too fast. The light blinked in and out through the canopy, stuttering like a failing bulb. His breath came shorter now, sharp in his nose, iron on the tongue.

Another flash of motion, now behind him. He turned too fast, lost footing, caught himself on a trunk that felt warm. Too warm. Bark flaked beneath his palm like scabbed paint.

He pressed on. Another shape ahead. Another flicker of moss-coloured hair. Always turning away. Always leading. His limbs ached. His thoughts felt misted, memory bleeding around the edges. Had he passed that tree before? That split in the trunk like a knuckle pressed through skin?

Everything looked the same. Everything looked wrong. The forest had closed behind him. Every direction looked like the last. He turned again. Nothing. Then again. Still nothing. The trail was gone. He felt it before he saw it; panic rising like bile. Every step he took now felt circular. Familiar roots. The same rock. The same lichen-slick trunk. The forest closing in, not with movement, but with sameness. He stumbled once. Righted himself.

Then suddenly; light.

Not ahead, but above. The faintest break in the canopy. He turned, followed it with uneven breath. And there, like a mirage, the trail again. Dirt, not moss. Flattened pine needles and the brittle crunch of homeward steps. The figure was no more. It had led him astray. But he found a familiar path.

Johan didn't run anymore. Although, his pace got faster and faster. By the time he reached the clearing, twilight again, dim and low. Freya sat near the empty fire-pit. No fire had been lit. The old pit remained cold and grey, ash settled deep in its cracks.

Freya sat cross-legged near it, brushing Lena's hair with slow, deliberate strokes. The girl leaned into her, wrapped in the fleece blanket, head tilted just slightly like she might doze off again. Freya's eyes didn't move from her daughter, but her hand faltered. Another small clump of hair had come away with the brush. Not much, just a pinch. But enough. She didn't say anything. Just closed her hand around it.

Johan stepped into the clearing. He wasn't carrying wood. Freya looked up. Saw his face. Something about it made her sit straighter.

"You've been gone over an hour, Johan! And where's the firewood?"

He didn't speak immediately. Just walked toward them, slower than usual, eyes darting between Freya and Lena.

"There's something out there," he said.

Freya raised an eyebrow. "A fox again?"

"No," he said, too quickly. "I mean, it wasn't an animal."

Freya stopped brushing. Lena moved her weight faintly, murmured something and then went quiet again.

"Something watching?" She asked.

Johan ran a hand through his hair, his fingers snagged. "No. It's not like that. I saw something. A figure. Woman-shaped. Half in the trees, like... Like the forest swallowed her halfway through."

Freya frowned, but didn't argue. "Did she speak?"

Johan shook his head as he started getting dinner prepared. Firewood was quickly gathered from the edge of the clearing as normal. No more wandering into the forest. They ate quietly that evening, if it could be called eating. Freya had insisted on something hot. Boiled water, packet soup, the last of the good bread. Johan managed a few spoonfuls before setting his cup aside. Lena cradled hers in both hands like it was just something warm to hold.

The fire spat gently in the pit. Freya tried to pretend the silence wasn't oppressive. Lena blinked slowly, watching the steam rise from her bowl. She lifted the spoon to her lips but didn't sip. Her wrist trembled. A small fleck of broth dribbled down her chin. Freya reached over instinctively with a cloth and dabbed it away.

A faint red bloom had spread along the curve of Lena's neck, just under her jawline. It hadn't been there that morning. Freya was sure of it. The rash had spread.

"Sweetheart," Freya said softly. "Tilt your head for me."

Lena obeyed without question. Her skin was flushed, slightly damp. The rash followed a broken pattern, like splintered veins beneath the surface. Freya brushed her thumb along the edge of it. It wasn't raised, not dry. Just a red, angry rash. Spreading like poisoned Ivy. Lena winced.

"Does it itch?" Freya asked.

"A little," Lena murmured.

Freya looked across the fire at Johan, who hadn't noticed. He was staring into the flames, arms resting loosely on his knees, fingers slack. Freya stood, almost too suddenly. "I'm going to check something," she said. "Be back in a minute."

Johan didn't respond. Lena barely moved, her spoon now resting upside down on her thigh.

Freya stepped into the darker part of camp, toward her pack. The forest loomed just outside the fire's reach. For the first time, it felt like it had moved closer. Freya didn't go straight to the tent. She walked past it. The trees broke in a thin line just beyond, where the slope tipped gently toward the lake. The air was cooler here. The water still, as if the glacier lake had forever been untouched.

She sat on a fallen log just above the shoreline, pulling the battery pack from her coat pocket and slotting in the phone. It buzzed weakly, the screen catching her reflection in the dark glass before it opened.

Six percent battery. No signal. Still, she tried.

Child symptoms rash vomiting fatigue

The spinning wheel held for too long. She waited patiently. When the page finally loaded, it gave her everything and nothing: allergic reactions, contact dermatitis, sunstroke, tainted water. A blog post on pine pollen allergies.

Nothing jumped out. She kept scrolling through as the responses got worse.

Someone had replied with a photo of a tick. A conspiracy theory: poisoned by dirt, an advert for Iodine. Nothing seemed appropriate. Instead she clicked instead on a 1177 link; the Swedish health guide. The page half-loaded, offered general symptoms but no answer Freya switched to her messages. Claire still hadn't responded. The photo had gone through, timestamped from the morning. No read receipt. No reply.

Freya looked out over the lake. The water didn't move. The light had faded from the tops of the trees. A bird called out once, then went quiet. She stayed a moment longer, then rose. Her knees cracked as she stood. The battery was down to five percent.

Back at camp, Johan sat alone by the fire. His knees drawn up, the journal propped against one thigh. Lena had taken herself to bed. Not unusual recently but very rare she'd be so eager to get rest at home. The flames had dulled to embers now, burning low and slow; more glow than heat.

He'd written the date. Nothing else. The ink bled slightly into the grain of the paper. After a long pause, he added:

Lena threw up again. She says she's not cold, but her hands shake. Freya's scared. I can see it in the way she moves

He stared at the next line for a long time before continuing.

> *I relapsed today. There was a bottle of whisky in a bag. Yet ever since, I feel someone watching. This isn't withdrawal. Doesn't feel like last time.*

He stopped. Crossed it out. He tapped the pen against his knee.

The trees are still. I don't like it.

He underlined the last four words, then smudged them out with his thumb. The page looked worse with the mark erased. He closed the leather journal softly. The sun had set to its usual position, just underneath the horizon. It's light still filling the sky with civil twilight.

Freya stepped back into camp without speaking. She didn't look at him, just walked past the fire and toward the tent. Her shoulders were stiff, arms folded against her chest. He watched her stand there a moment longer, just outside the tent flap. As if listening for something. Or waiting for the strength to go inside.

She didn't mention the messages. Or the lake. Or the rash. He didn't ask.

Ease

Silence felt less tense today. Not heavy with menace, nor threaded with unseen eyes. An indifferent stillness, stretching from birch-shadows edge to edge. Freya blinked herself into waking. Her body hesitated, slow to believe the new day. Light bled through the tent fabric. Its usual diffused grey, unwilling to give any actual sunshine. She lay still for a moment with her spine prickling. Eventually, she moved. Carefully. A quiet shrug out of blankets, bare feet brushing the chill mat beneath her. Damp air clung to the inside of her jacket as she pulled it on. She reached for the zip, and the tent's edge peeled back with a rasp.

Birch stood sentinel in every direction, yet they seemed so far away from the dirt-floored clearing. Lena remained cocooned in the purple tent. Curled in a child's instinctive shape, arms drawn close, Pebble nestled against her throat. Breath shallow and steady, seen by her silhouette rising and falling softly. No more muttering. No shivering. No cries dragged up from fever-induced dreams. Only the small, human sounds of sleep.

Freya glanced over with a nervous twitch of her lips, almost a smile. It should have been comforting. But the silence gave way to distrust. As if the forest was hollow. The quiet that comes after things have been abandoned. By both humans and animals. Even the trees. Freya stepped towards the fire pit. Cold ash mounded in soft folds where flame danced the evening before. No glow lingered. No scent of smoke. Yet beneath the soot-stained stones, heat clung thin and stubborn. She crouched, hand hovering above the centre. Always warm.

Stretching slowly, she felt the ache unwind through her back and into her skull. After many days, the pains felt familiar. The headache never quite left. It had simply become part of her mornings, like damp socks or brittle breath. She moved through a morning ritual. Checked the stove. Revised the water bottles. Counted the firewood. A routine assembled from stubbornness. Then finally, time for a morning coffee.

Behind her, a sound. Gravel under boot. Johan emerged from the orange tent, journal tucked beneath one arm. His eyes met hers, steadier than yesterday. Still pale, but not the ashen cast she'd grown used to. There was no heel drag. No hiss of breath through clenched teeth. For a moment, he looked like the man she used to know. The one who swung axes and split logs.

"Morning," he said, with a bounce in his voice. "You're up early."

"So are you," Freya replied, analysing him with an unreadable expression.

Johan nodded, glancing toward Lena's tent. "She okay?"

"She seemed to have slept. Properly, this time." Freya paused. "Didn't even call out once."

He crouched beside the fire-pit, fingers brushing one of the stones without flinching. He too was wondering about a toasty early morning coffee. They didn't say anything more for a while. Johan pulled out his journal and sat cross-legged on the nearest flat rock, flipping to a blank page. The sound of the pen scratching was soft but definite; each line a tether back to normality. Freya listened to it while the kettle warmed.

Behind them, the tent rustled. A soft groan, a yawn, then Lena's voice:

"Mamma... I want a toasted sandwich. With cheese. Real cheese."

Freya turned, surprised, as Lena poked her head through the flap, eyes squinting at the light.

"You hate cheese," Johan said, perched on his rock.

"Not anymore," Lena replied, rubbing her eyes with one fist. "But it has to be melty."

Freya managed a small smile. "We don't have cheese."

Lena sighed dramatically, crawling out with her blanket still wrapped around her like a cape. "Then just something crunchy. Not soup. No more soup."

It felt like a rehearsed tantrum of a child wanting to cause a little mischief. Freya knelt and caught Lena's face gently in her hand, pressing the backs of her fingers against her daughter's cheek. Warm, but not hot. Her eyes weren't bloodshot anymore. Her lips didn't tremble either. The rash, what Freya could see of it above the collarbone, had faded to the soft pink of a healing graze.

Johan looked up from his writing, folding the journal shut with a soft thud. "She's demanding food. Must be a miracle."

The kettle upon the newly re-lit fire-pit began to whistle. In the stillness that followed, nothing cracked. Just the low steam curl of water while the three came together in the cold early sun. After breakfast, or something akin to it, Freya declared the day a quiet one.

No hiking. No foraging. No shivering up wet paths to chase a mobile signal that only blinked alive when no one was looking. Just rest. Although Freya felt a little under the weather while the other two seemed to have recovered just fine. At least, they felt fine. Maybe there was a little too much worrying on her part, she thought. Lena didn't argue. She was still wrapped in the blanket like a cocoon, cross-legged beside the flattened fire pit. Her curls were a mess of sleep, and she'd drawn little faces into the dust with a stick: a line of heads with too many eyes and lopsided smiles.

Johan knelt by the fire pit, nudging a blackened stone with the toe of his boot. Warmth still crept up through packed soil. He felt his face easier than it had felt days, more relaxed. Freya seemed quieter too this morning; less tightly wound, Maybe because Lena no longer looked like a ghost. He glanced over. Freya and Lena were sprawled across a patch of moss, sketch-pads and pencils spread between them like a picnic. Arts and crafts had never been his thing.

"Feels like it's finally turning," he said, brushing grit from his palms. "She's got colour again."

Freya didn't answer straight away. She was focused on Lena's page, her face unreadable. Johan stood with a groan, rolling his shoulders. "Might try the lake again. If she wants something other than soup for lunch, I'd better go catch it."

Lena perked up. "Can I have the crispy skin bit? Oh! And last time you made the fire too hot," she added brightly. "It smelled like mummy's hair straightener."

"Noted," Johan replied with a smirk. He moved to grab his rod and the old knife he kept lashed in a belt sheath, then pulled on his boots with a grunt.

"If you see any dragons," Lena called, "tell them I'm busy."

Freya gave a quiet snort. "And not to touch your rock."

Lena nodded solemnly, lifting Pebble. "She bites."

Johan raised a hand in a lazy half-wave and stepped into the tree-line, disappearing down the slope that led to the lake. His boots made almost no sound on the damp forest floor. Freya watched until the last flick of his jacket sleeve vanished behind the birch trunks. The silence returned. Thick, and full of things that chose not to speak.

Lena dumped her drawing supplies on it with a sigh like an overworked artist and immediately began scribbling with a red pencil that had lost its eraser. Freya arranged herself slowly. Her legs out, back propped against her bag. Her spine ached more than it should've, but she didn't say it aloud. She just watched her daughter move. Lena hummed as she worked. Not the eerie tune from days past. Something lighter with more melody. Freya didn't recognise it although it sounded like something from a cartoon theme song or the opening jingle of a video that looped endlessly in their apartment back home.

"What are you drawing?" She asked, reaching over to brush a fallen leaf from Lena's hair. The leaf fell away with a small clump of hair.

They sat in a patch of grey-dappled light, the blanket spread over moss that never quite dried. Lena hunched over her sketchpad, a cluster of coloured pencils fanned out around her like knives in soft shades. Graphite, pale ochre, blood red dulled from use. She hadn't said much since Johan left for the lake. Just hummed under her breath and kept her hand moving.

Freya leaned back, arms crossed behind her head, watching the way Lena's face tensed in concentration. There was still colour in her cheeks this morning. That was something. Her breathing stayed quiet, un-laboured. That was something too. The first drawing took shape slowly.

Long strokes in black and dark green. A tree, or something meant to look like one. Crooked and split at the base. The trunk narrowed into a waist, bark peeling like skin. Strands of moss or vines trailed from the upper branches, draped like hair. Freya leaned forward, elbow braced against her knee. It wasn't just the shape that disturbed her. It was the *posture*. The figure stood half-blended into the roots of the forest, hips cocked slightly to one side like it had just noticed it was being watched. No face. Just a pale oval where one should have been; blank as space.

One arm reached downward, fingers impossibly long. The other curved behind its back, as though hiding something. Or holding something there. And then the figure had a tail. A fox's tail? Or a cow's?

Lena didn't comment on her art. She turned the page with a soft flick. The next drawing came faster. Harsher.

Freya watched the pencil judder in her daughter's hand. The graphite scraped and dragged. Dark, clustered lines crowded toward the centre of the page. A small figure. Thin arms. No feet. Her body almost floated above the ground. Around the head, the pencil marks thickened. Heavy black smudges where a mouth should have been. The face was a blur. A mistake? No. It had been done with intention. The shadows swallowed it. And at the bottom: the shoes.

Red. Carefully done, unlike everything else. Two small, precise shapes in fire-truck red. The kind Lena usually hated using. The pencil must have been pressed hard to get that brightness. That detail. Those shoes.

The story had changed versions. Drowned, buried, abandoned; but the shoes were always the same. The little girl with the red shoes who cried at night, the one who crawled behind tents and hated being seen. Lena had spoken of her Freya had always brushed it off as a nightmare. A tangle of folklore and cartoons. Lena paused, tilting her head.

Then turned the page again.

The third picture was different. Softer. Drawn in blue and ochre. It was the camp. Three tents, lopsided but recognisable. Johan's orange one, her own in dark blue, and Lena's smaller purple one between them. A stick-figure stood beside each: Lena first, herself in the centre, Johan to the right. But they weren't alone.

To the left of Lena, far off yet watching the red-shoed figure again. This time, her hand was extended. Not grabbing anything. Just there.

On the far right, half-hidden by a scribbled birch, was another silhouette. Taller. Lean. Her hair was long and grey and crawled all the way into the soil. Eyes missing. One arm hung too low. Reaching. Freya stared at the third drawing. Her mouth felt dry. Lena looked up then, calm as anything. Her pencil dangled loosely from her fingers.

"They follow the people they remember," she said.

Freya didn't speak. She wasn't sure she should. The clearing felt thinner suddenly, as though something was listening between the trees. Lena tapped the page, her fingernail clicking gently against the red shoes. "She was alone before. I keep her company now."

Then her hand drifted to the other side of the drawing. "She watches pappa," Lena said. "She doesn't blink."

Freya's voice, when it came, was quiet. "And the two of them... They're far away. Why?"

Lena's brow creased, as if the answer was obvious. "Because they're not staying long."

Freya's eyes dropped again to the sketch. "And me?" She asked carefully. "Where's my friend?"

Lena smiled, "You don't have one."

That should've stung, but it didn't. Not quite. Just left a hollow, weightless echo in Freya's ribs.

"Because I'm alone?"

Lena nodded, then returned to shading in the soil beneath the tents. "That's the safest."

A breeze passed through the clearing. Freya reached down and held the corner of the page to keep it from lifting. None of them spoke after that.

Further down the path, the lake held still. Water sat still. It reflected the grey sky like a mirror. No breeze skimmed across it. No insects stitched the surface. Just that cold, glassy silence; like the whole thing had been poured in one motion and left to harden.

Johan sat at the water's edge, boots tossed aside, toes splayed against a dry rock that jutted from the shallows. His line trailed into the lake like a thread coming undone. He hadn't baited it properly. He had noticed halfway through but hadn't been bothered to fix it. Fishing wasn't the point today. The rod balanced idly between two stones. He let it be, sat there, waiting.

From his jacket, he pulled the journal and pen. The pages had softened, edges curling with damp.

> *Day six. Weather's holding. Water's clearer than yesterday.*
> *I can hear my own breath again. Lena asked for 'real food'*
> *this morning. Said soup's for babies. She's got bite again.*

Johan paused with his pen lifted. A metallic tang clung to his tongue. Thin and sour. He pressed it against a molar, testing the shape of something. Pressure, dull and steady, bloomed along one side of his jaw. His pen moved again, slower now.

> *Freya seemed easier this morning. Still watchful. She*
> *seems more relaxed. Probably as Lena doesn't seem sick.*
> *That counts for something.*

Sweat gathered at his temple. He wiped it with a sleeve and set the journal beside him on the stone. He settled down onto one elbow, his gaze taking in the lake. Something flicked beneath the surface. Pale. Fluid. It vanished before he could catch the shape. The water held its calm once again. No ripple followed.

After a moment, the rod jerked. He bounced back to life, reaching for the rod. The line had gone taut, a clear weight pulling down through the water. He reeled with steady hands. The moment lengthened. Then the lake broke.

A brown trout burst from the surface, its body slick with lake-water and veined in gold. Copper-tinted across the shoulders, pale and speckled down the flanks. Roughly thirty centimetres, heavy through the middle, its flanks shivered with dappled muscle as Johan drew it in. He crouched low, gripped behind the gills, and held fast. The fish thrashed once, strong and clean, then stilled in his hands. Its eyes were dark and round, scales glossy in the light.

Something about that steadiness after let him breathe deeper. He laid his catch flat on a nearby stone and took out the knife. A firm press behind the gill slit, then a smooth pull down through the belly. Entrails slipped out in a warm coil. Liver full. He rinsed the body in lake-water, watching threads of pink drift off between reeds. Then he wrapped the golden-backed catch in a cloth and tied it tight, corners knotted with care. A small success.

Johan's mouth filled with saliva, sudden and sour. Hunger stirred low in his gut, but something else crept in with it; a sharp pulse along his gums. He shifted his tongue across the back teeth once again and flinched. The left molar felt swollen, as though the root was pressing upward from inside, looking for a way out.

He turned his head and spat. A smear of pink landed in the moss. He wiped his lip with the back of his hand and checked for more. No fresh blood. No sharp sting. Just that dull, bruising pressure working its way behind the gum-line. Perhaps a wisdom tooth. He'd never had them pulled, always assumed they would settle in on their own. Maybe this was just late.

He breathed slowly to indulge himself in the calmness around him. Yet, his eyes watered slightly. Pain climbed up behind his cheekbone in a slow, steady bloom. The sort of ache that made thoughts feel soft around the edges.

He crouched to gather the parcel, cloth still warm where the fish had rested. The knife folded into its sheath after a clean click. He tucked it back onto his belt, wiped his palm against the side of his trousers, and reached for the journal and fishing rod. The water, now behind him, lay undisturbed. No ripples. No insect hum. A mirror, cold and glassed over, pretending not to have ever moved.

He took the path back through the brush, careful with his steps. The fish weighed against his arm, heavier now. By the time he reached the edge of the clearing, camp had folded back into its usual quiet.

Lena sat cross-legged on the ground, sunlight edging around her shoulders. She clutched her sketchpad tightly, like it might vanish if she blinked. The pencil moved fast across the page. Erratic strokes, sharp turns. She didn't acknowledge her fathers return. The drawing caught his eye: a twisted tree, bark curling like skin, and beneath it, a shape with too many eyes. Blank, lidless circles, ringed in dark. Freya crouched nearby, folding a jacket into shape. She didn't speak as he approached. Her eyes flicked once to him, then to Lena, then away again. A greeting smile rose, but nothing more.

A wad of tissue stuck from Lena's left nostril, stained rust-red near the tip. She didn't seem to notice it anymore. That worried him more than anything else. Johan knelt by the cooler, unwrapped the fish, and laid it across a flat board. Its scales caught the light. Copper along the back, creamy near the belly, a soft scatter of red freckles glinting like damp coals.

"Did you pick at it?" Freya asked, moving to crouch beside Lena.

Lena shook her head, lips pressed together. "I sneezed too hard."

Freya reached gently for her daughter's chin and tilted her head up. The tissue was blotched with bright red. A nosebleed. Not heavy, but enough to coil something cold through Freya's stomach.

Behind them, boots crunched against stone and dried dirt. Johan appeared between the trees, shirt damp at the collar and a fish wrapped in cloth under one arm like a gift. He looked pleased with himself. A little colour back in his face, a line of sweat on his brow that didn't seem born of fever.

"Look what I caught," he said, lifting the bundle.

Lena brightened. "The crispy skin part?"

"If I don't burn it."

She pointed at her nose with enthusiasm, her eyes lighting up. "I sneezed too hard, pappa!"

Johan gave a mock-serious nod. "Dangerous outbursts, these forest sneezes. Trees don't like being startled."

Freya forced a smile, rose to her feet, and moved to help unpack near the fire-pit. Johan said nothing. If there was blood in his mouth, he ignored it, or convinced himself it didn't matter. He crouched again, washed the trout with some bottled up lake-water, and set to work.

They moved together without words, falling into the old rhythm from years ago. Johan steadied the trout with one hand, scraping gently along the skin with the back of the knife. Scales lifted in delicate curls, scattering like dry leaves across stone. Freya crouched beside him, fingers brushing his for a moment as she reached for the small tin.

Inside: a twist of wax paper holding salt, a browned sachet of dried dill, a few crushed juniper berries clinging to the bottom. She picked out what she could, rubbed the salt between her fingers, grainy and damp from the forest air.

Johan turned the fish, working along its spine now. Clean shallow cuts separated fish from bone as he began to fillet. His hands had steadied again. Muscle memory. Years of camping trips and caught dinners. When things between them were easier, or at least simpler. Just like old times.

Soon, the air thickened with the scent of hot oil, crisping skin and the slow render of trout fat. It spread across the clearing like something that didn't belong. Too rich and too good. A contrast from prior days. As if their bodies had forgotten how real food should smell.

Lena abandoned her sketchpad and padded over, blanket trailing behind her. Bare legs speckled with red pinpricks from kneeling in moss. She sat with knees hugged to her chest, blanket draped loosely around her shoulders. Her lips looked pale, but she smiled anyway. It almost felt normal. A meal shared. Firelight catching three happy faces again.

When the fish curled at the edges and the skin turned bronze, Johan portioned it with care. A tail piece, crisp and blackened, he placed gently onto Lena's plate. Thicker cuts for himself and Freya.

They ate without speaking for a while. Freya let the salt linger on her tongue. The flesh flaked apart perfectly, soft against the roof of her mouth. She found herself chewing slowly, unwilling to rush it. Johan used his fingers, licking each one in turn before returning to his share. Lena chewed carefully, lips parted slightly, eyes half-lidded. She didn't finish, but she tried. That was enough.

"Better than soup," Johan said, voice low around a mouthful.

Freya leaned back, elbows in the moss. "We might need to ration smugness next."

Lena grinned with her teeth peeking through. Her nose had stopped bleeding. A small relief. For a moment, the scene arranged itself like a memory might. End of summer. A breeze through birch tops. Shadows falling where they should. The right kind of warmth. Freya closed her eyes, just long enough to let the light reach through them. She felt it settle against her lashes, warm and strange. But she didn't let it stay long.

Lena stood up beside her. Her blanket dragged behind her like shed bark from a dying tree. She skipped away without excuse, mumbling about sticks and crowns and whether Pebble liked moss or needed somewhere dry to sleep. Her voice carried through the trees, soft and fractured. Then it vanished into the undergrowth.

Freya didn't stop her. Johan didn't look up.

Now only the fire cracked between them. Johan sat cross-legged opposite, arms resting on his knees, gaze downcast at his empty plate. His expression had cleared of effort. Calm had settled over him, loose and unfixed, like something borrowed for the moment. The kind that comes after storms have passed, though the ground still drinks the water. They hadn't spoken since the food. Eventually, Freya broke the silence.

"I forgot it was there,"

He didn't ask what she meant. He knew a tough conversation was coming. "I know."

They sat with the unspoken conversation.

"I didn't drink because of the place," Johan said. "Or even you. I drank because the silence felt like the part I'd always run from... The part where I have to stay and do things alone. I was never scared of being a bad father. I was scared of being one at all. Of waking up and knowing she needed me... And not knowing what I'd still have left to give."

Freya didn't interrupt. She didn't even blink. She listened intently whilst her eyes were entranced in the softening camp-fire embers.

"I drank to outrun it. Shame of being unsure. Weight of pretending I had anything under control."

He went quiet again. When he reached for his journal and set it beside him, it wasn't per-formative. Just instinct. A gesture of grounding. Freya watched the way his fingers hovered near the spine, like they weren't sure they belonged there.

"You're better when you write," she said softly "You don't close up so hard."

He didn't answer, but his shoulders dropped. Freya shifted onto one elbow, facing him now. "She doesn't need perfect. She needs honest. And for what it's worth..." Her voice caught slightly, but she cleared it. "You stayed. That matters. I couldn't handle watching you drink yourself to death."

Johan looked down. A muscle in his jaw ticked. No more words were worth speaking. The moment wasn't built for resolution, only understanding. The fire had long since settled into ash, the kind that held warmth but gave off no light. Freya crouched by an old tin, sweeping away fish bones with a stick, flicking crumbs into a shallow depression in the soil. Her hands moved efficiently, but her mind felt like it had been wading through syrup since lunch.

She'd found Lena's sketchpad left open by the edge of the blanket. The paper had curled at the corners. Her latest drawing sat half-finished. Another picture of the camp: the three tents in crooked scale. Beneath the middle one, Lena's, a spiral had begun to bloom. Thin, winding lines descending under the ground, glowing faintly yellow. Freya closed the pad gently. She didn't want to see where it led.

A sound came from the slope. Soft footsteps, a child's breath through trees. Lena appeared between the trunks, barefoot, with dirt streaked up both shins. She held Pebble wrapped in moss while she cradled in the curve of her elbow like a newborn. Her eyes looked glassy. Tired, perhaps.

"I made her a nest," Lena muttered. "But she didn't want to stay in it."

Lena's voice came slowly. Each word seemed pulled from somewhere deep, as if shaping them cost her breath. She lowered herself onto the blanket without prompting. One hand pressed flat against her side, fingers splayed like she was holding something in. Blood had crusted beneath her nostrils again. A dark smear stained the sleeve of her jumper. Freya crouched beside her, gently brushing tangled strands from her face. Her fingertips came away damp with sweat.

"You're warm again," she murmured.

Lena blinked slowly. "It's humming again."

Her gaze drifted downward and held, fixed on no visible point. As if trying to see through the moss, beyond soil and root, toward something that lived in the dark beneath. Her body wanted to move, but its motion lagged. Limbs followed like they'd forgotten how to obey. When she folded toward Freya, it was clumsy, weightless.

Freya caught her easily. She lifted Lena into her lap, careful not to jostle whatever bruised machinery worked beneath her skin. Warmth radiated through the thin cotton of her shirt. Her skin hovered close to a fever.

The light had drifted once again into an evening twilight. It no longer bathed things properly. Birch bark dulled to the colour of bone. Shadows stretched long. Lena pressed her face into the crook of Freya's neck, her breath shallow and uneven.

Freya stared outward, unsure what she was watching for. A flicker. A shape. A voice. Something had shifted in the calmness of dinner. The hush held weight.

Freya rocked without meaning to. A slow rhythm. Soothing. Instinctive.

Johan's voice cut through. "I'll get the fire going again."

Lena sagged in Freya's arms, her breathing shallower now. Small, irregular pulls of air, like she was wincing with each one. Freya smoothed a hand across her crown. Damp strands of hair clung to her fingers. She didn't wipe them away. Behind them, fire snapped back to life. Johan had built it carefully, almost with reverence. Log placement deliberate, symmetrical. Its glow didn't flicker; it pulsed. Heavy and orange, it smeared the air around it like oil brushed over water.

Freya stayed where she was, Lena curled in her lap. She wrapped them both in the unzipped sleeping bag, tugging it higher over the girl's shoulders. The fabric still held some warmth.

Lena's skin felt clammy while burning up. A tremor in her limbs hadn't eased. A thin thread of blood marked her nostril again. Freya dabbed at it with a folded damp cloth

"She's just tired," she whispered, barely audible. Mostly to herself. Mostly for belief.

Johan sat across the fire, tending to a strip of bark he'd been whittling into something for no reason at all. His lips were pale. Not as pale as the child's, but pale all the same. Freya saw him press a knuckle to his mouth and hold it there too long.

He blinked. He looked at his hand. There was blood on his fingers. But even a little was too much. It was bright and clean and fresh from somewhere it shouldn't be. He wiped it onto his jeans like it was nothing. The wind picked up just enough to move smoke sideways. It stung her eyes. Lena let out a dry, hollow cough. Freya shifted to settle her more fully on the ground beneath.

"She needs sleep," Johan said, barely above breath.

Freya nodded and moved Lena gently in her arms. Together, they carried her across the soft earth. Past cooling embers and scattered pine needles to Lena's tent. Inside the tent, air held a faint trace of damp wool. Freya eased Lena down into the sleeping bag, tucking it up beneath her chin. She reached for Pebble, still faintly warm in the corner of the tent, and tucked it beside Lena's ribs like a charm. Something that might mean comfort. Lena murmured something, words too slurred to understand. Her lips barely moved. Her eyes stayed shut.

Freya crouched a moment longer, brushing the fringe from her forehead. One palm rested lightly on her chest, waiting for the slow, thin rise of breath. It came, but too softly. As though Lena was already practising absence. She pressed her lips to the girl's temple and lingered there. Outside, firelight pulsed through canvas walls, rising and falling in tired rhythm. She pulled the zip partway closed and stepped into the dark again.

Johan sat just beyond the ring of light, elbows on knees, face slack with something heavier than exhaustion. Freya lowered herself beside him, close but not quite touching. The fire swayed gently in place, a dull orange rhythm like a heart trying not to stop. Freya watched the flames dance. Eyes catching on the smallest twitches of firelight. The silence between them wasn't cold. It had just worn thin.

"If she's worse tomorrow," she said, voice quiet, "we go."

Johan nodded, as if the weight of the decision had already settled in his bones. More like someone finally conceding to what had already been decided.

"We'll leave," he said. "If things get worse."

His voice held, but something within didn't match. Drawn out like fabric pulled too far across a frame. A quiet cadence of a man too tired to disguise the shape of what he felt. Between them, the truth had already settled. It hung in wafting smoke. Lena would resist. The car's engine would falter again, stuttering through its final insistence.

They sat in silence, except a continuous crackle from the fire in twilight. Freya leaned into Johan, shoulders grazing. Johan stayed still. His breath slowed slightly, relaxed.

She let herself breathe deeply. Scents of wood-smoke and a faint metallic bite. She wondered if he noticed it too. The fire cracked once. Beyond that narrow ring of light, trees hovered over the clearing, pressing in.

"Thank you," she murmured.

"Not just for agreeing. But for being here at all. For staying with us."

Thermal

Morning came, only shown by the slight increase of light as the evenings twilight subsided.

Light from the risen sun shone through the opening, not quite grey but not warm either. Just pale. As if something had drawn the hue out of the world and left only shape behind. Freya was the first to awake.

She was already crouched at the side of Lena's tent, half-zipped, inspecting the girl's arm in the hush of early light. Her fingers were gentle, clinical. Lena's rash had returned. It was angry now. Blistered along the edge like something had burned the skin from inside. The girl rolled onto her side and murmured something about "quiet humming." Freya stayed a moment longer. She covered the rash again, smoothing the fabric down to Lena's side. Each movement slow. Not gentle. Intent.

The zip was noisy in the quiet, each tooth locking into the next like a seal being made.

Johan was slow to emerge. His shadow lingered inside the orange canvas for a full minute before the zip finally gave a reluctant rasp and he stepped out, squinting. He looked worse. There was a stain at the edge of his lip. Dried, faint, but red. He wiped at it with the back of his hand without comment. His eyes had that glassy tension again, like the world was too bright in places and too dim in others. He knelt by the smouldering remains of last night's fire, coughed once into his sleeve, then began stirring the ash like it might have answers buried in it.

Freya watched him from across the clearing, arms folded.

"Feeling okay?" She asked at seeing the sight of Johan.

Johan didn't look up. "I'm fine. Just need a coffee."

Freya said nothing to that. She moved instead to the edge of the gear pile in the orange tent and unzipped one of the duffel's, pulling out a sealed pack of crispbread and a half-empty bottle of juice. It was warm to the touch, even though the air had that thin morning chill. She placed both near the flattened log, then turned away again.

Lena emerged not long after. She walked like her limbs had forgotten the sequence. Too much sway in the shoulders. Not enough in the knees. There was no greeting from her. No smile. No *hello*. She collapsed beside the juice bottle, peeled the cap off, and drank three mouthfuls before coughing hard into the dirt.

The cough started low, buried in her chest. One hard sound followed by another, then a pause. A pause that held too long, like the body couldn't quite decide whether to keep going. Then she buckled forward, both hands catching herself in the damp soil. The bottle rolled away unnoticed, its contents sloshing gently as it settled against a tuft of grass. Freya ran towards Lena, her knees hitting the earth beside her.

"Breathe slowly. In through your nose," she instructed calmly. But

Lena didn't lift her head. Her breath came in short bursts now as she struggled to regain breath after each reach.

Johan was slower, rubbing his eyes with the back of his wrist before stumbling upright. He hovered on the other side of the girl, one hand resting on her back. His touch was shaky. He looked up at Freya like a man checking if something had broken all the way through.

"Did she eat anything weird?" He asked, too quickly.

"She didn't eat," Freya replied. "She barely touched dinner."

Lena coughed again, then froze. Her fingers had curled into the soil. Her shoulders trembled. When she finally turned her head, her face looked drained.

"Mamma..." She whispered. "It's louder in the morning."

Freya blinked. "What is?"

Lena leaned sideways into Johan, her breath catching against his jumper. Her head dropped to his side, heavy, like sleep was pressing from inside her skull. One hand gripped the fabric at his waist. Her eyes stayed half-open but lost focus, caught somewhere behind the trees. She spoke again. A sound more than a sentence. Johan shifted his weight, held her upright. His hand moved across her back, light and uncertain.

"She's just tired," he said.

He was staring at the patch of earth where she'd coughed. The soil had darkened. Wet grit clung to her fingers, her knees. Freya crouched across from them. Her voice came low, with no sharpness in it.

"No. She's worse."

"I'll clear the fire-pit," Johan eventually replied, ignoring Freya's comment.

Freya nodded once with a raised eyebrow and , but didn't move. She was already thinking about the bags. She moved with the deliberate quiet of someone who had already made a decision. Her hands sorted through gear without hesitation: blanket, bottles, Lena's thinner shoes, half a roll of biscuits folded into a crinkled zip bag. Nothing dramatic. No shouting or arguments. Just a quiet protest preparing to leave.

The fire-pit had sagged in the night. One of the stones had tipped, the whole ring slumping slightly as if something beneath had dragged the ground in. A charred length of birch still sat in the centre. A bed of ash below had turned the colour of cement. He stood over the pit for a moment. Then reached for the trowel in his tent. The handle felt heavier than he remembered. Perhaps it was heavier, perhaps it was fatigue.

Freya passed behind him, her steps quiet but present, boots breaking the fine crust of ash and pine matter. Johan pressed the spade into the pit. The blade bit easily through the top layer, bringing up loose ash mixed with dark grit. The texture felt wrong beneath his boot. Too soft for the season, too damp despite the dry air.

As he dug, the earth began to darken. Beneath the fire-bed, the soil had turned rust-red in places, broken by streaks of oily black liquid that clung to the spade. The texture thickened as he dug, less like earth and more like something melted and left to congeal. It looked bruised. Some patches held together like clay, while others broke apart into a strange, heavy powder. His hands adjusted on the handle, and he pressed down again.

The soil offered no structure. It gave way in thick, wet sections, shearing off along hidden seams. Where he expected grain, there was slump; the ground seemed to slip inward, folding around the spade like pulp. Each strike of the spade met the same texture. A yielding pressure followed by a sudden ease. The ground didn't push back.

On the next lift, something caught. A smear of earth clung stubbornly to the blade, dragging behind it a darker lump. Sharper than root or stone. It dropped with a low thud beside his boot. Johan crouched closer to inspect.

The fragment sat lodged in the soil, barely visible beneath a smear of ash and grit. Johan leaned closer and brushed it clear with the back of his knuckles. The surface was dulled to a dark brown, coated in earth that clung like grease. One corner jutted free at an uneven angle, the edge slightly distorted. Warped. It wasn't jagged, but it hadn't broken clean.

He worked his fingers under the edge, loosening the weight of it. The soil let go with a slow pull. When it lifted, he was surprised by the heft. It lay across his palm, warm and misshapen, curved along one side like the outer skin of a pipe or a housing. The underside was uneven, bearing a raised line that tracked close to the edge. A seam, or a join. It didn't feel like scrap. There were no weld points, no jagged edges or bolt holes. Just a single piece, formed with purpose and then forgotten.

The metal seemed heavier than it should be. Dense, like lead, or maybe tungsten. It sat oddly in the hand, as though the weight had gathered inwards. He turned it over and caught the edge of a shallow gouge that crossed the grain, almost melted smooth at one end. Faint scoring covered the rest of the surface, a fine pattern of abrasion that shimmered slightly beneath the grime.

One corner was smeared with something darker. It clung to his fingers. Sticky, but dry.

He pressed his thumb to the centre. The metal gave off a low heat, steady against the skin. It had been in the ground a long time, but whatever warmth it held hadn't gone with the seasons. He looked back down at the pit. A line of soil had slumped in where he'd pulled the shard free. Just beyond it, something wider dipped into the earth. The same curve. The same tone. Still buried. He placed the fragment beside his knee, keeping it within reach.

"Freya," he said, steady and quiet. "Can you come here?"

Freya approached at a cautious pace, brushing her palms along the sides of her thighs as she moved. Her boots sank lightly into the softened ground near the pit. His eyes fixed on the hole that he'd dug, gesturing toward it as Freya arrived.

"There's more of it down there," he said. "Same shape. Looks like it keeps going."

Freya crouched beside him and peered into the cavity. The dirt along the edge had slumped slightly, exposing another section of metal beneath. It wasn't wide, but it bent inward along the same curve. The grain of the soil around it looked different, more compact, as if heat had drawn it tight. She leaned closer, squinting at the depth.

Johan began to make sense of what he was seeing, "Could be casing. But it's thick. Probably insulated."

Johan reached for the spade. He set the blade against the far edge and pressed down. The first cut was shallow. The second bite struck resistance. It didn't feel like stone or root. Something solid pushed back against the steel. He adjusted his grip and forced it deeper.

The metal gave way with a sound. A dull knock, followed by a low, breathless crack. Then came the hiss.

It rose through the soil in a steady line, pale and thin. A thread of steam curled upward into the air between them.

Freya moved without hesitation. She reached across Johan, arm extended, and covered the breach with the sleeve of her jumper. The steam struck fabric instead of their faces. The plume grew at once, pulling a sour stench into the air. The ground beneath it pulsed with heat. She caught the scent behind her teeth: burnt plastic, scorched earth, a chemical tang that coated the tongue.

Johan dropped back onto one hand, eyes fixed on the breach. The fissure ran like a hairline crack across the exposed curve, barely visible at first, but widening as the soil collapsed around it. Another section of the object slid into view, sloughing free from the dirt with a thick, wet sound. Light caught on its surface.

A strip of faded yellow arced along the casing. The paint had thinned with age, patchy and mottled beneath streaks of grey. Just beneath it, something darker bled through.

Freya held her stance, one arm still raised. The warmth pressed harder now, drawn through the fabric of her jumper, soaking slowly into the skin beneath. She shifted her weight, blinked against the sting rising with the steam.

The soil slipped again, pulling a fresh edge of the casing into view. Johan leaned forward and reached for the spade, but stopped halfway. His fingers sank into the earth instead. The soil at the breach stuck to his skin in streaks. Thickened, greasy, dark. It left a residue that caught in the creases of his knuckles.

He wiped it away in slow passes, brushing along the curve where the surface dipped. The grime came off in layers, smeared thin by the back of his hand. Beneath it, the casing had dulled to a matte grey, the sheen eaten away by corrosion and time.

Then something snagged beneath his knuckle. A fleck of colour. He leaned in. Paint. He scrubbed harder, hand slipping in slick soil. Yellow pushed through in broken patches. Flaked. Peeled. Worn thin by age. Underneath, a shape emerged: black. Stencilled. Three arms radiating from a central point.

Freya jerked back as the symbol caught her eye. Her arms rose instinctively, hands reaching to drag Johan from the pit.

His voice cracked. "That's a radiation symbol."

Her grip tightened around Johan's arm. Freya stepped back to brace. Johan's boot caught ash. The rim gave. Soil broke loose beneath him. He fell forward. One knee hit the ground hard. Both arms stretched out. Left hand struck grit. Right plunged into steam. A burst of vapour caught him across the face. Hot. Chemical. Sharp. It clung fast.

He gasped. Air flooded in.

Vapour tore down his throat and into his lungs. Bitter behind the teeth. A dry cough broke the still. His throat flared. Each breath clawed inward. The sound cracked short.

Freya grabbed his coat and hauled. He rose unsteady, jaw slack, right sleeve soaked through to the elbow. Steam beaded along his cheekbone. His eyes had dulled. The last of the vapour thinned. It drifted into the clearing, no longer rising. Only warmth lingered, folded into the air.

Johan stood in place. His eyes stayed fixed on the exposed arc. Soil had slipped back across the surface, half-masking the metal in grey. Ash clung to the rim. Heat no longer moved, but the air still felt wrong. Like something old was waiting for its moment.

Freya turned away.

She packed fast. The smaller duffel already open. Bandages. Bottles. One blanket crumpled into the corner. She zipped it closed in one motion. No glancing. No checking. Only what she could carry.

Johan stepped back from the edge, slowly, like the act of leaving needed permission. His hand wiped across his mouth. It came away clean. Still, he tasted it. Metal. The sting of old coins. Dry and sour. His chest rose once, then stopped halfway.

Freya had already crossed to the tent. Lena lay on her side, knees drawn partway up, one hand curled beneath her chin. Her face looked thinner. The skin around her eyes had paled to something cold. Freya knelt beside her, resting a hand on her shoulder with careful pressure.

"Lena." Her voice barely passed the air. "Älskling, we have to go now."

The girl turned slow. Her eyes opened partway, dry and unfocused. Freya reached again, slower this time, but Lena moved first. Her hands pushed against the mat, trembling under the effort. Her legs folded beneath her in the wrong order. She sat upright with a shallow breath.

"I can walk," she whispered.

Freya didn't correct her. She wrapped the blanket around her daughter's body, tucked it tight, then lifted her in one motion. Lena didn't resist. Her head pressed against Freya's chest, breath soft against her collarbone. She turned to leave. Then paused. Pebble still sat near the sleeping mat, nestled against the hoodie.

Freya bent and picked it up, tucking it between the folds of the blanket.

Johan was waiting at the tree-line. Both bags were on him now; one over his shoulder, the other pulled tight against his chest. His mouth was half-open, still in shock. No sound came. He pointed with his chin toward the slope.

"This way."

Behind them, the clearing had settled again. The air still carried its scent: chemical, faintly metallic, the kind that clings behind the nose long after it's gone. The casing had slipped beneath the surface once more, half-covered by the soil that had tried to hold it.

But the clearing hadn't let them go. The air behind them felt loaded, like it was holding its breath for their return. They walked quickly. Footfalls against pine needles. The soft thud of boots skipping over roots. Branches brushed against them without notice. Their breath came light, shallow. The path was only a path because they remembered it. A dip in the earth where the trees opened enough to pretend to know their direction. The same slope they'd followed down days ago, when Lena had run ahead laughing. Now it was only distance. Johan took the lead.

Johan's boots dragged more than they lifted. His breath had thickened. Not quite a wheeze, but close. Each step looked forced, shoulders tight, muscles locked like tension alone might hold his body together. He kept both bags strapped across his frame, one on each shoulder. Too much weight for the slope, but he carried it without complaint. Occasionally, he glanced back, eyes flicking over his shoulder to check for Freya.

Freya followed five paces behind. One of Lena's arms looped around Freya's neck, but it hung without pressure. No real grip. Just the shape of one. Her breath still warmed the skin just below Freya's collar, but her body felt cooler now, as if whatever heat she'd had was being drawn steadily outward. Freya adjusted her hold. Not to lift. Just to feel her move.

"How much further?" She asked, voice low.

Johan didn't turn.

"It's the same way we came. Twenty minutes, maybe."

Freya looked up. The light had flattened. Grey across the treetops. No sun. Just a haze that sat low against the sky, direction-less.

"Doesn't feel like twenty minutes," she muttered.

Johan gave no answer. They kept moving. The slope beneath them had steepened, though neither could say if it was the hill or their legs that had changed. Their muscles had forgotten how to climb. Each incline stretched longer than the one before. The trees were closing in.

Ranks of pine on either side thickened with every dozen steps, their trunks darker now, packed tight. What had passed for a path had unravelled. No more worn soil. No tracks. Just moss, root, and the sense that something had walked here once, but hadn't returned.

Freya looked back once, on instinct. A thread of unease unwound through her chest. Nothing looked familiar anymore. The trees were too evenly spaced. The rocks lay in the same patterns; a scatter, a slump, a rotten log with an empty centre. It was the kind of repetition the mind filled in on its own. Not enough to say for certain. Just enough to make you doubt.

She slowed. Lena shifted in her arms, the blanket slipping at one shoulder.

"Mamma..." Lena's first words in a long time. "I want to walk."

Freya crouched down carefully and set her on her feet. The girl swayed once, legs slightly bowed, and righted herself with effort. Her face was flushed. A bright fever spread across her. Red patches blotched the skin beneath both eyes. There was a thin line of dried blood under one nostril, cracked and caked at the edge. Her hands trembled when she reached out to steady herself against her mother's arm. Freya didn't argue. She wrapped the blanket tighter around Lena's shoulders and kept her close as they walked.

Johan was further ahead. His posture had buckled. The packs dragged unevenly against his spine, tilting his frame. He stepped like someone on uneven ground, even where the earth was flat. Once, he reached to brush a low branch aside and missed it completely, hand grasping at air.

"Wait," Freya said.

He stopped slowly, like the command took a moment to travel through him. One of the duffel's dropped to the ground with a soft thud. He kept the other on his back.

Freya stepped forward with Lena, still supporting the girl. Her tone stayed calm.

"Let me see your phone."

Johan turned. His eyes were rimmed red. "Why?"

"I just want to check something. Please."

He hesitated, then reached into his coat pocket. The phone was warm to the touch. Too warm for something that hadn't been used all morning. She pressed the power button once. Nothing. She held it longer. Still black.

"Battery's gone," Johan muttered. "It was on earlier."

Freya handed it back without answering. She pulled her own phone from her inside pocket, pressing the button as she brought it up. The screen blinked on, flickered, the logo ghosted then vanished. For a moment, she thought she saw a bar of signal in the corner. Then nothing. Just the reflection of trees across the dead glass. She stared at it before sliding it back into her jacket.

"Both dead," she said.

Johan didn't speak. He sat down on a low rock and leaned forward with his elbows on his knees. His hands hung between them. Sweat had soaked into the top of his t-shirt. Lena stood between them, arms buried deep inside the blanket. Her eyes moved from tree to tree like she was trying to spot something in the gaps. Freya crouched beside her. She brushed a hand over the girl's forehead, thumb resting at the temple. The skin there was clammy. Beneath it, the faintest pulse fluttered while a tremor ran down Lena's side.

"How far did you say?" Freya asked, glancing up.

Freya stood and turned, looking back the way they'd come. But there was nothing there. No trail. No thinning of trees. No point of reference. Just forest. Johan didn't answer right away. His eyes were on the ground. His skin had gone a shade paler again. Thin-looking; drawn too tight around the cheeks. He hadn't moved from the rock, but something about his shape looked different now. Shoulders slightly hunched, hands curled loosely between his knees. His head hung low, neck drawn in like a man sitting through a cold wind. He wasn't looking at her. Not at anything.

Then his gaze lifted. Not to meet hers, but past her. Beyond her shoulder. She stilled, halfway to reaching for the pack. His eyes had widened, just slightly. His head angled like he was tracing the shape of something. Something far off, or too thin to fully catch. Freya turned to follow his focus. The woods stood in place. Just pine trunks and stone, scattered brush, moss catching the last of the light.

"Johan?" She asked.

He blinked. Something flickered through his face, too quick to name. His expression slackened, the sort of blankness people wear when they've stopped hearing things properly. A breath slipped through his nose, slow and thin. He gave a short shake of his head. Not a refusal. Just something to clear the air.

His eyes stayed elsewhere. Freya stepped in. The backpack strap snapped into her hand. She pushed it against his chest with more force than necessary.

"Don't do that," she said. "You were staring at nothing. I thought you were about to collapse."

He took the bag. No comment. No change in pace.

She turned back to Lena. The blanket had slipped slightly. She adjusted it, pressing one fold beneath the child's arm. Lena's fingers had curled in on themselves, light and cold, like they'd lost their purpose.

Freya's breath caught. Just enough to lock behind her ribs. Her arms held the weight, but everything else felt one movement away from failing. She didn't know how long she could trust her own body to keep behaving like it was supposed to. They walked.

The slope pitched harder than she remembered. Moss slipped beneath her boots. Roots snagged in the dark soil. Freya moved out of habit, every step recalibrated as it landed. Her lungs burned cold at the edges, her chest tightening. Lena moved beside her in small, uneven steps. Her head hung forward, chin tucked to her chest. Each breath came thin and quiet. Freya kept close, one arm ready if the girl began to fall.

The forest narrowed around them. Trees thickened on either side, pulling the light out of the air. Branches dipped low, their tips matted with old needles and clusters of grey lichen. The path, such as it had ever been, had vanished beneath ferns and broken stone. Freya pressed forward, picking her way by memory and instinct alone. Behind her, Johan's footsteps shifted. At first they followed hers, then wandered. A soft drag. A pause. The faint scrape of a boot twisting against something unseen. Freya glanced back.

He was still upright, still walking, but his head was turned. His eyes swept across the trees to their right, slow and unblinking. His mouth had fallen open slightly. His focus wasn't on the trail. She turned forward again.

Lena walked ahead, but her movement had changed. Her knees bent out of rhythm, feet landing with the hesitation of someone testing unfamiliar ground. Her arms hung at her sides, loose and slow. She moved like the memory of walking had outlived the intent. Freya stayed close behind, one hand ready to catch her if she slipped. Freya reached out and steadied her without stopping. Her palm touched Lena's shoulder. It felt thin beneath the blanket.

Behind her, Johan's steps faltered again. A pause. Then two more steps. Then none. He'd stopped. Freya turned her head, half-expecting to see him bent double or clutching his side. But he was standing straight. Still facing the trees. Then he tilted his head.

A sound came from somewhere to his left. A voice. Soft enough to be missed, unless he'd already been listening.

"Johan? Eyes here. The forest doesn't like you." A voice like Freya's taunted him.

He turned slowly toward the ridge. His heart lurched once, then steadied into something slower, heavier. The voice had already vanished, but the words hung in the space behind his eyes, clear as if they'd been whispered an inch from his ear. Ahead, Freya hadn't flinched. She kept moving with one hand braced against Lena's back, her focus pinned to the path. Her mouth was set tight. Every movement was spare, functional. She hadn't spoken.

Johan looked toward a ridge. It dropped into a shallow crease between the trees, a slope thick with pine. The trunks were older here. Closer. The ground was hard-packed, scattered with dry needles and splinters of bark.

A smell rose in the stillness. Subtle. Mulch-heavy. Damp wood and leaf mould, like earth that had soaked too long beneath fallen rain. It clung to the air with a low sweetness, the kind that stuck behind the teeth. The soil beneath him told a different story. Dust sat between the roots. Every step had broken dry ground. But the scent followed anyway, close and warm, like something buried had begun to breathe again.

He rubbed his thumb across his palm. The skin was raw. Beneath the rawness, it felt hot. Not from friction, but like a fever boiling him inside.

He adjusted the pack strap on his shoulder and pressed forward. For a while, the feeling dulled. Then it returned. So did the voice.

"Johan? You're not going to make it."

He froze again. Turned fully, eyes scanning the ridge behind them. Still nothing. No wind. No birds. Just pine trunks and rock. He turned back toward the others.

Freya hadn't paused. She was moving Lena past a tangled knot of roots, guiding her carefully with an outstretched arm. The girl walked mechanically, feet shuffling, head low.

Johan called out before thinking. "You said something earlier."

Freya didn't look back. "huh?"

"Just now. You said something. About the forest not liking me."

That stopped her. She turned partway, her face unreadable at first. Then her mouth opened, not with an answer, just disbelief. She stared for a second longer than necessary.

"What are you on about?"

Johan held her gaze. "I heard you."

"You didn't."

"I did. You said..."

"I haven't said a word since the ridge."

They stood in the narrow break between the trees. Just far enough apart that the silence felt stretched. Freya held his gaze a second longer than she meant to. Johan looked away first. He shifted the pack higher on his shoulder and walked on, brushing past her with the same weightless pace he'd had since morning. Freya followed. One hand moved automatically to Lena's back. The hush behind them didn't lift. It settled back into the trunks and the undergrowth like it had never been broken. Johan stopped again. Just for a breath.

"Did you..." He started. His voice was flat.

Whatever he meant to say never made it out. Johan turned toward the ridge again, eyes locked on the tree-line. Moss ran darker along the roots, thick where it pooled in the crease of the dip. The air pressed harder. He swallowed. Then walked on. Freya's hands wouldn't still. They had started trembling. Each breath felt like it had to be taken from something else.

Johan spoke in front of her.

"We keep heading downhill. If we find that rock formation..."

"No." Her voice cut in, sharp. "We passed it. Twice. Or something like it."

She stopped. Turned slowly. The trees around them stood too close, their trunks bleeding into shadow where the light had thinned. The pine stretched in every direction, branches low and heavy, no sky between them. Johan stayed quiet. Lena stumbled at Freya's side, her shoulder bumping against her mother's hip. One hand reached out, unfocused, fingers brushing fabric without grip.

"Mamma?"

Freya brushed the girl's hair aside, her voice gentler than before. "You're alright."

Johan sat down just ahead of them. He didn't fall. He just let himself sink to the ground. His elbows rested on his knees, head in his hands. He looked up slowly, eyes glassed over.

"We've lost the path. This isn't the way out."

Orbit

All three took a moment to observe what was around them. Only trees filled their view in every direction. Something pressed deep on their shoulders. It wasn't the trees, although even those felt wrong now too. It pressed against their skin as if it were a hot yet humid day. Warm in places it shouldn't be. The sky above filtered in through the canopy in dull bands of grey, too flat for morning, too bright for night. Nothing moved. Not even wind rustled the trees. Only the crunch of their boots on old moss and the rustle of gear shifting on sore shoulders.

Freya led this time.

She walked ten paces ahead with a map crumpled in one hand, compass clutched in the other. Her stride was stiff. Focused. Behind her, Johan kept pace. He limped slightly. Either from exhaustion or the lingering ache in his left leg, though he hadn't admitted to either.

Lena followed between them, unusually silent. Her small boots dragged now and then. The toe of one catching roots she usually danced over. Her rabbit hung limp from one hand. Pebble, forgotten about for the moment, was zipped into her coat pocket. Her eyes tracked the trees. Not with the wonder she used to. Now it was with suspicion.

Like they might move if she stopped looking.

"We need to veer west at the lake," Freya started to speak for the first time since Johan had wandered. "If the second lake is behind us, then the slope here should carry us across the lower ridge. It should align with the utility road."

Johan grunted non-committally.

"How long have we been walking?" Lena asked quietly.

Freya glanced at the sky, as if it might offer anything useful. "Not long, Älskling. An hour maybe."

"It feels like longer," Lena muttered.

Freya refused to argue back. She didn't want to admit that her sense of time had warped too. Her watch had stopped sometime during the night. Johan's had by the morning also.

The phones were long useless too. Black screens and dead batteries. Freya had tried restarting hers until the button caved inward from pressure. Now it lived in her coat pocket like a brick made of glass and circuits. Johan slowed slightly. His steps started to feel heavier.

"Remind me again why we didn't stay put?" He asked, more to provoke than contribute.

Freya didn't look back and she spoke. "Because staying put is what people do when they're ready to die."

"Bit dramatic."

"No, Johan. Dramatic would've been setting the tent on fire. This is just survival."

Lena tripped slightly but caught herself. Neither parent moved to help. They were too far apart. She stood, brushed her hands against her jacket, and kept walking.

The path narrowed. Pines grew closer together, straight-backed and thin, their trunks coated in lichen and dust. Bark split in narrow seams, some fresh, some furred with age. The ground rose slightly beneath their feet. Moss clung to the slope in thick folds, softened at the edges with old pine needles. There was no clear track now, only the pressure of direction. The light dropped away by degrees.

"We'll hit the lake soon," Freya said to herself.

"You said that twenty minutes ago," Johan muttered.

To their left, the tree-line fractured into a gentle slope. A rare incline. It pulled against the flat monotony of trunks that had stretched for hours. Freya adjusted her pack, shoulder straps cutting deeper than before. The ache had settled into her muscles days ago, but this was something more. A burn that pulsed from bone. She turned slightly, checking behind.

Lena had stopped walking. Her mouth opened. No words formed.

Freya slowed. "What is it?"

Lena blinked, hard. As if dragging herself upward through thought. She rubbed both palms across her face.

"I thought..." She said, voice thin, "there was a woman. Over there."

She didn't raise her arm straight away. Her eyes stayed fixed on the trees. Then, slowly, she lifted one hand, pointing toward a narrow gap between trunks. A place where pine needles stirred faintly. Caught in a trickle of light. Nothing else moved.

Lena shook her head, not even sure herself what she saw.

Johan sat on a low rock, elbows slung over his knees, hands slack between them. His head hung forward, not in rest, but in effort. As if each vertebra had become heavier by degrees. His eyes were half-lidded, drawn to a patch of moss near his boots. The expression didn't hold focus, but it didn't drift either. Fixed. Like something deep inside him was listening.

A bird called overhead. High and alone. The note cracked through the stillness, then fell away abruptly, almost embarrassed. Freya stepped forward and reached down to un-clip one of the smaller packs from Johan's hip. She meant to lift some of his weight. Let him rest.

But before her fingers touched the strap, he moved.

His head lifted. Slow. Yet, his eyes didn't meet hers. They tracked beyond her shoulder, still locked on something deeper in the trees.

She froze. "Johan?"

He didn't blink.

His jaw loosened, barely parting. A breath held between intention and voice. His focus narrowed to a point past the visible, as if the forest had peeled open to show him something it hadn't offered her.

Freya stepped into his eye-line. "Johan?"

Lena made a low noise behind her; a small cough. Freya turned in time to see the girl sway, then double over, her hands pressed to her knees. Freya dropped to her side just as Lena vomited. A thin, stringy bile, yellow and flecked with foam. Her knees collapsed underneath her. Freya caught her and eased her to the ground. The girl's arms twitched in her sleeves. Her breath came fast, shallow, barely drawing in. When Freya looked up again, Johan was gone.

His hands swung loosely at his sides, fingers curling and uncurling without rhythm, brushing at branches he no longer moved to avoid. She was always just ahead. Not close. Not even fully visible. But present always.

He hadn't seen her face. He never will. A pale braid swings behind her. It had hung there before he looked. Pulled tight down a back too straight to be natural. Her shoulders taper. They will vanish soon. She walks without touching anything. The trees lean away. The under-brush folds under her step.

Johan follows.

There was no decision. His feet begin to move. Something in the shape of her spine told him he would always follow. The air swallows every sound. Just his breath, catching in his throat. He had breathed easier once. He is forgetting how.

He walks anyway.

The ground moves beneath him. It felt spongy, springing back slow. Heat rose through his boots. The moss had known he was coming. He stepped again. He will leave no imprint. The rot rises sweet in the back of his nose. Sap and something softer. The smell is thicker now.

He blinked.

The trees were moving out of the way. Or they had already. Bark slid into bark. Grey wrapped grey. He stares.

Nothing focused. He had known how light should bend. That memory won't help him here.

She moves between two trees.

He lost her. His heart kicks once. Then twice. The silence was going to wait. He didn't call out. He stands still. His arms twitch. His chest stayed tight. He was about to stop breathing, but only briefly.

She returns.

The braid is first. Then her shoulder. Then her elbow folded inward like it was hinged differently. He sees the shape, not the body. He felt calm again. Like something important had un-paused.

He tries to speak.

A sound leaves his throat. It wasn't a word. It won't become one later. She doesn't turn. But she hears. He knows that deep in his ribs. The bones are always first to understand.

He starts walking toward her. He had already fallen. The ground will come closer again. His foot catches on the log. He is going down. He remembers hitting the ground. His palms reach bark. They will sting later.

This place had never belonged to them. Not to Freya. Not to Lena. Not to him. It was always hers. She had lived beneath it. Waited. They built their camp on her den. Lit fires above her cradle. Dug into her side. Pulled the thing she kept asleep.

She wants him to see.

He stumbles again. His knee will give. A root lifts. He doesn't see it. He does now. It catches his boot. He falls harder. The ground snaps up. Bark bites his skin.

His hand splits open. The blood hasn't reached the surface yet. It will.

His vision swims. He coughed. He hasn't finished coughing. One, then two. Something touches the edge of his tongue. Wet. Warm. He wipes it away. His wrist smears red. It had already been there.

Blood.

Only a little. Later, there will be more blood on his wrist.

His body slips further. The signals stretch. Every message arrives late. His name would sound wrong if someone called it. His muscles pull against each other. One trembles. Then both. He smiles.

She is there again. Close now. But still no face. Her braid sways as she moves. It swings like a rope in water. Smoke folding back into itself. She is walking ahead of him. He knows he will follow.

He tries to speak. The shape never forms. No sound. His mouth stays open. He presses up from the moss. His hands shake. His eyes won't focus. The blur spreads wider.

His knees collapse. He is already falling again. This time, it was softer.

His cheek touches moss. The fibres bend beneath him. He does not rise.

He stays.

Breath shallow. Ears full of static. The world swaying gently to the rhythm of a body losing centre. He thought he heard footsteps behind him. Slow, barefoot, deliberate.

He blinks.

Lena is there. She sits beside the figure. No older than a baby, legs bare, hands limp in her lap. Her eyes look past him. She does not speak. She will not speak. Her hair was lighter. The way it was later in life. He will reach out. He doesn't. The moss presses into his fingers.

The woman looks down at the child. One hand rests on her shoulder. A gesture soft enough to mimic care. She might already have taken her.

He sees her stand.

Yet the baby does not move.

There is something ahead now. Further, beyond the next row of pines. A small rise in the soil. A large stone extruding from the top. It feels recent. Placed a month ahead. The shape holds in his vision; a mark on the earth. The length of a child.

He is walking before he understands.

The moss hasn't reached it yet. There's time. Roots still grip outward, searching.

He sees a second. A stone seven decades old. The earth is more settled. Spores of pine-cone-cap rise from the soil, pale and still.

Another child's grave. He would look closer. The surface warped. The carving shallow.

Letters swim in the blur of his vision. *1953; Jo...*

He squints. The name won't hold still. *Jonna. Or Joe. Or Johan. Inte!*

Bakom stenen. His breath falters. He will not go closer. He coughs once. More blood is on his wrist. The sound snaps in his throat.

He has awoken a demon from its core.

He *begins* to run. He would be faster. His boots sink deeper. His legs forgot their rhythm. He sees her ahead, Hon går före. Turned away **now**, the braid lifted slightly in the breeze. Her *figure* **is** long. Wrong.

He lifts the axe. The grip was worn smooth for years. Isotoped-fused **muscles** remember before his brain does. He steps toward *the* tree that was in front, He swings. **The** blade ~~should~~ bite. It <u>doesn't</u>. *There* is no hit. There **was** ~~no~~ axe.

He stares at his hands. They ache with weight *that* ~~isn't~~ there. Cherenkov must be glowing in his grave. Oppenheimers laughing. The tree ~~wasn't~~ there. He *aimed* at "*Skogsrå*". That's what fifteen gray will do to ya. You'll speak **her** <u>name</u>. A fox's tail was tickled and it awoke a dragon.

She moves again. He aches **throughout**, like cancer <u>in</u> his bones. The damage is irreversible.

She left. She is gone. But he stayed.

Breath shallow. Ears, static, full. Wlord *swaying* gnelty to <u>the</u> reethum; bdoy losing ctener.

His breath slows.

Slower...

Slowly...

Calm...

Calmer.

Freya felt the movement before she saw it; a twitch in Johan's shoulder. A shallow breath catching on the inhale. His eyes opened slowly. The pupils were unfocused at first, darting across her face as if trying to place her.

"You're back," she said softly.

He blinked once. Then again. His jaw worked as though trying to form a word, but nothing came.

"Don't speak yet, Just breathe." Freya continued, forcing a worried smile.

He tried. The breath that came was ragged, but it held. Freya placed a hand against his chest, steadying him as he shifted upright. His arms trembled under his own weight. Johan's skin had lost what little colour it had left. A greyness clung to his cheeks, the kind that didn't lift with rest. His lips were dry. Cracked. His throat twitched as he swallowed hard.

"I..." He started, but winced mid-breath.

"You had a seizure," Freya said. "You collapsed."

A small, jolting motion came on from his head. It looked like it cost him more energy than it should have.

"I thought... I was walking."

"You weren't."

He lowered his head.

The weight of it hung between his shoulders. Freya reached for the water bottle, unscrewed the cap, and held it out.

"Slow sips."

He took it with both hands. His fingers were still trembling. Behind them, Lena hadn't moved slightly. Freya glanced back. The girl was curled on the moss, her breathing shallow but even. The forest around them was still. Unnaturally so. Even the light filtering through the trees felt too white, too distant. Freya looked back at Johan.

"We need to move soon," she said. "We need to get to the car."

Johan nodded again, slower this time.

"I can walk," he muttered.

She helped him slowly to his feet.

Freya shifted Lena's weight in her arms as Johan steadied against the tree. He hadn't spoken again since the last sip of water. His breathing came soft and irregular. A pulse beat high in his throat.

Lena hadn't made a sound in twenty minutes. Her limbs sagged with fever-weight. Freya had tried to seat her upright earlier, but the girl had slumped sideways within minutes, muscles loose. She held her closer after helping Johan. Lena's body curled in against her ribs like something delicate and warm.

They sat in moss dappled with dust-light. Branches above no longer moved. Johan blinked slowly, eyes drifting toward them. Freya watched his gaze land on Lena. It didn't move away.

The girl's skin gleamed faintly. Sweat clinging to cheeks flushed too red. Her breath reached shallow. Eyes stayed shut.

Freya adjusted her hand at Lena's back, fingers pressing gently to feel the motion of lungs. Johan knelt beside her. His voice barely held shape.

"I didn't mean to," he whispered. "I thought I saw..."

Freya met his eyes. No blame passed between them.

"I know," she said. "But we need to move soon."

He nodded once. No sound. The forest ahead narrowed fast. They moved in a single line, Freya leading.

Lena slipped on wet rock, one foot catching on stone slick with moss. She caught herself with open palms, then stood again. Slower, chest working harder now. Each breath rasped with a faint whistle beneath it. Most of their walk was in silence, until one moment where Lena broke.

"Pappa, why were you shaking?"

There was no possible right answer to respond with. Water next to their trail held still. Its surface as smooth as glass. The sky reflected back in a bruised silver. No wind touched the edge. Freya stepped toward the bank and paused.

"We eat here. Ten minutes."

Johan eased his pack to the ground without a word. His shoulders sagged. Face drawn in on itself. Freya opened the food pouch. Passed out what remained: oat bars, bruised fruit, water turned lukewarm in their bottles. Metallic. Faintly sour. Lena took her share and studied it without expression. She turned the apple over slowly, thumb tracing the skin. Freya unwrapped a bar but didn't eat. Her eyes stayed on the child.

Johan bit into his apple. Chewed with slow, rhythmic motion. His lips had cracked further; pale against the red pulp. The fruit hung in his hand, browning at the edge. He sipped from the bottle, then pulled back, grimacing. A string of spit followed as he leaned forward and spat into moss.

Lena lifted her apple. Took one bite. The sound was soft. Muffled. She chewed once. Twice. Then stopped. Her hand opened slowly. A chewed apple dropped into her palm. Her gaze didn't follow it. She stared off to the side toward something near, but unseen.

Freya leaned closer. Lena's mouth moved. A slow shape of discomfort. She shifted her tongue against her teeth. Then she winced. When her voice came, it was barely there.

"It hurts."

Freya kept her voice steady. "Show me."

Lena raised one hand and touched her cheek. Then her upper palate.

Fingers pulled back stained in red. Freya reached forward, tilted her chin. Lips parted slightly, reluctant. Inside, flesh had bloomed raw. Ulcers marked the corners and gum-line. One had broken across the inner mouth; blood already dried at the edge.

Freya wiped gently with a sleeve. Then reached for a packet of crackers. She opened it in silence. Lena took it and held it in her lap. Her hands didn't move again.

Freya drank from her bottle. The water tasted like old metal. A sharpness coated her tongue. She swished the water around then swallowed. A tingling bloomed beneath her gums. When she wiped her mouth, her sleeve came away stained faint pink.

Lena curled forward, and was sick.

Freya caught most of it in her hands without thinking. The sound was thin. Liquid. More effort than result. Lena didn't sob like most children would. She trembled, chin pressed to her chest, arms wrapped tight around the rabbit teddy like it could anchor her. Freya rubbed her back. Her own breathing had quickened without her noticing. She reached into the pack for a cloth, found only one of Johan's spare shirts, and used that instead.

Johan hadn't moved. He sat still, one hand hanging loosely between his knees. His other wiped absently at his nose. The blood had already started, a slow line that threaded down to his lip and across the corner of his mouth. His eyes became fixed on trees ahead. Starring at nothing, and responding to nothing. Freya looked at him. He pressed his palm against his nostrils, tilted his head back. The blood soaked the web of skin between his fingers. Still staring absently.

Lena moved against Freya's side. She mumbled something her mother didn't catch, then reached for her bottle. Freya offered the cap instead, filled it with a small measure, and held it steady as Lena drank. The girl swallowed twice, then turned her face away. The stillness pressed in again. Even the sound of the lake had vanished. The water sat like glass behind them.

"We need to keep moving," Freya said.

Johan nodded. He didn't look at her. Freya wiped her hands once more in the spare shirt and dropped it on the ground. Freya tightened the pack straps across her shoulders and waited while Johan struggled to his feet. He staggered slightly, caught himself with a hand against a fallen trunk. He hesitated for a few moments, looking around at the trees.

"I just need a minute," he muttered, already stepping away. "Back in a sec."

Freya didn't ask where. She crouched beside Lena again. Lena's skin had grown hot under the jacket. Her breath thin and damp against the inside of the collar.

Johan moved to a secluded spot, just out of sight. He didn't go far. The silence behind him swallowed his footsteps. He paused, resting one hand against the tree trunk, trying to breathe through the churn in his gut. The cramps returned fast. Low and sharp, cutting sideways through his abdomen. His legs trembled. He crouched instinctively, pressing his shoulder to the tree for balance.

The pressure gave out almost at once.

He closed his eyes. The release brought no relief. Only heat and a sickly slickness that clung too fast, too loose. He didn't look down. He could feel it. He could smell it. Liquid. His body felt hollow afterward. Empty in a way that frightened him. His hands were shaking again. He wiped with an old shirt scrap from his jacket pocket, then wrapped it tightly and buried it beneath loose soil and needles, fumbling with numb fingers. The stain was already soaking through.

He sat back on his heels, resting briefly against a tree trunk. His vision blurred at the edges. For a few seconds, he stayed there, crouched in the half-shadow, breath shallow and fast. Then he stood. Slowly and carefully. He walked back to the two waiting for him, stumbling around. Freya looked up as he reappeared.

"You alright?"

He didn't meet her eyes but nodded.

She held his gaze for a beat longer than he expected, then nodded once.

"Fine," she said. "Straps on. We need to move."

Johan adjusted the shoulder of his pack and glanced at Lena. Lena didn't speak. She followed when prompted, face pale, a flush creeping across her cheeks that wasn't from the cold.

The air had grown heavier since they stopped. Damp and scentless. The kind of weight that made breath feel like something to carry. Freya watched Lena closely as they set off. Her steps were unsteady now. Her arms were limp at her sides, rabbit dragging behind, dragging in the dirt. Freya adjusted her grip on the compass, though she hadn't trusted it in hours. The needle no longer held direction. It constantly drifted side to side, never truly telling its direction.

Still, she chose a bearing and began walking. She called Lena to ensure she was following. The compass in her hands started to feel like it burned. Like the metal was melting in her hands. Her hands shook more than before. Freya told herself it was exhaustion. She had noticed it as they passed through a narrow corridor of pines. A tightness beneath her knuckles, like sunburn just beginning to declare itself. She looked down. Her fingers were reddened at the joints. Pale fluid sat along the creases. A blister had begun to rise along the webbing of her right palm. She wiped it on her trouser leg and didn't say anything.

The path curved gently uphill. They crossed over what might once have been a dry run-off or animal trail. It looked vaguely familiar, though everything had begun to share the same dullness of tone. Moss underfoot, bark greying at the edges, lichen like old growth on stone.

Lena stopped walking a few paces later and crouched. Not to rest. Or to complain. She just seemed to forget she was meant to keep going. Starring blankly ahead with an expression of confusion. Freya doubled back and lifted her without a word. The girl folded against her without resistance. She weighed less than before, or perhaps Freya had stopped registering the difference. They pushed forward. Moments later, Johan stopped. Shoulders squared. Gaze fixed ahead.

Freya stepped to his side and followed his line of sight. For a few seconds, the scene ahead refused to settle into shape. Just another glade of crushed moss. A few branches stripped of bark. A frayed curve of nylon tangled at the edge of a fallen tree.

Then she saw the tent. They had returned.

The approach was different. That orange canvas slumped deeper than before. One wall had given way completely. Support poles no longer held tension. They drooped inward, bent at uneven angles. Pegs lifted from the soil as though pulled from beneath. The blue tent leaned crookedly into the roots of a nearby pine. A fresh layer of pine needles buried half of it. Branches from above hung lower now, weighed down with moisture. The entrance zip curled inward, snagged on the edge of the flap. It looked paused. Mid-motion. Lena's purple tent had collapsed in on itself. One corner vanished into a soft cavity in the ground. Watermarks striped the canvas in faded streaks, dye bled from the seams in ragged lines.

The kettle still sat by the fire-pit. Unmoved, but transformed. Its metal dulled to a washed-out pewter. The soot beneath had whitened, almost chalky. Ash spread in a thin halo, as if the memory of heat had bleached it over time. The log where Johan once sat had begun to tear itself open. A wide split bloomed at one end, showing pulp wet and fibrous like a tendon. What had once been a seat now felt like a rib cracked under pressure.

Freya lowered Lena to the moss at the very edge of the clearing. The girl crouched without protest. Her hands dropped against her knees. Her face turned toward the fire-pit but her eyes did not follow. She blinked once, then again, both movements delayed. Her mouth stayed shut.

Freya stepped forward.

Earth had fractured along pale seams. Hairline lines radiated outward through the dirt, brittle and fine. The texture resembled scorched pottery, over-fired and hollow. In the centre of that broken soil sat the object.

The casing. A low, heavy mass of metal, matte and uneven. Tarnish spread across its edges in a slow fade. One side bore a fracture. Slightly wider now. Moisture no longer clung to its surface. The soil beneath shone faintly, a wet gleam that refused to darken. Bleached and glistening.

Freya moved closer. Her hand began to itch. She looked down. A fresh blister swelled across her thumb, waxy at the centre and yellowing toward the edge. Another near her palm had broken open. Fluid gathered in the crease between fingers. Behind her, Johan stayed at the edge of the clearing. He kept his eyes on the tents.

"I don't understand," he said, barely above a whisper.

Lena had sunk down fully now. Her eyes had become dull and distant. Freya stood and turned in a slow circle. The tree line looked unfamiliar, but the ground told the truth. Her bootprints from earlier was still there. Softer, blurred by mist, but unmistakable. They had circled.

Johan crouched on his knees, breathing loud through his nose. His forehead shone. Sweat beaded above his lips.

The line of dried blood beneath one nostril had turned rust-brown, flaking with each breath.

"I can't do this," he said. "She's sick. You're worse." He wiped his face and stared at the moss. "We're not getting out of here. You realise that, right?"

His voice came flat. Stripped of pattern. Like a phrase worn out through too much repetition. Freya pressed a hand against her ribs. The pain there had ripened. It sat dense beneath the surface, pressing outward as though something inside her was trying to swell through the muscle.

"We're walking in circles. And now we're back here... With *that*."

He didn't speak its name. He lifted one hand in its direction without turning his head. Then he looked. Truly looked. Something underneath his expression dropped. The muscles behind his eyes changed shape. His face took on the quality of someone recognising a thing far too late. His fingers reached for his forehead. When they came away, they left a line across his skin. A trace of heat and salt and dust. He turned slowly toward her.

"Your hands," he said.

She didn't need to answer. She could feel them. Skin stretched tight across each knuckle. Wetness pooling in the creases. The soft sting of tissue separating. Johan let out a sharp sound. It might have been laughter once, but it came hollow. Dry at the edge.

"This was your idea."

He blinked slowly. Then turned away. His head moved without purpose. Freya stayed where she was, eyes scanning the trees for an answer that didn't exist. The track ahead seemed familiar. A bend in the tree-line. A slant in the light. Perhaps that led to the car. Perhaps not. She raised her hand and pointed, unsure if she wanted reassurance or agreement. Johan's gaze followed. Blank. Nothing anchored behind it. She understood he didn't know either. Together, they chose direction over reason. Movement over certainty.

Lena was lifted to her feet, her weight scattered through Johan's arms. She swayed, slow and silent. Her balance failed for a moment, but her feet held. They moved forward. No rhythm. No momentum. Only the forward drag of necessity. The forest ahead thinned, but Freya didn't trust the light. The last time the trees parted, it had only led them back.

Johan supported Lena with both arms. Her feet dragged occasionally. She hadn't spoken in several minutes. Freya kept glancing back to check her chest still rose and fell. The air pressed close around their faces. Damp but lacking scent. Freya's fingers ached. The blistering had grown worse. She stopped trying to use her right hand to adjust the straps of her pack. It couldn't grip properly anymore.

The terrain had flattened out into a carpet of pine needles that felt the same no matter where she stepped. Freya tried to stay focused on the way the trees leaned to keep her sense of direction. The ridge-line had vanished a while ago.

Johan stumbled. Lena's weight tipped with him. He caught her awkwardly, breath hitching. He muttered something about her feeling heavier, though he couldn't tell if it was her weight or his failing strength. He adjusted her in his arms. After a few paces, his knees wavered. His skin had dulled to a sickly grey. Blood had begun to crust again beneath his nostril. He nodded at the moss, a quiet concession.

Freya moved to help. Together, they eased Lena to the ground.

The girl sagged sideways, eyelids fluttering. Not quite conscious. Freya pressed her palm to Lena's cheek. Heat radiated from beneath the skin. One eye blinked, slow and uneven. Vision vacant.

"We're close," Freya murmured. Not to reassure. Just to say something that might hold.

She scanned ahead. The light became somehow, but unfixed. Beyond the trees, a shape waited. Broad, pale, too regular for forest. A cut in the undergrowth. A clearing, maybe. She passed her pack to Johan and lifted Lena again. This time the girl didn't move. Her limbs dangled. Breath barely brushed against Freya's collar.

Something flashed ahead. A glint. Steel or glass. Cold light reflecting through the trees. Freya moved forward. Between two leaning trunks. A low branch scraped her shoulder. Her arms ached, joints locked tight around the child's weight. Each step felt skewed, uneven. She shifted her grip and kept going. The incline dipped gently.

Then the trees parted.

No sound announced it. No change in air. The forest simply peeled back. A ragged edge of gravel and packed earth appeared beneath her boots. The road was there. Silent. Flattened. Bleached by cloud-light.

And resting just ahead, half-shadowed by pine, sat the Volvo.

Meeting

The Volvo sat just beyond the tree line, skewed awkwardly where the forest yielded reluctantly to the road. Its body remained intact beneath the murky green paint, coated thickly in a pale film of dust. Tyres still plump but crusted with mud. On the bonnet, No rust marred its surface; no visible damage appeared. Yet, the car felt undeniably changed.

It stood with unnatural stillness, as if holding a secret or a breath too long. Condensation clung unevenly across the rear window, leaving a single cleared patch as if someone had tried desperately to peer inside. A flawless line of pine needles parched on the roof, untouched, orderly. Pollen traced delicate veins across the windscreen, like frost trapped in summer. Everything appeared normal.

Freya halted, her legs trembling faintly beneath her. Moments later, Johan staggered to her side. His breath remained shallow, sweat beading across his pale forehead. He said nothing, only stared vacantly, before collapsing awkwardly onto the ground. Lena, fragile and barely responsive, lay beside him. Her eyes opened in brief slivers, struggling against exhaustion.

Taking a deep breath, Freya moved slowly toward the passenger side, fingers unsteady as she tugged at the handle. The door yielded with a reluctant groan. Inside, the car was warped. The car had been covered from the inside in a fine layer of dust. Their Thermos rolled aimlessly in the foot-well, and the first-aid kit had burst, bandages stained yellow.

With mounting dread, Freya rounded to the driver's seat, hope dimming with each step. She inserted the key and turned. Silence. She twisted again, desperation edging into her movements, yet the engine remained lifeless.

"The battery's dead," Johan murmured hoarsely from behind, voice barely audible over the deafening quiet. "Or the wiring. Or both."

Freya remained motionless, fingers stuck momentarily to the wheel's. Her body felt heavier as she emerged from the car. Johan didn't lift his gaze, shoulders slumped, one arm wrapped loosely around Lena, keeping her upright. The girl's cheek rested limply against his leg, lips parted, breathing uneven. Her eyes had drifted shut once more, their dark circles deepening with each passing second.

"She needs help," Johan whispered, his voice raw and fragile.

Freya nodded slowly, reaching out with trembling fingers to brush Lena's forehead. Fever burned beneath her touch.

"The village isn't far," Freya's voice carried a tremble as she tried to think of another way. "Two kilometres at most."

Johan looked up. "Are you sure?"

"We saw it on our way here, remember?"

Gently, Freya lifted Lena once more, the child's slight frame painfully easy to hold. Johan pushed himself upright, wobbling as though gravity had doubled. He steadied himself, scooping up their final bottle of water, his eyes trailing back to the car as if it had betrayed them. The road stretched ahead, a line of pale dirt between the trees. Straight. Familiar. The last thing she trusted before this entire trip.

The road revealed itself slowly. Trees that leaned closer now than they had on the drive in. Dirt layered with dust. The tyre ruts had almost vanished under a thin pelt of needles. The utility track looked more like a fire break than a road. But it was there.

Freya stepped first.

Lena's weight shifted against her collarbone, one leg dragging limp against Freya's side. She was too light. Freya adjusted her grip. Her arms trembled with the effort, not from weight, but from something deeper. Her hands, swaddled in the torn cotton of a T-shirt, pulsed with heat. The fabric stuck faintly where skin had ruptured. Blisters had broken in the last half hour. She could feel it, an ache made visible.

Behind her, Johan moved like something half-carried by gravity. One foot. Then another. He kept to the centre of the path, his head low, shoulders hunched like winded prey. His left hand dragged the bottle. His right trembled every fifth step.

The forest and overcast clouds had thinned just enough to see the sky. A pale seam of blue running above. Mid-afternoon, though it carried none of the warmth. This far away from the camp, birds could be spotted again. Although they were quiet. Freya's boots made no sound. Her thighs burned from the incline, but she didn't stop. She couldn't. If she stopped, she wasn't sure she'd start again. Lena murmured something. A fragment of a word, maybe.

Her lips brushed Freya's collarbone, head shifted minutely.

"Lena?" Freya asked, too quietly.

The child didn't respond. Freya walked faster with Johan struggling to keep up behind.

A slope rose in the road. Gentle but deceptive. Freya's eyes began to blur. She blinked hard. Once. Twice. The burn of salt at the corners. Her arms ached. Her ribs ached. Her breath felt thin. Behind her, Johan coughed. A low, wet sound. Freya didn't look back.

Another bend in the road. Then another. The forest held the shape of silence. The kind of hush that comes after something sharp. A pause after a scream. Freya shifted Lena again to get comfortable, though it didn't help. Her sleeve caught on the child's cheek. Too hot, too dry. Lena's eyes were half-open. Her irises unfocused, her lashes stuck to the skin beneath.

Freya breathed through her teeth. "You're alright," she said, though she wasn't sure who she was talking to.

Behind her, Johan faltered. A muted thump. Not quite a fall. More a collapse of strength. She could hear him gasping for air, each inhalation rasping like sandpaper. Then, painfully slow, his steps resumed, hesitant and heavy. The earth beneath them had lost its strange warmth, becoming brittle and unforgiving.

Another incline. Freya's foot snagged on something. A root or rock hidden in shadows. She neither saw nor cared. Her knee trembled violently, threatening collapse. But desperation steadied her, Lena's weight shifting awkwardly in her numbing arms. Her muscles screamed in protest. Her mouth felt as dry as tinder, the metallic taste of fear thick on her tongue. Sweat trickled slowly down her sleeve. Blood from Lena's gums, persistent and unforgiving, stained the fabric dark red from elbow to wrist.

Yet, she pressed on.

Behind her, Johan halted again, choking out a ragged cough. His skin radiated heat, unnatural against his pallid complexion. He fumbled the cap of their final water bottle, tipping it shakily against parched lips. Water spilled over his chin as he gulped desperately. He coughed again, weaker, sputtering water mixed with blood. He said nothing more, eyes glassy, fixed on Freya's wavering silhouette ahead, the only anchor left in his dissolving world.

Freya kept her focus fixed forward. One step. Another. Rhythmic steps despite the fatigue. Her vision narrowed to the dirt track stretching endlessly beneath weary boots. The path persisted. Gradually, the oppressive forest loosened its grip. The trees parted hesitantly, giving way to open meadows bathed in weak, dappled sunlight. Grass clipped low, orderly yet alien after their chaotic ordeal. Pines framed distant cabins. Their wooden boards stained a faded crimson, peeling paint reminiscent of dried blood. Rooftops pitched sharply, ready to defy snowfall of harsh winter months. Windflowers clustered defiantly by stone walls, their sweet fragrance carried on whispers of a gentle, untainted breeze.

Below them, the forest retreated slowly, revealing the lake's expanse. A sheet of placid water, reflecting a world that no longer made sense.

It stretched vast and flat in the distance, silvered beneath the afternoon light. Its far shore faded into pine and mist. The surface barely stirred. Only faint ripples near the reed-beds disturbed the stillness. Övre Gålvattssjön. Freya couldn't recall its name, but its shape remained clear in her memory. Gentle waves, like a trapped ocean.

The distant tree-line shimmered, everything suspended, as though time had lost its footing and never bothered to correct itself.

Nestled against the lake's edge was the village. Red cabins roofed in grey slate clustered along gravel roads like scattered seeds. Some cabins stood older, their eaves sagging, moss creeping slowly upward from their foundations. Others appeared freshly painted, fences half-completed, tools abandoned mid-task. A solitary moped leaned against a birch, mirrors faintly catching the sun. Laundry swayed behind one cabin, shirts hanging limp like empty human shapes.

A narrow lane ran through the village, winding gently like an artery, shaped more by habit than design. A white enamel sign tilted at a curve. Strandgårdarna. The lettering faded from the weather, nearly unreadable beneath grime. One bolt had rusted loose from its bracket. No cars. No voices. Only the soft hiss of wind through pine needles, and a faint, rhythmic creak of old timber shifting. The village appeared half-asleep.

Freya's knees trembled again. The downward slope should have eased her burden, but her thighs burned sharply. Her chest ached. Carefully, she adjusted Lena higher against her side. One of Lena's arms swung limply, knuckles brushing Freya's jacket. Lena's breath whispered softly against her neck. Slow and weak like the ticking of a clock nearing its final hour.

Johan stopped beside her. He stared blankly at the rooftops as if expecting them to shift under his gaze. Sweat darkened the collar of his shirt, spreading down his spine. He lifted a hand briefly toward his brow, then hesitated, letting it fall heavily back to his side.

Ahead, a bleached bicycle lay on its side beside a postbox. Further on, a garden sat neatly kept. Lawn mown tight, chairs arranged around a stump sawn flat into a table. An ashtray rested on its surface, half-full. The curtains in the nearest window hung open, but the room beyond was dark.

Freya stared down the lane, waiting for a sign. Somewhere beyond the houses, a dog barked once. Then silence returned. They stepped forward. Gravel shifted beneath their boots with a sound that felt too loud for the stillness.

A gate clicked open. It belonged to a small cottage tucked behind low birch and spruce, its paint dulled with age. The garden brimmed with foxgloves and nodding geraniums, their colour vivid beneath the pale sky.

A man stood at the gate, stooped slightly over a wheelbarrow stacked with fresh-cut wood. Broad across the shoulders, his frame carried the quiet weight of habit. Flannel sleeves rolled to the elbow. Arms freckled. Callused hands. On the porch, a woman rinsed her fingers beneath an outdoor tap. Water trickled over her wrists and dripped from her knuckles.

She turned first.

Silver hair pulled into a neat braid. A lavender jumper worn soft at the seams. Blue work trousers that matched the slate roof behind her. Her eyes met Freya's and held steady.

"Hugaligen," she said softly, stepping down from the porch. The word came without surprise. Just concern. She took in the scene with the stillness of someone used to emergencies. "Come here. Put her down gently."

Freya moved without hesitation. Pain surged through her arms as she lowered Lena into the man's outstretched hold. He accepted the girl with care, one arm steadying her weight, the other resting lightly behind her shoulders. He murmured something too quiet to catch, then glanced down at Lena's face with a small smile.

The woman's attention became focused. Her gaze landed on Freya's hands. The fabric wrapped around them had darkened. Moist where the blisters had split.

"Have you burned yourself?" She asked.

Freya tried to answer.

The man cleared his throat. "Margit, She's in shock."

The woman, Margit, paused for a moment. Then she turned, already walking toward the open door.

"Come inside," she called. "Bring her in."

Their cottage was low timber, walls timbered in pale grey, windows trimmed white. Inside, wood-smoke lingered by the hearth, with the faint tang of boiled potatoes. A coffee machine hissed away dripping. The floor creaked under Freya she made her way in. Lena and the older man close behind.

Margit keeled by the child who had been placed on the couch, still barely responsive. She checked pulse and forehead. Her face held something between concern and confusion. Someone confronted by serious injury.

"She's hot," Margit said, voice calm. "But these appear like burns you'd see from a flare or embers. She shouldn't burn up all over"

Freya watched the woman "It burned me instantly, just from the smoke it gave out," Freya said softly.

Margit straightened and gave Freya a gentle, sad look. "You're in shock," she said. "Those..." She touched Freya's arms again,

"...You'll need proper dressings. But I can fix them."

Freya's chest tightened. She would take help, even if it came with questions. Margit turned her attention back to the child, taking her pulse.

"Pulse is thin," Margit murmured.

She leaned closer to examine Lena's face, gently moving a strand of hair away from the girl's temple. The hair fell out into the woman's hands. Clumps had been falling out subtly for a while, leaving a balding patch. Her fingers moved with quiet assurance, the steadiness of someone who had touched too many fevers in too many rooms. The sweat on Lena's skin had started to dry in patches, leaving a dull sheen across her face. Margit's gaze drifted lower. She eased back the collar of Lena's shirt, revealing the rash creeping down the child's neck. A scattering of red-brown welts, some glistening where the skin had split. She said nothing at first, but her mouth set into a frown.

Freya had taken a seat in an armchair next to the couch where Lena laid. Feeling the damp press of cloth against her palms. The fabric had started to stick again. She was afraid to peel it back now. Afraid to see how deep the damage had gone. Her elbows ached from holding too long.

Outside, Johan sat where he had first stopped, on the edge of the porch. His posture had collapsed in on itself. One arm hung slack across his lap. The other cradled the water bottle loosely against his thigh. He hadn't lifted it in minutes. He had barely any vision and no energy to call for help.

Freya glanced toward him, being able to see him at the back door from the living room. His back rose and fell, but unevenly, as though breath had become something measured. She watched the side of his jaw, waiting for any sign that he was watching them in return. But his head stayed bowed.

"Would you mind checking on him?" She said quietly. "He's... He was worse than this earlier."

Margit glanced toward the porch without rising. Her eyes lingered. She gave a small nod and turned to where Johan still sat, slumped just outside the door. She looked to her husband. A silent gesture. He moved at once, stepping through the doorway. The man reached down and took Johan by the arm. Helped him up, slowly. Johan rose. One step forward.

Then a knock. Dull, hollow. Knuckles against wood. A thud. Final. Heavy.

Freya moved before thought caught up. She turned. Johan had collapsed against the porch post, his body folded awkwardly, legs twisted beneath him. One hand scrabbled faintly across the floorboards, fingers grasping nothing.

The man crouched beside him, one hand braced against the rail, the other outstretched but uncertain.

Johan's head jerked. Once. Then again. His spine locked tight. Chest lifted in a sharp arch. Mouth pulled open in a grimace that left his eyes strangely still. Then the tremor came. Subtle at first, then rolling down his arms, just like before. A heel struck the wood, scraping loud and wrong. Like a match dragged far too long.

Margit's voice broke, remaining calm. "Seizure," she said. "Get something under his head."

The man slid the folded cloth beneath Johan's skull as his jaw clamped and shuddered. Freya watched from just inside the living room. There was nothing to do but witness. It lasted less than a minute. When it stopped, Johan went limp. His breath returned in short bursts. His eyes opened. Blurred. Unfocused. He mumbled something, though the words caught in his mouth like broken glass. Margit knelt beside him and placed two fingers to his neck.

"His pulse is racing. Rolf, call 112. Tell them it's three patients. One child barely conscious, A Seizure, And Burns. Possibly something more systemic."

Rolf stepped back from the door, one hand already going to his jacket pocket. He pulled out a mobile, screen cracked through one corner, and turned slightly toward the gravel lane as he raised it to his ear. His voice, when it came, was steady. A low murmur, the kind built from years of not needing to panic.

Freya leaned against the wall. The cool plaster pressed between her shoulder blades. Her breath felt uneven in her chest, as if there wasn't enough room inside her anymore to do everything at once.

Margit helped reposition Johan. His breath, each more shallow than the last. A string of sweat threaded down the side of his face. His hand twitched once, then stilled again.

"Did he hit his head when he went down?" Margit asked.

"I don't know," Freya replied. "I didn't see."

The woman stood slowly and wiped her palms on her trousers. She glanced over at Lena who hadn't moved. The blanket Margit had tucked around her had slipped slightly from one shoulder, and the skin beneath looked pale and waxed. Her lips were parted. A shallow dryness marked the edges. Rolf stepped back inside, phone still pressed to one ear.

"They're dispatching from Östersund. Helicopter," he said. "It'll be about thirty minutes."

Margit gave a slow nod. "Did they ask for vitals?"

"They asked everything. I told them what we could. Said we were near the lake."

Freya turned from Lena and looked at Margit. "I need to explain."

Margit looked at her closely. Not just listening but weighing something in her mind. Freya swallowed. Her throat felt lined with dust.

"We were camped near the smaller lakes. About six kilometres west. Past the waterline. We followed an old road. Not marked on any of the maps. It ended in a clearing. A low one. There was heat, from the ground. And no birds. Just... Stillness. Everything was too quiet."

Freya reached up and unwound part of her sleeve. The cloth had dried into the broken skin beneath. She peeled it back slowly, carefully. Flesh opened again where it stuck, raw in the creases of her palm. Cold air met the wound with a clinical sting. Rolf had stepped further into the room now, a hand braced loosely on the table.

"Radiation," he said. "That's what your man called it. The triangle. Trefoil."

Freya gave a small nod. Margit looked at her husband, her voice quieter than before.

"That old path above Gålvattssjön. Didn't you say the military used it once? For weather stations?"

Rolf didn't answer at first. His eyes had fallen on Lena's sleeping form. He looked older than he had minutes ago.

"I helped build one. Eighty-three we started, I think. A lot of weather stations through here and up through Lapland were built with the same design. An RTG for remote access, even in the winters. Good for research. I heard the whole thing was knocked down by eighty-six after a bunch of researchers abandoned the thing."

Margit took a small step back. A quiet calculation of someone fitting one truth against another. Freya stayed silent. The pain in her hands was less noticeable now. Or perhaps simply overwhelmed by the heaviness that had entered the room. The realisation that none of this had been sudden.

Time passed slowly. Freya eased herself into the chair by the door, shoulders stiff, her gaze distant. A slight tremor ran through her limbs. Whether it came from cold, fatigue, or something deeper, she no longer knew. Rolf stood motionless for a while longer. The weight of it all had settled on him too. Three strangers were brought into his home, all of them ill. One barely breathing. Another unconscious. The third unravelled and burned. His worry was quiet, but it shaped his face in hard lines. A kind of guilt hung behind his eyes, as though some part of him had already guessed what might have been left behind.

He stepped away, almost gently, and walked out into the garden. Outside, Rolf's head tilted toward the eastern tree-line. The birch leaves had started to quiver, though there was no wind. The sound grew. Freya recognised the pulse of rotors. She had not realised how long it had been since she had heard anything mechanical.

She moved to the window. The light slanted hard across the grass, catching every fleck of dust in the glass. Two helicopters came in low, one behind the other. Bright yellow with green. One larger, one leaner. Their shadows moved ahead of them like spectres, rippling across the trees, through the fencing, into the gravel. The house shuddered faintly when they passed overhead.

Margit opened the door and stepped onto the porch. The field at the far end of the property had already begun to flatten. Grass whipped sideways. A plastic bucket rolled along the fence-line, then lifted briefly and vanished out of sight. Freya followed her out. The air stung now. Every loose particle thrown up from the soil spun in waves. A fine grit coated her tongue. She squinted against it, raising her bandaged hand to cover her mouth.

The first helicopter touched down. The side hatch opened before the rotors had fully settled. Two medics jumped down, carrying packs between them. One glanced toward the house and spoke into a shoulder radio. The other pointed toward Johan, who was now half-upright against the porch rail. Rolf knelt beside him, hand on his shoulder.

Another medic stepped down from the second helicopter. He wore a high-vis jacket marked with regional emblems, reflective strips catching light in the haze. The uniform was red and deep navy, streaked with pale dust along the seams. A headset looped down to his collar. His boots were wet up to the ankles.

"We need to assess them where they are," he said. He pointed toward the house. "The child first."

Freya stepped aside. Margit held the door. The medic stepped through, followed by a second with the stretcher. Inside, the air felt too still again, too separate. Freya watched from the hall as they checked Lena. One knelt down and spoke softly, though the girl didn't respond. The other medic uncapped a pen and wrote something on the back of his glove, two short numbers. Then clipped a monitor to the girl's finger. It beeped once. He placed a mask gently over her mouth and nose. Her skin looked greyer now.

"She's febrile," the medic said. "Low response. Rash visible across torso and neck. When did the symptoms begin?"

Freya tried to speak but her throat caught. Margit touched her arm lightly. "Four days ago," Freya said. "No, maybe five. She was tired at first. Then sick. She got a bit better. Then worse when we found some sort of radioactive box."

The medic nodded. He looked a little flustered as he looked over to the other medic. "Manifest Stage of Acute Radiation Syndrome?" He spoke with the other paramedic who gave him an assuring nod.

Freya stood aside as they lifted Lena onto the stretcher. One of the medics spoke briefly into his radio. The words didn't reach her. Another team had reached Johan. He had tried to rise on his own but failed. Rolf had helped lower him onto a stretcher, guiding him gently with both hands.

The first helicopter's rotors began to move once more. One of the medics signalled toward the other. Freya saw the exchange in glances, the way they checked over Johan's vitals again. Their hands moved fast but without flinching. Johan's eyes were open, but unfocused.

Freya stepped forward. One of the responders stopped her with a glance.

"You're Freya?" He asked.

She nodded.

"We're taking you all to Östersund. We can't risk longer transit yet. They're prepping the trauma bay. They'll be waiting."

Freya looked toward Lena's stretcher. The medic had covered her with a thermal sheet as she was taken into the first helicopter

"What's wrong with her?" Freya asked. Her voice sounded distant.

The medic paused. "We don't know everything yet. But she's exhibiting signs consistent with acute radiation exposure. You all are. Possibly high dose. If the exposure source was recent, we may still be within a critical window."

The medic's voice softened slightly. "We'll stabilize everyone. Then reassess for transfer to Stockholm, if needed."

Margit stood by the doorway. Her hands were clasped tightly in front of her.

"Her burns," Freya said suddenly. "Mine too. They weren't from heat."

The medic gave the faintest shake of the head. "They'll be treated as contamination until ruled out."

Outside, the blades of the first helicopter turned slower now, ready but waiting. The stretcher bearing Lena was lifted inside first. She didn't move beneath the foil, her face pale where it was visible beneath the oxygen mask. One medic climbed in after her, adjusting straps and tubes quietly. Johan followed soon after.

They moved him on the second stretcher. One of the paramedics paused at his shoulder, spoke briefly into his ear. Johan didn't answer. His fingers curled faintly against the edge of the blanket. His face had taken on a greyness Freya didn't recognise.

The door was pulled shut behind them. The thrum of the rotor grew louder as it gathered speed.

A medic turned to her, gesturing to the second aircraft where the blades had started to rise again. "You'll follow in the next one," she said. "They'll be ahead of you by ten minutes at most."

Freya nodded. She didn't know what else to do. Rolf stood at the edge of the grass, shielding his eyes from the dust. Margit was beside him, arms folded tight across her chest, watching the tree-line as though something else might emerge behind it. Margit gave a single nod as Freya passed, a motion both kind and help-less.

The seat belts clipped in with a hard snap. Her hands throbbed beneath the gauze, nerves catching at every bump and motion. The medic inside offered her a blanket but she didn't take it. The door sealed with a dull hiss. Rotors span. Lift-off. The ground, green and bright, fell away as the sky became closer. Freya looked to her left. In the distance beneath the forest. An opening. A patch of dirt. Three tents.

Inside the cabin, the noise pressed against everything. It was con-stant and uneven. An engine struggling against its own rhythm. Freya sat with her back against the wall with her hands elevated slightly in her lap. Her fingers had started to throb with a more regular pulse now. Like though something beneath the gauze was trying to force its way out. She turned her attention to the medic.

The medic sitting opposite her seemed younger than Freya; mid-twenties, Light brown hair tied back under a navy cap. Thin, carefully shaped eyebrows that gave her expression a kind of fo-cused neatness. Her face was calm but alert; the sort of face that had learned how to hold still in other people's panic. Her uni-form was clean at the collar but dusted down the sleeves, and her gloved hands rested loosely against her knees, ready to move but in no rush. Her boots were strapped tightly, military neat. Her badge read Linnea, just below the patch marked *Region Jämtland Härjedalen.* They didn't speak at first.

The world moved outside the window in blurs of pine and low marsh. The sun had begun to lower, softening the edges of everything. Clouds stretched thin and uneven above the horizon like pulled wool. Freya watched them pass by.

Linnea reached across the small space and checked the bandaging at Freya's left forearm. She didn't ask permission. She peeled a small section back, inspected the colour beneath, then replaced it with practised care.

"No fresh bleeding," she said. "That's good."

Freya looked up but didn't respond. The hum in the cabin rose as they banked slightly. The seatbelt dug into her collarbone.

"Do you know how far ahead the others are?" Freya asked.

"Six or seven minutes. Maybe eight."

"And they're... Okay?"

Linnea tilted her head slightly, weighing their options.

"They're alive. That's the baseline right now." The medic looked out the window, then back. "The girl was unresponsive when we lifted. But still breathing on her own... Although fever's climbing."

"Lena," Freya said quietly. "Her name is Lena."

Linnea nodded once and started some paperwork; patient intake forms. She paused again, still looking down at the paperwork "She's small. And young. The smaller they are, the faster it gets them."

Freya looked down at her hands. Dark moisture bled through the bandage near her thumbs, soaking into the cuff of her shirt with a creeping, rust-brown edge. "Will she make it?" She asked.

Linnea was quiet for a moment. She tapped her pen a couple of times before continuing her paperwork un-phased. "I don't know," she said.

Freya looked up sharply. Linnea met her gaze without flinching.

"I'm not going to give you a maybe," Linnea continued. "I'm not trained for comfort. If it's bad enough to cause skin changes and collapse this fast, then yes, it might not be good. That doesn't mean no either."

The words hung between them. Freya's breath caught somewhere in her throat and didn't move. She nodded, though it felt mechanical.

Outside, the trees blurred past. Roads appeared. Farm tracks. Fences. The shapes of lives that had kept going while hers had stopped. Somewhere in the far distance, she thought she saw a car moving. It looked impossibly small.

"Your partner is with her now, she'll at least feel less scared with that." Linnea said after a moment.

Freya turned her head. "Ex-partner."

Linnea smiled, brief and dry. "Right. My mistake. You've got that look people get when they've been trying not to murder others in a confined space. I get that look when my friends put me in a novel."

Freya let out a sound. Not quite a laugh, but not far off. Linnea nodded, pleased enough with herself.

"They'll keep them together," she said. "Östersund's good for trauma. They'll be seen straight in."

"Is that where she'll stay?"

"For now. But if it's confirmed radiation, she'll go south. Karolinska's got the isolation wards. And better coffee."

Freya nodded again. A smile came a bit easier this time. The engine wurred down tone as they began to descend. The cabin stilled in that way things do when the sky stops holding them up. Linnea tightened her belt, then leaned forward to secure the supplies beneath her seat. Through the port window, the trees came closer. The city unrolled in fragments. Rooftops, roads, antennae. A large glass-fronted building stood just beyond the approach, its helipad ringed in yellow on the lake. Linnea checked the latch on Freya's belt and gave her a brief glance. The landing was smooth but loud. The skids touched down with a jolt that seemed to echo up through her teeth. Then silence, except for the slowing of the blades.

A nurse waited just outside, masked, gloves pulled high up her forearms. Behind her, a stretcher. The doors opened. Cool air rolled in. Freya blinked at the sudden light. Everything smelt of disinfectant and fuel.

Linnea unbuckled her straps. "You good to stand?"

Freya nodded, though the motion made her head swim. She stepped down into the floodlights. The hospital stood tall above her, glass and steel. Somewhere inside, machines were already humming for Johan and Lena. Nurses walking briskly between wards. She closed her eyes as they wheeled her forward.

In the dark behind her lids, the image came back. Distance beneath the forest. An opening. A patch of dirt. Three tents.

Arrival

Gravel grew sparse where the utility road ended, giving way to pine roots pushing through ruts like exposed ribs. Rainwater gathered quietly in shallow dips. A Volvo stood off-centre, the driver's door nudged almost closed.

A folding trestle table stood erected beneath taut green tarp, each corner weighed by heavy black sandbags. Paper maps lay clipped down with metal fasteners. Two Geiger counters rested inside a plastic case, one already humming a steady warning. Radiation badges had been methodically arranged in careful rows beside a clipboard. Three readings circled firmly, one scratched out, re-placed by another marked provisional. Set-up had finished over-night, ready for investigation come morning.

Beside a logistics truck, two men stepped into pale yellow hazmat suits. Fabric appeared almost translucent were stretched taut. Stiff seams folded sharply at elbows and knees, broad hoods fixed onto rounded collars. Black visors narrowed their faces to insecticide anonymity. One man slowly pulled a zipper upward, pausing briefly as an intake hose clipped firmly into its filter pack. His companion crouched already, tightening boot straps, breath fogging faintly inside his visor. A diesel generator idled softly behind the last vehicle, its faint pulse drifting quietly through thinning trees. Nearby, another figure adjusted gloves without looking, already retreating behind reflective glass. Their suits bore no insignia; nothing but shape and deliberate movement. Their presence stilled every sound, making even forest silence deepen.

Three figures prepared in hazmat suits advanced single-file down a narrowing trail. Their boots slowly sank into the under-brush that yielded softly, swallowing each step. Birch pressed closer as they pressed further. Branches caught silently at their sleeves. Pine needles whispering faint secrets. Behind them, their path faded gradually until swallowed completely, road and daylight lost to dense shadows and thickening leaves. Early-morning twilight seeped steadily into the spaces between trunks, turning greens to muted greys, colours bleeding quietly into darkness.

Mosses grew patchier here, brittle and yellowed, edges curled inward as if recoiling from an unknown harm. Even air seemed heavier, pressing gently against visors, breath growing shallow inside enclosed masks. Their steps slowed involuntarily, caution instinctively taking hold. A silence fell deeper around them, broken only by muffled footfalls.

Minutes stretched unnaturally before arriving at camp's boundary. It appeared smaller than maps had promised, shrinking inward as trees loomed closely at its edges, trunks leaning like curious mourners at graveside. At its centre sagged a single green tent, pole snapped sharply, fabric collapsed inwardly as if wounded, gasping for breath. A single child's shoe rested half-submerged in damp earth near an extinguished fire-pit, laces undone. Beside it sprawled a sleeping bag dragged open, its fabric crumpled and empty. Near the tent's entrance lay vomit, visible against pale ash. Nearby, a Geiger counter clicked steady ticks. Not quite frantic, but enough for concern. Just loud enough to sharpen nerves, a whisper of something unseen but undeniably present, quietly seeping radiation into soil, skin, and silence alike.

Erik Nyström stood near the centre of the clearing, sleeves damp to the elbow. The weight of command settled quiet on his shoulders. His voice and bearing marked him as *Överstelöjtnant*; Lieutenant Colonel, CBRN command. He wasn't the sort who needed volume for his orders to be followed.

The hazmat material hung heavier on him than it did on the younger men. Pale orange, streaked dark at the knees and along the lower back where he'd crouched earlier to take soil samples himself. His boots were caked thick with dirt. He held a dosimeter at arm's length, slow and steady, like a man waiting for news he already understood. A secondary unit was strapped to his wrist. Its screen faint behind scratched plastic. The hand-held meter ticked once, then again, then sharper the third time. He adjusted the range setting with one gloved thumb. No reaction on his face. Just a blink.

He glanced sideways at the clipboard tech standing nearby, then looked back toward the tree line. Still nothing moved. When the new team emerged, suits rustling faintly as they crossed into the open space, he didn't raise a hand.

"Start your sweep from the south side," he said, the voice inside the mask flat and clipped. "Mark anything that spikes above the background. Photograph every quadrant before you touch it."

One of the new arrivals nodded. The tallest moved toward the crushed tent. Erik turned slightly and spoke to someone behind him, a younger man with a clipboard.

"Log every pass on the minute. If it moves, if it melts, if it's warm, we take it."

The man nodded, pencil already moving. Erik moved to the centre of the camp. Right where the metal container had been dug up earlier that day.

"What we got so far?" He questioned, reaching his arm out expecting another clipboard. An officer gave him a report on a clipboard. The clipboard was damp around the edges. A plastic cover had bubbled from the heat in the truck. Erik flipped it back and read without speaking.

DEVICE:

RTG - Nuclear Radiothermal Generator; Small Steel casing, corroded. Model unlisted.

Likely origin: Weather station field deployment, early-80s.

Recovered at ~30cm depth, adjacent to tent site.

ISOTOPE:

Primary: Strontium-90

Casing breach confirmed.

Decay heat intact. Estimated activity: 2.4 TBq

Dose at source: 2 Sv/h ; Dose at 1m: 250 mSv/h

Soil saturation in the core zone. Beta emitter.

Contamination within 3 - 4m.

EXPOSURE RISK:

Surface contact = severe beta burn potential.

No alpha risk. Inhalation improbable.

Internal dose vector: ingestion or mucosal contact.

Bioaccumulates in bone. Avoid contact. Deadly exposure probable.

Erik ran a gloved thumb along the edge of the clipboard. It squeaked faintly. He didn't look at the officer beside him. He let the page settle back, then passed the board off without meeting the man's eye.

"Strontium," he murmured bitterly, the word catching like gravel in his throat. "Someone buried a generator and didn't bother logging it. That's our legacy. A country of indifferent fools."

The bitterness in his voice lingered, a quiet accusation hanging thickly in the air, unchallenged. He moved forward again, pausing over the rusted metal container. His Geiger counter clicked faster now, a subtle, unrelenting reminder of invisible danger. The team's eyes were fixed silently on Erik, yet his own gaze remained trained solely on the casing; corroded, dented from some forgotten impact, nearly half a metre long and lying askew in disturbed earth.

"Good luck maintaining healthy bones after exposure to this," he continued whilst observing.

His words were hollow, lacking any comfort or hope. They settled heavily into silence. Nothing but the clicking of Geiger counters. No one spoke; what reassurance could they possibly give?

A younger team member stepped tentatively forward. His voice trembled slightly, betraying anxiety born from inexperience. "Sir... How bad is this, really?"

Erik didn't respond immediately. Instead, he carefully adjusted the gain on his Geiger counter, watching as the needle twitched steadily upwards. His expression tightened imperceptibly. The rusted metal, dull grey beneath layers of corrosion, bore scorch marks along one side. A faded identification tag clung stubbornly to the casing, its text rendered illegible by years of neglect and exposure.

"It's not great," he said at last. His voice steady but cautious. He glanced toward the younger team member before looking up toward the sky as a breeze stuck. "But it's not terrible. Could be much worse."

He straightened slowly, turning to gaze back at the waiting vehicles, their outlines blurred softly by shadowed branches and creeping twilight.

"At least it's enclosed," he continued with an attempt at reassurance, "Better than an open core at Forsmark. If it ever comes to that, we'll be evacuating entire counties, not just clearing up camp-grounds."

He paused, raising his gaze staying upwards, as if hoping to find clarity in the indifferent expanse of the afternoon sky. A weary sigh escaped him, heavy with frustration, weariness gathered from repeated tedious tasks and endless bureaucratic repetition.

"Still, the IAEA's going to have a bloody field day with this one," he murmured, more to himself than anyone else, resignation settling firmly in his shoulders. Erik turned slowly, his eyes settling heavily on another of the men in hazmat suits. "And the campers? Where are they now?"

***

The hospital room carried an oppressive scent of plastic; thick, sterile, and cloying. It was the smell of medical dressings sealed tightly in packets and warmed gently by artificial heat, mingling subtly with disinfectant and the sterile air of clinical indifference. Fluorescent lights above hummed persistently, their monotonous drone filling every quiet gap. One fixture flickered erratically, casting brief, jittering shadows across the ceiling before stabilising reluctantly. Off-white tiles, discoloured slightly at the edges, stretched in perfect uniformity overhead, adding to the oppressive sterility. The room's atmosphere felt thin, dry enough to scratch at the back of the throat, making each breath rasp slightly.

Freya's eyes were half-open, fighting against a film that blurred the world around her. Shapes appeared soft-edged, indistinct, as if glimpsed through misted glass. She attempted to blink clarity back into her vision, but her lashes stuck stubbornly together, gummy and heavy. Her head felt swollen with pressure, as though packed too tightly from within.

Her hands were first to awaken, bringing with them a pain that rose in hot, rhythmic waves. Each pulse felt strange. Something restless, trapped beneath her skin, crawling to escape. Numb fingers remained immobile, joints stiff and resistant, encased beneath layers of bandaging that muffled all sensation but pain. The pain burned like they were still bathed in flames. A muted scratching sounded from her left. The idle scribbling of a pen moving mechanically, capping and uncapping between quiet pauses. Beneath these small noises lay the steady hum of machinery, an alien rhythm, out of sync with her own heartbeat.

She became aware then of tubes taped securely along her forearm, tugging faintly against her skin each time she swallowed. Freya cautiously turned her head, the motion slow and hesitant, with the room lagging behind her movements like a delayed echo. She saw a partition wall, a pale fabric curtain hanging limply from a curved rail, and beside it stood a monitor displaying numbers she couldn't decipher, blinking and beeping softly in a pattern she did not recognise.

A table sat near the bed, its surface crowded with small labelled bottles. One held a liquid of muted pink, another beaded with droplets of condensation, moisture running in slow trails down its glass surface. Freya opened her mouth to speak but anxiety tightened her throat.

A nurse entered without sound, as though part of the sterile quiet itself. Mid-thirties perhaps, with features softened by long practice in control. She wore pale blue scrubs beneath a translucent crinkled plastic apron. Her hands were embraced with purple latex. No smile greeted Freya, but neither did she avert her gaze. There was a kind of watchful stillness in her bearing. A quiet endurance of countless hours spent in rooms just like this one. The sort of person who knew exactly how to move around grief, confusion, and pain without being swallowed by it. She paused a moment longer than necessary, reading something in Freya's eyes before crossing to the bedside.

"You're in Östersund," she said, checking the monitor with a glance. "They brought you in just after yesterday afternoon."

Freya blinked. Her throat ached a little. "Lena?" She asked. The word came out raw but clear.

"She's here," the nurse said, not missing a beat. "Two floors down. They've moved her into paediatrics for observation. She was asking for you earlier."

Freya exhaled. Her chest still felt tight. A held breath releasing. The nurse moved to the IV stand and adjusted the flow. A small click, then the hiss of a fresh syringe being slotted into place.

"You've had contact burns. Mostly palm-side, some tracking up the forearms. Beta radiation. We've started antibiotics and fluids. You're stable enough for transfer."

Freya glanced down. She couldn't see the damage, only the shape of her arms inside the thick wrappings. A faintly pink where the bandages thinned, stained at the knuckles. Her fingers were swollen. Her thumbs stuck out awkwardly, bandaged separately. The nurse checked the saline level and made a note on a clipboard she pulled from the wall.

"They logged your dose at just over two sieverts. No marrow impact so far. No lung exposure. That's good. But the hands will take time."

Freya closed her eyes.

"We'll be flying you to Karolinska University hospital tonight," the nurse continued. "Stockholm. The burns unit there has more capacity, and they're better equipped for contamination cases."

"I want to see Lena."

"I know." The nurse's voice didn't shift, yet an unspoken understanding ensued by a pause. "But we're waiting on your clearance panel. You've still got trace surface readings. It's precautionary."

Freya turned her head to the side. The partition wall met the floor with a thin line of plastic. Beyond it, the faint sound of a cart moving. The nurse unwrapped part of her right hand. The skin beneath was raw, the colour of overripe fruit, slick where an outer layer of skin had peeled away. Blisters had collapsed. A fingernail was missing. Freya didn't look any longer than she needed to. She stared at the ceiling. The nurse applied gel from a foil packet and re-wrapped the hand in a fresh layer of bandages.

"She's sleeping," the nurse said gently, referring to Lena. "They gave her something to sleep."

Freya felt something close to her ribs tighten. The weight of being still here, while her daughter was somewhere below, just as wrapped and just as watched.

"She's not alone," the nurse said. "I'll be back before your transport."

She adjusted the blanket at Freya's side, checked the IV one last time, then moved the curtain halfway closed as she stepped out. In the corridor, the hum of filtered air replaced the heart monitor's rhythm. She peeled off one glove as she walked, rolled it in her palm, and reached into her pocket for her badge.

Two floors down, through an isolated wing, a door waited. Yellow-taped and coded with *radiation hazard*. The paediatric ward had been cleared in a hurry. Most of the rooms stood empty, equipment unplugged, carts wheeled into corners. The doors to each unit were marked with biohazard tape and whiteboard scrawl. Lena's room was at the far end, just beyond the secondary filter doors. The nurse keyed herself in and stepped through.

The air was drier here, filtered more aggressively until it lost all trace of weather or breath. A portable scrubber hissed from the far wall, its steady exhale soft but unrelenting. Lena lay in the centre of the bed, disturbingly still. Sheets had been drawn tight around her, too tight. They were tucked in with the kind of precision that implied she was not expected to move. Her small frame barely lifted the fabric. One foot had slipped sideways beneath the hem, heel exposed, toes curled faintly inward like something forgotten mid-motion. Her hospital gown sagged at the collar, revealing the delicate ridge of her collarbone. Her skin remained dull and greyed.

The IV line disappeared into her right arm, skin there blotched with old adhesive. Its edges lifted where sweat had gathered and dried in ridges. Tape had been layered, then layered again, clumsy where it tried to hold failing flesh together. Above her, the monitor traced shallow pulses in dim green. A hollow rhythm, consistent but reluctant. The oxygen mask had slipped beneath her chin, resting now like an afterthought. No one had removed it. No one had put it back.

Across the pillowcase, strands of hair were strewn not in wisps but in clumps. Root-heavy. The kind of shedding not seen in sleep, but in decline. They had clung to fabric and to one another, forming small, irregular nests at the edge of her head. Nesting where her skull met cotton, as though trying to return to something before movement.

The nurse moved carefully. She brushed the hair back with a gloved hand, then wiped the strands away with a tissue from the tray. She paused, gently lifting the pillow edge to check for moisture. It was damp underneath. Sweat, mostly. A faint pink stain where her cheek had rested and bled. Lena's face was pale. The rash had spread further along her jawline. Patches rising just below the ear with purple spots appearing. A paediatrician had noted it as "non-specific erythema," but the nurse had seen it before.

She glanced across the room. A sealed plastic evidence bag lay on the counter, zipped and labelled. Inside, a rounded stone, faintly damp. Pebble. It just sat there. One googly eye still attached. Staring. Wrapped twice. Marked for pickup. No one had touched it since.

The nurse returned her focus to the bed. She checked the cannula for occlusion and tapped the screen to log the readings. Lena moved slightly. A twitch at first, one finger, then a flutter at the corner of her mouth.

The nurse stood for a moment longer. She reached out, adjusted the blanket at the girl's shoulder, and gently brushed the last of the hair from her cheek. Her oxygen mask was readjusted, then the nurse turned away. The light over the bed dimmed slightly as she passed. She closed the door behind her with both hands, careful not to let the latch catch loud.

Freya was propped upright as she awoke a couple of hours later. The bed had been angled slightly, a second pillow added behind her shoulders. The bandages on her hands had been changed again. Tighter. Neater. The pain was sharper. More defined; a constant throb that came and went like pressure behind the eyes.

A tray table had been folded to the side. Two men stood beside it. No coats. No hospital attire. One carried a clipboard. The other held a black notebook and a pair of gloves. The older man stood with his weight balanced evenly, feet placed with precision. His posture was shaped by years of duty. He looked built for structure. Even out of hazmat suits or military uniforms, the lines of service still held him. His face wore the imprint of rank long carried. Lines pressed deep around the mouth and upon the forehead, tension settled just behind the eyes.

His shirt was standard-issue blue, collar worn pale along the seam. A plain belt circled his waist, polished smooth near the buckle. Shoulders remained squared. Hands rested calmly, one over the other. The name badge clipped to his chest caught a glint of light. *Erik Nyström.*

Hair had greyed unevenly across the scalp, thinning where it lifted from the crown, damp near the temples from the filtered air just outside. There was experience in how he watched the room. He understood what kind of silence this was.

The younger man stood a step behind him. Neatly dressed. A notepad gripped in one hand, the pen poised but unmoving. His expression was stern, but inexperienced. A civilian suit on a daunting task.

"We're not here to take long," Erik said. "Just to understand what happened at the site."

Freya didn't speak right away. She shifted herself to get more comfortable. She tried to wet her lips with her tongue but her mouth remained dry and metallic.

"We camped for five nights," she said eventually. "It was quiet. It looked safe."

"And when did you find the object?"

Freya let her eyes drift to the ceiling for a moment. One of the panels had water damage near the edge. A faint, brownish ring.

"Johan dug something out near the fire-pit. Said he hit metal. He cleared it with a spade, I helped as it hissed."

"Did it look new?"

"No. It was rusted through. A seal had cracked. I told him to leave it."

"And your daughter? How long was she exposed?"

There was no reaction from the two men. The man behind the clipboard wrote something down with a face fit for poker. Freya swallowed hard, tearing up at the eyes.

"I don't know. She was tired, but she wasn't frightened. That was the worst part."

Erik nodded. "You handled the object directly?"

"No, we were close trying to figure out what it was when it broke"

"For how long?"

Freya looked down at her wrapped hands. No one spoke for a moment. The monitor beside her beeped softly. Silence continued to fill the space with Freya not knowing how to answer. Erik noticed the tears building up behind Freya's eyes. With the majority of his life in service, he knew he had hardened these sorts of encounters; so much that he was unsure on how to comfort civilians anymore.

"It's a radiothermal generator," Erik broke the silence, making a dull attempt at being comforting, "A forgotten one. From a weather station decommissioned in the mid 80s. Strontium-90 casing. Bad shielding, if any. It should've been logged and removed."

Her hands ached. The left was worse than the right. There was heat rising under the gauze, a kind that didn't fade. Erik cleared his throat.

"You'll be moved to Karolinska within the hour," Erik said. "The burns team is already briefed."

They turned to leave. Erik hesitated once, then followed the other man outside. Freya listened to the door close. Soon after, nurses changed Freya into something that didn't feel like clothes. A transport gown, stiff at the seams, cut too high at the collar. The sleeves had been rolled back awkwardly to accommodate the bandages. Her arms had been propped on folded towels to keep the swelling down. She still couldn't move her fingers properly. The right one twitched involuntarily now and then.

The nurse this time was younger. No name tag. Brisk in that overly gentle way some people had around patients. "Transports nearly ready," she said. "Just waiting on the ambulance crew."

Freya didn't ask where they were taking her. That part she knew.

"I want to see my daughter," Freya said.

The nurse didn't pause. She was already adjusting the chart. "Still under contact restriction," she replied. "It's precautionary."

"Her surface counts are climbing," she continued, attempting to provide hope. "They're moving her into full paediatric isolation. No direct access, no room entry. I'm sorry."

Freya sat back, stunned by the clarity of the refusal. For a moment, the world sounded thin. As if the air had pulled itself tighter. "I want to see her. Please."

A pause. Just long enough to count as consideration.

"I'll check," the nurse said, and left without promising anything. When she returned, a man in a navy vest stood beside her. A radiation symbol crest at the chest, FOI stitched beneath it. One of the defence research team. Masked, gloved, voice sealed by protocol.

"You can view her through observation glass," he said. "No closer." His voice was cold and calculated. They wheeled her down corridors she didn't recognise. Past empty beds, a closed coffee kiosk, a line of vending machines all flashing the same red error message. Her bed moved with the slight tremor of poor wheels. The IV bag swung faintly above her head.

They brought her to a room that smelled like antiseptic. One wall was glass: thick, lead-lined, double-sealed.

Behind it: Lena.

She was still asleep, comatose by medication to help with the pain. Curled on her side beneath a thin blanket, hands tucked to her chest. An oxygen line trailed from her nose. Her hair had been plaited since the last time. Sectioned. Combed into small divisions to monitor hair loss. The crown of her head showed the scalp. The lighting was soft. The kind that mimicked dusk. Lena's chest rose slowly. Then fell again.

Freya pressed her bandaged hands into the blanket across her lap.

"She doesn't know I'm leaving," she said.

"She'll follow in the next day or two," the man replied calmly. "When her blood-work stabilises."

She watched the shape of her daughter's body beneath the sheet. One foot bent inward, toes against the mattress. A tiny blister sat at the corner of her mouth. It had been less than a minute before Freya was being wheeled off once more, leaving Lena behind.

They wheeled her out through the lower level, into a corridor where everything smelled of steam and bleach. Linen carts lined the walls, piled high with sheets still warm from dryers. Mop heads hung from metal hooks, dripping slowly into stained plastic buckets. The air was humid. Motion-triggered lights blinked overhead in quick succession, buzzing faintly as they flared to life, then fell dark again as she passed beneath them. One by one, they receded behind her like distant buoys slipping underwater.

At the ambulance bay, the concrete held the warmth of spent rain. It smelled of rubber tyres, and diesel. A stretcher jolted slightly as it changed hands. Two paramedics waited just beyond the sliding glass. One gave a nod, face unreadable behind his mask. The other leaned forward to adjust the brake pedal before guiding her up the metal ramp. The wheels clattered. Every vibration moved straight through the frame and into her spine, a series of dull shocks she could neither brace for nor escape.

Inside, the ambulance glowed under a strip of pale overhead light. Walls curved into each other. Sterile white, bleached clean. Every surface was either buckled in or bracketed down. A defibrillator sat holstered by Freya's head. A radio crackled softly from the front console. Voices came and went. Clipped exchanges, short bursts followed by termination beeps. Other calls were being answered. Other names, other incidents. Teams dispatched to scenes she'd never see. She lay still, listening to problems that did not include her. One of the crew checked her IV line, fingers pressing the tape near her elbow. The other clipped the stretcher into place with a solid, final click. When the doors shut, the interior dimmed to a sterile dusk, a kind of artificial quiet that hummed in her teeth.

The drive took fifteen minutes. She tracked it not by time, but by what passed her window. Östersund slid sideways outside the glass, glimpses of familiar buildings, roads she knew, side streets she didn't. The roundabout with the cracked sculpture near the yoghurt café. A petrol station where the sign had folded in on itself during a storm last year. Then nothing she could name. Street-lights blurred in long ribbons. The motion felt unreal, like being carried backwards through a version of her own life. City lights from the window disappeared as they crossed the bridge. Another fifteen minutes of darkness.

They turned off near a metal gate that hissed open at their approach. The wheels met tarmac. At the far end of the runway, a hangar opened onto floodlit concrete. The plane stood waiting. Its body, a clean white except for the faint grey outline of a Swedish roundel on the tail. The glass over the cockpit caught no light. It reminded her of the business jets that had once moved consultants and politicians between quiet cities. This one had been stripped down to its function.

Inside: one hospital bed, two folding seats, and the smell of alcohol wipes soaked into brushed aluminium. The air was too dry; processed. The turbines ticked as they cooled. A high, stuttering rhythm that seemed to linger even after the noise stopped.

A set of folding stairs had been lowered to the tarmac. Two crew members stood beside them: gloved, masked, layered in jackets against the drop in temperature. Neither said her name. One nodded. A smile that Freya couldn't see under their masks. They wheeled the stretcher forward without a word. Freya tried to lift her head to see the sky. It was pale and wide and fading slowly. The kind of light that never fully left, this far north.

Inside, the cabin was narrow. One stretcher bay that she was placed onto. A long medical rack lined the opposite wall. White cabinets, clipped oxygen tanks, a bank of muted monitors. Tubing and straps coiled from the ceiling like spare thoughts.

Her hands twitched beneath the bandages. No one said when they'd leave. The engines started up. The vibration from the engines behind her vibrating the floor and cabinets beside her. A deep hum passed up through the stretcher into her ribs. A second tone joined it. A soft beep. Someone murmured to someone else behind the partition.

She thought about Lena. Not a word. Not a shape. Just the weight of not being there. The door closed. The lights dimmed. The pitch rose beneath her.

She didn't cry, but her chest felt hollow as the plane lifted. And the ground, once again, slipped away beneath her.

Return

The aircraft touched down in Stockholm just before half ten. Bromma Airport, subdued and half-lit, sat hushed against a rain-darkened runway. Moisture still clung to the tarmac, glistening faintly under sodium lamps.

She was shown little of the arrival. Her stretcher moved briskly, lifted straight into a waiting road ambulance. A new crew appeared, masked in unfamiliar eyes and powdered gloves, clipping her straps into place. They spoke only her name. Then motion resumed: long wet curves of road, tunnel lights dragging overhead in pale stripes, bridges rattling faintly beneath tyres. Streetlamps blurred into ribbons, their glow bending oddly through the scratched plastic of the window. A green neon pharmacy sign trembled across her vision, warping into an hourglass shape before it vanished behind the glass.

Karolinska Hospital emerged without fanfare. Vast pale blocks of sealed windows loomed above, faceless and exact. The ambulance reversed into a bay, doors opening to a new gust of disinfected air mixed with the sour tang of plastic warmed by friction and fuel.

Space constricted inside. Corridors tightened into long ribs of linoleum polished to a weary sheen. Overhead fixtures hummed faintly, one stuttering once before steadying again. Shoes whispered beside her in muted rhythm, their soles rubber-soft. A hand gloved in latex pressed lightly near her elbow, steadying the frame as if she might float away if not anchored.

The smell was immediate. Not the human sourness of the emergency wing in Östersund; clean chemicals, over-washed surfaces, gloves still carrying the scent of powder. The air was dry. Processed. They passed through a short airlock. Doors opened inward, then closed behind them with a hum. Her ears popped gently.

"Radiation protocol still active," someone said. A clipped voice, male. "Double filter line engaged."

Freya turned her head slightly. It felt heavy. She caught glimpses of the people surrounding her. A paper gown, a radiation badge, a pressure valve set into a wall-mounted cabinet. She was wheeled into a room with the door already open. It was cooler than the corridor. The walls were a pale grey, the paint dull. One high window to the outside, frosted glass. One window on the opposite side. A viewport into the corridor.

A bed already waited. Sheets drawn tight. A monitor blinked faintly, patient but indifferent. Beside it, a portable vitals unit stood humming with quiet light. Oxygen and suction ports sat labelled but unused. On the side table, a towel folded square, still holding the crease of hands that had set it down not long before. Everything felt recent, as though another body had been here minutes ago and scrubbed away without trace.

The nurse moved around her without a word of introduction. She looked older than the others, though not by years. Fatigue had carved its own lines at the edges of her eyes, the sort earned by hours of standing still beneath artificial light. A pedal clicked beneath her shoe, the frame rising a notch. She checked the tubing at Freya's wrist, then fitted a fresh cannula above the bruised skin where the last one had sat. Tape pulled. Freya winced, her skin sore with the raw tenderness of repeated intrusion.

"Still running fluids," the nurse murmured. "Normal saline. A litre overnight."

Her scanner chirped against the bracelet. A single muted tone. The sound felt less like care than inventory. Freya let her head roll again, slower this time, trying to map the space around her. A soap dispenser bolted to the wall. The edge of a yellow sharps bin catching the glow. A narrow clock, its second hand moving with barely a sound. Quarter past eleven. She tried to pin herself to that fact, but time felt distant, drained of meaning inside these sealed walls.

Overhead, the lights had been dimmed. Half-power, tinted faint blue, a poor imitation of night. The hue pressed down with its false calm, pretending at darkness but never granting it. Shadows pooled in corners, but none of them were deep enough to be safe. For a moment, it reminded her of the endless twilight out by the lakes. That same feeling of being caught between one hour and the next, body suspended in a day that refused to finish.

Plastic whispered as the curtain came around her. A small call button set gently onto the blanket, feather-light against her palm. The nurse's footsteps retreated, rubber soles slipping into the hush of the corridor. Freya was left alone, walled off by clear folds that blurred the edges of everything. Not unlike canvas. Not unlike nights when wind had pressed the tent walls flat to her face.

"You'll see the burns team in the morning," she said. "Sleep if you can."

Freya blinked. Her eyes stung at the corners. The door sealed with a hiss when the nurse left. No other words were exchanged. The pressure shifted in her ears again. The air vents near the ceiling purred softly, keeping a rhythm that didn't match her own. Her hands itched under the dressings. She closed her eyes fully.

In the dark behind her lids, Lena's voice returned in echoes. The last clear thing. *"It's warm. It's louder when you touch it."*

Sleep came eventually.

A thin column reached across the floor tiles, climbing halfway up the base of the wall. The morning light had started to shine through the outside window, softly waking Freya. Freya lay still, half awake. Machines beeped steadily, a pulse of fluid pushed into her arm. After a few moments of gathering her thoughts, the door's soft suction broke the quiet. Two figures stepped in. Gowned and masked. One carried a tablet. The other pushed a wheeled tray covered in folded cloth and sealed containers.

"Good morning, Freya," the taller one said. His voice came flat through the mask "I'm Dr. Levin. Burns team. This is Nurse Hellström."

The nurse offered a nod Freya didn't need to return.

"We're going to check your dressings this morning," Levin continued. "We'll talk after we've had a look."

They moved quietly and quickly. Freya's blanket was peeled back. Her arms lifted gently from their padded rests. The air met her skin with a faint chill. It felt damp at the edges. The first bandage came away slowly. Gentle pulling was felt from the bandages letting go of scabs and hairs as they exposed the burns underneath. The skin underneath pulsed faintly with the sudden exposure. She turned her head, but not far enough not to see. The skin was red. Stripped in places. A few edges sloughing. The swelling had gone down. What remained looked like damage layered rather than spread. The aftermath of heat.

"Not terrible," Levin murmured. "Not great, but we've avoided full-depth dermal loss."

Freya flinched as the doctor pressed near the base of her thumb. She let out a small wince of pain, greeted by a nod and a slight smile from the doctor. The nurse applied a gel from a silver sachet. The cold was immediate. Then stinging, then numb. She wrapped the hand again, firmer this time, with soft cotton and mesh. Then repeated the process on the other side. When both were bound again, Levin stepped back and tapped notes into the tablet.

"We'll monitor response over the next 48 hours," he said. "If recovery trends hold, we won't need to think of skin graft. But that can change... Circulation and tissue quality are variables."

The bandages now felt heavier, though less hostile. Freya breathed a slight sigh of relief. Perhaps if her injuries were subsiding, Lena would be okay too.

"What about Lena?" Her voice caught slightly. "Is she here?"

Levin's pause was slight, but she noticed it.

"She's in transit," he said. "They're managing her arrival separately."

Another pause ensued whilst the doctor tapped away at the tablet in his hands. "You'll stay on fluids today. Morphine is coming down. Oral paracetamol to start once your panels confirm clearance."

Freya turned her face to the ceiling. The light overhead had warmed slightly, but only in tone. Levin tapped once more into the tablet, then stepped back. Then he was gone. The nurse remained just long enough to check her vitals one more time. A soft beep at the monitor, a glance at the fluid level.

"You'll be seen again this evening," she said, then pulled the blanket over Freya's arms before leaving. The door sealed softly behind her.

She ate because she was told to, not because she was hungry. The tray arrived with a knock that barely registered, left on the side-table without comment. A lidded bowl of soup, lukewarm. A bread roll sealed in crackling plastic. Something pale and trembling faintly in a dessert cup; custard, maybe. She peeled the film back with one stiff thumb and let it drop to the tray without folding.

The spoon clicked against porcelain, too loud for the room. Five mouthfuls forced down before flavour collapsed into texture. The soup wasn't hot enough to burn, not cool enough to swallow without thought. It just lingered, heavy, like something foreign. Morphine dulled the edges. Her hands still ached inside the dressings, but the pain had become rhythmic, a steady throb that pulsed up into her forearms when she breathed too deeply.

The air tasted dry. Filtered through vents she couldn't see, only hear. A soft hum, sharp enough to notice when everything else stilled. She began to time it against the IV pump beside her. Three clicks through the line to every single breath of the filter. Then again. The cycle held her thoughts still.

Her eyes shifted, catching the small wall-mounted television angled down toward the bed. The screen sat black at first, a faint green diode glowing beneath it. She pressed the remote with her thumb. Static. Then colour. News anchor's voice, cut by field footage.

The clearing.

It showed only briefly, but she recognised it instantly: that circle of bare soil ringed by birch, now cordoned with tape strung between poles hammered into the ground. White suits moved carefully across the frame, masks gleaming under a washed-out northern sun. Behind them, the lake shone like a mirror.

"...Confirmation that the site, once a weather station, was abandoned during the late Cold War era. In 1986, responsibility for the clean-up fell to GeoSiftra AB, a subcontracted environmental services group. Records indicate the company was led by Vic..."

Her attention was refocused to a conversation outside her room. Two voices broke the rhythm. One male, low and clipped. The other female, mid-sentence, impatient.

"...Can't move him like that..."

"...What did the last panel show?..."

"Her counts are worse than..."

"...You can't sedate both..."

Freya sat up slightly almost too fast as a wave of dizziness surrounded her head. The voices were just outside the door now, but neither belonged to anyone she recognised. She held still, listening.

"Paediatric bed's not isolated yet..."

"..We'll have to separate..."

"Just get her stable..."

Then silence again. Footsteps dissolved into distance, a door further down clicked, then closed. No return. No one entered. Freya turned her head, pressing her forehead against the chill of the bed rail. Metal steadied her skin for a moment, as though cold could anchor her. Her breathing came shallow, uneven. She tried to force rhythm back, counting down in her head. Six. Five. Four.

Nausea had lifted. That at least was something. Relief came thin, like water over dry stone. She held herself still, letting minutes stretch, or maybe longer. Time had become without shape. Only when the pump clicked again did she notice she'd lost the measure, that her own tally had drifted away.

The tray still lingered untouched, soup now filmed and cooling in its bowl. She reached for the spoon, hesitating. On the surface, a reflection formed: her mouth, colourless, half parted and unfamiliar. It looked less like herself and more like a mask slipping free. She turned her face aside before the image could settle.

At the foot of the bed, a fresh blanket had been folded earlier with clinical precision. She hadn't touched it. Her eyes kept drifting back, tracing the edge of the fabric. The urge to move it, to unfold it, tugged at her. As though such a gesture might mean something. An act of will, a declaration of still belonging here. She did nothing. Instead she rolled onto her side, spine curving toward the wall.

From that angle, she could just catch the outline of the door. Closed. Sealed. The world pressed in behind her forehead; pressure thickened, not enough for tears, but enough to sharpen sound, to make every shift of fabric, every breath of air, too near.

She closed her eyes and searched for something concrete to hold.

Anything to bind herself to memory. She reached for Lena's voice, but sound failed her. Only words remained.

The ground hums. The sun is warmer underneath.

A flush of heat rose behind Freya's eyes. Her throat tightened, sudden and sharp. She wanted to stand. Not to move but just to prove she still could. Instead, she pulled the blanket up to her chest, and tried to breathe in slowly.

She thought of asking again... Pressing the call button... Asking if Lena had arrived, if she was okay. She already knew the answer. *You'll be informed when we can.*

That had been the phrase. Meant to reassure, not silence. Yet had done neither. Freya turned her face back to the pillow and let it rest there. A single tear had let slip. No panic, but fear of not knowing what will be next. If her daughter would even survive. The voices outside hadn't returned. The world beyond the door went on without her. She kept listening, just in case.

Later that afternoon, the first of the two ambulances rolled into the covered bay without lights. No sirens. No running. Just the low crunch of wet tyres and a hiss as the brakes locked in place.

Inside, a stretcher. Johan.

The rear doors opened to fluorescent light. Two paramedics stepped down expressionless. One lifted the chart clipped at the foot of the stretcher. The other tightened the fluid bag already swinging faintly from its pole.

"Male, twenty-eight," the lead medic said. "Strontium radiation source. Estimated proximity exposure seventeen gray. Vomiting onset in the field. Collapse confirmed post-site. Subject is comatose."

He was pale. More grey than white; the colour of fatigue that came from bone marrow, not muscles. The oxygen mask across his face was fogged. Blood pressure cuff Velcro just above the elbow. IV in place. Monitors running off a portable case, ticking low and slow.

His hands were visible. One trembled slightly, just at the fingers. The other lay limp against the edge of the sheet. There were lines drawn in pen on his forearm. Temporary field markings for IV site rotation. Beneath that, an old wristband. Östersund hospital.

A registrar in green scrubs met the bed as it entered the corridor. She barely glanced up from a clipboard.

"Bloods?"

"Thrombocytes dropping. WBC at 0.7. Starting him on G-CSF."

"Push dose?"

"Just confirmed."

A nurse nodded and moved to the line. The ampoule clicked open. The plunger slid home without resistance. The bed bumped as they turned the corner. Johan didn't flinch.

"Manifest stage?" The registrar asked.

"Yes. Pupil sluggish. Gastrointestinal syndrome suspected; no haemorrhaging yet. Seizures reported."

The corridor split. Two doors had been prepared. Both marked with laminated red signage, handwritten updates taped to the glass: *STRÅL-04* and *STRÅL-05*. Radiation Isolation units. The walls were too clean. The scrubbers made a soft hiss that swallowed footfalls. They pushed him through into the first room. A second nurse keyed the door. It sealed with a low mechanical sigh. The room's pressure stabilised. The monitors were reconnected. No one used his name. The room remained quiet. From the window to the corridor, another bed was quickly pushed past with nurses running behind.

Lena.

The paediatric stretcher moved fast, flanked by two nurses and a medic with a clipboard pressed flat to his chest. The girl barely filled the space. Her body had been turned slightly to the left, shoulder sunken, spine curled under the thermal wrap. Sweat clung to her hairline in beads. Her jaw was slack under the oxygen mask, lips parted just enough to let the condensation rise.

One nurse kept her hand on the IV pole as they moved, stabilising the line. The butterfly needle taped at the wrist was already yellowing at the edges, skin beneath it pale and sunken.

"Seven years old," the medic called ahead. "Sedated in Östersund. Temp peaked over forty on transfer. BP unstable."

"She's not regulating," someone else said. "GCS has dropped since departure."

They cleared the glass of STRÅL-04: Johan's room. The blinds hadn't been drawn yet. A pale form under a hospital sheet, monitors blinking through layered haze. None of the team turned their heads.

Lena's arm slipped sideways off the padding. One nurse caught it mid-fall, folding it gently back under the blanket. The skin was slick with sweat and tacky to the glove.

"Neutrophil count?" A nurse with a clipboard asked one of the paramedics helping them in.

"Zero."

"Confirm G-CSF on standby. Push after vitals."

"We're not there yet," someone said. "Might be sepsis."

"She's showing every sign."

"Radiation fever *and* sepsis?"

"Probably both."

A nurse leaned closer, eyes narrowing at the bruised tones seeping across Lena's side. Skin mottled in irregular patches. Bruised-blue fading to violet, stretched thin over her ribs. No bleeding yet, but the pattern carried its own quiet alarm.

"She's shifting into the manifest stage," the registrar murmured, clipped and certain. "Stabilise her before marrow collapse takes hold."

Without pause, STRÅL-05 opened. A heavy door swung inward at a staff badge, no request for entry spoken aloud. Negative pressure hummed already, a faint hiss drawn through a ceiling vent, dragging each breath away. Walls pressed close, painted sterile white but still carrying the faint, metallic chill of machinery.

Monitoring pads had been readied in advance, adhesive strips curling slightly at their corners. A wall-mounted thermometer sounded a polite beep from behind its curtain, a reminder that heat never left these rooms unmeasured.

Together they lifted Lena, movements brisk but practised. No wasted adjustment. Her frame sagged into the centre of the sheets, knees bent lightly by their own weight as though strings had been cut. Latex hands worked without hesitation. A mask lowered, fitting snugly across her nose. Tubing clicked, valves sighed as oxygen found its channel. Another nurse tugged at the sodden gown, peeling fabric carefully from clammy skin, then slid a thermal wrap beneath her shoulders with the quiet reverence of routine.

The registrar stood apart, eyes moving across a chart as though the paper might confess more than the girl before him. Pen scratched, paused, then moved again. His gaze returned briefly to Lena. Her chest rose, shallow. Fingers twitched once against the blanket.

Freya, watching from beyond the glass, pressed her bandaged hands uselessly to the barrier. No warmth passed through. Only the reflection of her own gaunt face, staring back at her from the plexi-glass.

"Let's be clear. This is Acute Radiation Syndrome," she said. "Early GI syndrome. Plus suspected neutropenic sepsis. Platelets borderline. "

"Transfusion?"

"Prep type-matched. If she dips, we push."

"She'll dip."

"Then prep two units."

A new cannula had been fed into the ankle, taped neatly. Blood seeping faintly through the tube not yet connected to anything at the other end. The skin there was blotchy, paler than the rest of her leg. Her veins had risen. Fluids followed. She didn't move in her sedation.

One of the nurses adjusted her hand on the pillow. Her fingers were lax. The nails had discoloured slightly. Not bruised, but drained of tone. Her palms were pale yellow. The skin along her wrists had thinned enough to show the shadow of veins. The rest of her body lay still, covered only at the chest and knees. The fever had raised a rash across her lower abdomen. Small patches, pinpricks of red and purple spread under the skin. Her belly rose and fell with each breath, but not evenly. Sometimes it caught midrise, stuttered, then resumed.

Her hair was damp, or what remained of it. Broad bald patches exposed pale scalp, raw against the light. Clumps hung loose, threatening to give way at the slightest touch. A nurse had gathered the worst back from her brow, but stray strands still clung to her cheek, stuck fast by sweat. Beneath the oxygen mask, her lips had parted, parched and split at the corners. Dried blood traced one nostril, a fine rust line against the pale of her skin.

Her arms had been secured with loose straps across her stomach, elbows spread outward like abandoned wings. At the joints the skin had begun to flake and peel, whether from heat or thirst it was impossible to tell. Her legs angled away from one another, feet turning inward, too heavy to correct themselves. Only once did her left toes move, a single faint twitch. After that, stillness.

The monitor displayed its verdict in tiny, indifferent numbers. Ninety-four. Then ninety-three. A pause. Holding. Each change followed by the unblinking pulse of a machine, a shrill yet tired note marking the rhythm of her survival. No other motion. No other sound.

Blinds drew across the inner window, hiding the corridor. Door sealed with a mechanical sigh, a final lock settling into place. Lena remained within her small square of air, breathing faintly, the mask misting once then clearing.

Freya felt herself fall back, further than before. A corridor away and yet unreachable. Walls seemed to recede around her, pushing her deeper into the mattress. She lost the measure of time. Minutes collapsed together, stripped of sequence, leaving only weight. What she remembered with any certainty was the scratch of the blanket behind her knees, bunched in the wrong place. That had been earlier, or perhaps far longer. She tried to hold on to it, but her mind slid away, refusing to settle.

Her chest ached in strange ways. A weight sitting on her. An interlude before suffocation. The suffocating feeling of grief. A feeling too early for a name.

The door opened without warning.

A nurse entered. She didn't bother introducing herself, didn't even look directly at Freya. She was young. Precise. She moved quickly, practised. Carried a chart like a shield. She tapped at the machines linking up to Freya; an extension of herself now. The blood pressure cuff was rolled into place and inflated with a low mechanical whine. Another machine connected. The nurse reached for the oxygen sat probe, clipped it onto her finger. Another machine connected. Freya let out a quiet sigh.

Plastic. Gloves. The soft beep of monitoring.

Freya's eyes traced the corner of the room without focus. As the blood pressure monitor started to squeeze, she became aware of her own breath again. Shallow and controlled. The armband squeezed tighter still. Readings were jotted down by the nurse. The armband squeezed almost unbearably.

Freya closed her eyes for a second. The band released. She gathered herself to speak.

"She's here, isn't she? Lena."

The nurse made a small note on the clipboard at the bottom of the bed. No response was given to Freya's question. So she continued.

"And Johan. You've brought them."

No reply followed from the nurse. Freya continued once more.

"I want to see her. Just to…"

She stopped herself. The words didn't want to be formed properly. The nurse didn't meet her eyes. She adjusted the dressing at Freya's elbow then rechecked the catheter at the side. After the checks appeared to have been done, only then, the nurse met Freya's eyes.

"They're under full isolation," she said finally. "We can't permit exposure."

The nurse offered no argument, no explanation. She checked the line, marked the numbers in a quiet hand, and withdrew.

Freya stayed where she was, gaze fixed on the IV pole in the corner. Tubing lifted and sank with each pulse, the chamber trembling faintly as fluid slipped through. She studied it as if watching might keep the rhythm alive. Air vents whispered again, their constant hiss sliding back into the walls. Twice she forced herself to swallow before her chest would open enough to take breath. Every thought circled back to Lena.

The door opened. The same nurse returned, a wheelchair steadied between her palms. She disconnected the drip from its stand and clipped it to a smaller pole fixed to the chair. Footrests were drawn down with a metallic click. Sheets brushed aside. She waited with a softened smile, eyes steady on Freya.

Sitting up felt heavier than it should. The nurse guided her forward with practised care, easing her into the seat inch by inch. Legs resisted, stiff and unwilling. Bandaged hands throbbed with each shift of weight. When she finally settled, the nurse adjusted the blanket across her knees as though anchoring her in place.

The door released with a sigh. The corridor stretched ahead. Freya began to move, the chair rolling under a steady push. Yet no one had spoken of where she was being taken, or what waited beyond those next doors.

The corridor smelled of bleach. It was long and white. Without corners or sound. Freya heard the wheels beneath her chair; soft rubber turning over linoleum. The nurse pushed the wheelchair ahead. Silent but sure. They stopped halfway down a secondary wing. A viewing bay. The glass panel spanned wall to wall, fitted flush into the plaster. Markings had been scrawled in dry-erase pen on the outside: dates, initials, acronyms she didn't recognise.

The nurse stepped aside and left Freya with the window. She stood up and leaned in.

Lena was asleep.

Not nestled or curled. She lay straight. One arm down by her side, the other across her stomach. A fine dressing wrapped the wrist and up the arms. Tape ran the length of the IV port. Another line had been clipped to the foot. Saline or antibiotics possibly, she couldn't tell. The tubing arched over the side carrying dark red liquid from a bag overhead.

Her hair had been pulled back. Someone had tried to neaten it. Although, most of it was gone now. Thin tufts remained above the ears. The pillow beneath her was bare. All except a few loose strands of curly blonde wire. Hair that had continued falling since she was last checked upon. There was a rash across her temple; faint but growing.

The colour crept into the skin unevenly, as though it were being painted by something from underneath.

Freya raised a hand and placed it flat on the glass. The surface was cold. Her reflection wavered there for a moment. She barely recognised Lena. Far from the jumpy, excited child she had been a week before. She whispered something. It didn't reach the room. Not even to her own ears. The nurse touched her shoulder lightly. Just once. They moved on.

The chair slowed beside a second viewing panel. Freya leaned forward.

This room carried another weight. Ceiling vaulted higher, light sharpened to a harsher edge, every surface stripped of warmth. The arrangement resembled a test chamber more than any ward of recovery. Johan lay in the centre, body set half-upright by the angle of the bed. Pillows and folded blankets pinned him into posture. Nothing suggested rest. He had been positioned. Breathing issued shallow and reluctant, the cadence of machinery rather than will.

His decline was starker than the last glimpse in the air ambulance. Skin had drained to a muted grey, jaw slack as if carved from wax. Cheeks collapsed inward, deepening hollows that memory could not account for. Purple bruises pooled beneath both eyes. The sclera dulled to a sickened yellow, a hue that hinted at permanence, not illness. Chest lifted and fell with a rhythm that belonged to struggle, every inhalation reluctant, drawn for him rather than by him.

Freya placed her bandaged palm against the glass. Heat smudged into faint vapour on the surface, a mark already fading. No stir answered. His head remained fixed, eyes closed, lashes flat against mottled skin. Even in silence, strain seemed to run through him, a body tethered by invisible threads, reluctant to release but with little left to hold.

Her mouth twitched toward a smile though the muscles betrayed her. Still, she shaped the words, lips moving soundlessly. *Still here.* The words were not for him. They were for herself, for Lena, a fragment to hold in the absence of reply.

Tears crept, not with force but inevitability, until her vision fractured. Tubes and wires blurred into pale streaks, shoulders dissolved into watercolour. For one aching instant she believed him already gone. Only the metronomic stutter of a monitor insisted otherwise.

A touch at her arm pulled her back. The nurse's voice dropped low, softened by something close to pity.

"We should let him rest."

The return journey felt shorter, stripped of anticipation, corridor shrinking to white and silence. Air carried its filtered chill, sterile, manufactured. The IV line was reconnected with a soft click. Pumps released themselves at irregular intervals, a damp mechanical sigh each time a valve exhaled. Freya no longer heard them as machines. The sounds had become the room's own breathing, steady and indifferent.

She lay on her side, back turned to the door. The nurse offered no words, only brief adjustments: a line checked, blanket smoothed, then departure marked by quiet retreat. The mattress still carried traces of antiseptic, overlaid by something human. The faint residue of skin. A reminder that her own body had become part of this place, absorbed into its catalogue.

Her face pressed into the pillow, half-buried. Her bandaged hand moved once. Not deliberately. Just the body repositioning itself. The bandage dragged and pulled her skin against the sheet. She watched the room in the low twilight from the window. This twilight was darker than up north. Almost like it would finally soon be night-time again. Soon enough, she closed her eyes.

And tried to remember the sound of Lena breathing beside her. The slow, unconscious rhythm. Back when there had been tents and quiet and warmth. When breath was just something that happened. But the rhythm didn't come.

She had been told by a doctor she'd be better in a week or so. She hardly believed it for herself. She definitely didn't believe it for Johan or Lena.

Release

The sky outside her window refused to change. Some mornings thinned to a pale imitation of blue, other afternoons collapsed back into grey. Nothing ever shifted fully. The horizon stayed smudged by a single line of cloud, as though some careless hand had dragged chalk across glass. Beyond it, rooftops lined themselves in orderly rows, glass and steel laid out in clean geometry. From here the city looked immaculate. Untroubled. Arterial roads carried cars in patient streams, traffic gliding like blood unsure if it should clot or not.

Inside, sterility clung to every surface. Alcohol wipes. Bleached cotton. That manufactured citrus sting sprayed after every round of cleaning. Her IV stand had been taken down three days ago, left standing in the corner like a forgotten coat rack. A folded blanket remained on the visitor's chair, untouched, creased exactly as the nurse had left it. Hospital-issue clothes, pale and shapeless, lay ready on the bedside table.

Freya sat hunched at the mattress edge, flexing her right hand. The grafts held. Skin still felt tight, stitched wrong, tender where old burns had cracked and peeled away. Pink patches remained raw and unnatural, but she could curl her fingers now. She pressed her thumb to each fingertip, testing.

It hurt, but no longer sickened her. That counted for progress.

Laughter cut through the ward from an adjacent room. Something about gowns being reused. The tail end of a joke clattered through the corridor like dropped cutlery in a morgue. Freya didn't smile. She ran her other hand absently through her hair instead, tugging free two strands at a time. Fewer now. Recovery of a sort. Each strand landed against the linoleum, curling like a discarded fishing line. She counted them without realising.

By late afternoon the light had crawled low across the floor, turning sterile tiles the colour of old parchment. The door pushed open without warning. No knock, only the hush of skin against steel and hinges too slow to matter.

Her nurse, Emelia slipped inside with the same measured pace she always carried: competent, and hushed. She stood smaller than most, compact in her frame, hair so pale blonde it seemed silver where it caught the sterile glow of hospital lights. At first glance her eyes were unsettled: one green, one brown. The odd pairing made her gaze feel doubled, as if she weighed two versions of a person at once. *Heterochromia*, Freya recalled, the word clinical and strange on her tongue. Yet nothing in Emelia's manner suggested oddity. Her face held only a practised calm, the composure of someone who had walked too many hospital corridors to be startled by suffering anymore.

She brought a cup of water in one hand and a plastic cap of pills in the other, capsules rattling like loose teeth. She nudged the life monitor at the bedside with her knuckle, barely looking at the screen as her eyes swept Freya instead.

"Grafts are settling," she said, voice flat but kind enough. "Neutrophils are up. You'll be cleared for hand therapy tomorrow. You're doing well."

Freya gave a small smile, though her mind was elsewhere. She already held the water, cupping it carefully with both palms, as though the glass might break if she breathed too hard. The ache in her joints persisted. The bones beneath still refused to feel entirely her own.

"You're off watch now," Emelia said, scanning the tablet with practised flicks of her thumb. "Vitals have held steady for three days. Physio will come by in the morning. Might even have you walking without an escort before the weekend."

She lingered a moment, weight shifting onto her heels, the hem of her trousers tugged up just enough to reveal socks patterned with tiny cats arching their backs. The domestic softness jarred with the clinical light.

"Lena's team filed for closer contact," she went on. "They're holding off physical clearance until her blood-work improves. But..." Her voice caught briefly, "they're hopeful."

The word clanged inside Freya. *Hopeful.* It carried no promise, no solidity. A balloon filled with nothing but someone else's breath.

Her throat tightened. She forced herself to ask, voice thinner than she intended. "And Johan?"

Emelia's eyes softened, but her tone stayed neutral. "He hasn't woken. Still in a coma. Vitals are holding, but there's been no change."

No change. It landed like a stone. Freya's stomach twisted around it, her body understanding more than her mind wanted to. No change meant limbo. No change meant waiting. It meant he could slip further away while she sat here counting fallen strands of hair like prayers.

Emelia closed the tablet with a soft tap, thumb brushing the edge of the case. A thermometer appeared in her hand as if by instinct, though she never raised it. Instead, she glanced toward the curtained window.

"Storm tonight. Nothing serious. Just the kind that scrapes at the glass."

Freya nodded. She watched Emelia leave, her cat socks flashing before the door sealed shut with that vacuum hush that always made these rooms sound like lungs inhaling and never exhaling.

Freya stayed perched on the mattress edge, unwilling to lie down again. Her palms pressed to her thighs, feeling the new skin tug against its scars. Two days since the bleeding stopped. She could hold a cup now. She could brush her hair without crying out. She could thread a zip. Yet all those small victories landed weightless. None of them could touch the dread curdling in her chest.

But it didn't feel like healing. It felt like cheating. Behind her, the walls clicked and hummed: slow, mechanical rhythms. Filtered air, oxygen pumps, the soft beep of someone else's warning. It was strange how loud it all seemed now that she was out of the forest. How artificial the living sounded here.

The room had dimmed by degrees. The overhead light ticked faintly; a kind of mechanical tinnitus that had become the backdrop to everything. The glow from the street-lights outside leaked through the fabric of the closed curtains. A diluted yellow that bled across the floor in a tired diagonal. It made everything feel underwater. As if the room were sinking slowly, and only she had noticed.

She looked around the room. Her dinner tray sat untouched on the counter. The soup was cold, the bread stale around the edges.

A single grape had rolled away and settled near the water jug like it was trying to escape. She didn't bother with it. Instead, she pulled the blanket down and slid beneath it without the usual hesitation. No pulse oximeter tonight. No IV stand ticking beside her. Just the low-grade buzz of climate control and the faint rhythm of rubber soles in a hallway beyond.

She curled on her side toward the curtain, fingers hooked into the pillow's seam. Too smooth. Too laundered. Surfaces held no memory, no trace of her weight. The room smelled faintly of bleach and plastic, sharp and citrus-clean. Designed to soothe, it only reminded her of emptiness.

A heaviness sat in her chest, heavy as iron. It pressed down on every breath. Anticipation, not grief. Waiting for grief. Each inhale scraped, ribs resisting the rhythm. She tried matching her lungs to the steady hum in the ceiling, chasing calm in borrowed cadence. Her body refused, and sleep slid over her the way cold water soaks cloth; creeping until she could no longer hold it back.

The ground beneath her shifted to moss, damp and springing beneath her feet. Bare toes pressed into lichen that gave way like bruised fruit. She had not walked here, yet she moved, drifting through a twilight forest. A gown clung to her legs, hem trailing heavy with moisture, sleeves swallowing her arms. Her hands glowed raw and pink, skin stretched too thin.

Above her, pines and birches rose like pillars in a drowned cathedral, branches swaying in a hush that pressed against her ears. Twilight clung to the canopy, suspended in a blue-grey veil. Each step deepened the silence, pine needles catching on her soles.

A child's voice threaded the stillness. Lena's voice.

Rida, rida ranka...

Her heart lurched forward before her body followed. She stumbled through trees, branches sliding across her arms like ropes. The air thickened, resin and damp pine mingling with the sting of burnt hair.

Hästen heter Blanka...

The gown tore against a branch, fabric trailing like shed skin. The song drifted ahead, soft as breath through cloth. The forest opened into a clearing. Circular, sunken, its centre dipped inward like a shallow grave. Moss breathed warmth beneath her feet. Pebbles pressed upward through the soil, hard as bone.

At the edge of the clearing stood a woman.

Her hair spilled in sodden ropes of moss, trailing along the ground. Driftwood skin knotted around her arms and shoulders. She stood taller than any living figure, still and unblinking. A presence carved from wood and shadow.

Her head tilted slowly, angled toward the song.

Far han red till skogen svart...

Lena's lullaby circled the clearing. Beyond her, between two trees, a man moved away. Johan. Shoulders hunched, steps deliberate, his path certain. He did not look back. The knowledge hit Freya like recognition long rehearsed: he was already leaving.

Her lips formed his name, but sound never reached the air. The ground tipped beneath her. Moss and needles shifted like sand sliding downhill. She leaned forward and the earth swallowed her step. Bark scraped her tongue. Soil pressed against her teeth, rich and metallic.

The woman turned. Her hair peeled aside, revealing a hollow

back, a cavity shaped like a tree eaten from within. A coarse tail brushed the moss behind her legs. She carried no breath, only presence.

The lullaby faltered, then returned. This time muffled, as though sung from beneath water.

...aldrig kom han åter snart...

Freya reached forward again, but her body betrayed her. Limbs heavy, throat tight, she sank where she stood. Johan's figure slipped deeper into shadow until he was gone. The clearing folded inward. Hospital light burned back into view. Ceiling panels. White walls. She woke in her bed with her heart racing, chest hollow.

Morning pressed pale squares of light across the linoleum. She sat upright before the breakfast cart clattered in the corridor. Her reflection in the steel bed-frame stared back sunken and sleepless. When the knock came, soft and practised, she was already drawing the blanket aside.

Emelia stepped in, her pale hair catching the light.

"Dr Kihlberg approved it," Nurse Emelia said, slipping the thermometer back into her pocket. "You can sit with her. Half-hour, and no direct contact." She hesitated long enough for her mismatched eyes to settle on Freya's face. "You remember the infection protocol."

Freya nodded too quickly. Her body was already in motion, slippers pulled on with clumsy haste. The rubber soles clung to the floor, whispering against the linoleum as if even the ground wanted to slow her down. Breakfast sat untouched on the tray. Plates, lids, a carton of milk; all forgotten. None of it mattered. The only thing that mattered waited behind a sheet of glass.

Her pulse thudded hot in her throat as she followed Emelia out. The nurse carried her tablet, steady and clinical, but Freya carried something louder. Her silence felt brittle, crackling under every step. She pressed her hands against her gown to keep them from trembling.

The lift doors closed with a hush that seemed too soft for what it contained. As the carriage sank, she counted her heartbeats, faster than the machine's descent. Each floor passing brought her closer.

The isolation wing was quieter than she'd braced for. Thin air seemed to swallow every sound before it travelled. A machine beeped in soft triplets somewhere behind a sealed door. A cough scraped out, muted by glass. Above them, one fluorescent tube stuttered and flickered, buzzing faintly like a dying insect.

Freya quickened her pace despite the drag in her muscles. Every step felt both too fast and too slow. She could almost hear Lena already, the memory of her voice threaded through the sterile corridors like a lullaby waiting to surface.

Lena's room carried its warning before the door even opened. A laminated sheet hung crooked against the glass, corners curling where tape had lifted. Beneath it, a transparent flap of plastic sealed the threshold, Velcro peeling back with a faint rasp as Emelia drew it aside. The sheet crinkled in protest as they stepped through.

Freya paused inside the perimeter, breath caught. The air hit her with the sharp sting of antiseptic layered over something sour; dried sweat, plasticised bedding, that faint iron tang of blood scrubbed too clean. Surfaces gleamed with a polish that felt unnatural, as though nothing human had ever been meant to touch them.

The room was spare, built for function rather than comfort. A single bed dominated the space, its white sheets taut as bandages. To one side, a tray of untouched food sat abandoned near a half-drawn curtain, where shadow pooled against the linoleum. Between Freya and the bed, a wall of clear plastic sealed floor to ceiling. It stretched smooth and impenetrable, edges fixed with wide bands of hospital tape, humming faintly when the ventilation shifted. It was a barrier designed for safety, but to Freya it felt like a veil stitched from punishment.

She crouched, bringing herself level with the small figure beyond.

Lena lay curled toward the window, her profile outlined in the pale spill of morning light. Her hair, once a wild halo from the forest wind, had nearly disappeared. Her scalp showing in irregular patches. Tubing trailed from the crook of her elbow to a drip, another line fastened neatly against her ankle. The steady blink of a pulse monitor pulsed beside her hand, a rhythm far too fragile.

"Hi, älskling," Freya whispered. Her voice snagged in her throat.

The child turned, lids fluttering open as she awoke. For a moment her pupils drifted unfocused, then steadied. The effort alone seemed monumental.

"Mamma." The word was more sigh than sound, a thread of air caught in a drone.

Freya's mouth pulled into a smile before she could stop it, though her fingers pressed tight into her knees, knuckles white. She had no words ready. None that felt enough. The silence between them felt brittle, ready to shatter.

"You're here," Lena murmured, her voice almost a secret. "I dreamed you were in the lake."

Freya swallowed, her own memory answering before her tongue did. "You too."

Mother and daughter stayed like that, mirror-still on either side of the plastic veil. Lena's small hand twitched against her stomach, then lifted slightly, trembling before it fell short. Her breath misted against the barrier, a faint ghost of her outline on the sheet. With visible effort, she raised one finger and pointed, slow and deliberate. Freya turned, following her daughter's gaze.

Outside, the hospital garden lay still. Beyond the gravel path and trimmed hedges, a man in green overalls swept a rake through shallow standing water. A low channel, fed by sprinklers and runoff. Lena's hand fell.

Freya turned her head back to face the girl. Lena's eyes remained on the window. Her mouth parted slightly, then closed again. Whatever she'd meant to say had passed. Or hadn't arrived yet. A soft cough stirred the air behind her. Footsteps. Then stillness.

"It's quieter here," she said, not quite to her mother. Not quite to the room either. The words barely shaped themselves. More like something remembered aloud. Freya stayed seated with her eyes fixed on her daughter.

Lena's voice again, softer: "Not humming so much."

The monitor continued its patient rhythm. A blink of green. A pause. Another. Lena's gaze was on the window now, not blinking.

"That's not the real river."

No emphasis. No question.

Freya kept her gaze on Lena's face, watching the flutter of her eyelids as though each blink might anchor her to the world. Voices pressed through the wall. Muffled at first, clipped by the insulation, then sharper as though the words had found her directly.

"…Unresponsive since early morning."

The phrase slipped into her chest like a chill draft. Her skin prickled. She blinked hard, turned her head toward the sound.

"…Cardiac arrest."

There came the shuffle of paper, a voice dropping low, the heavy cadence of facts exchanged between colleagues.

"…We called the time at…"

Her stomach tightened. She didn't hear the end of the sentence. She already knew.

She rose too quickly. Blood fell away from her head and the floor tilted beneath her. For a moment her knees threatened to buckle. She steadied herself against the plastic chair, fingers whitening against the armrest. Then the door opened.

A man stepped inside. White coat, edges pressed crisp. Clean-shaven, hair clipped short at the temple, spectacles catching the glare of ceiling lights. His shoes squeaked faintly against the linoleum. He looked around forty. A professional face that had learned to quieten its muscles before entering any room. Prepared. That was worse than pity. His eyes caught hers. He tilted his head a fraction, inviting her out into the corridor, away from Lena's bed.

The hall was too bright. Fluorescents buzzed overhead, panels lined in neat formation. A cart rattled past somewhere distant, wheels shuddering with each seam in the tiles. The smell changed the moment she stepped out: antiseptic stronger here, sharper, undercut with boiled coffee from the nurses' station. The air had that faint dryness of ventilation left too long without reprieve.

"We did everything possible," he said, words modulated with practiced gentleness. "Complications overnight. Multi-organ failure. He never awoke."

Freya felt pressure close in around her ribs. Her arms pulled inward, one hand folding around her elbow. She nodded once, a motion that felt borrowed, as though she had copied it from another life where she had been asked to agree with something meaningless.

"He went quietly," the doctor added, as though quiet could be a comfort.

Her jaw throbbed. She had clenched without realising, molars grinding together until pain spread up into her temples. A hollowness stirred deep behind her sternum, peeling open with a slow weight.

Her eyes found Lena's room across the hall. The curtain had been drawn across the glass, a sheet of fabric held in place by protocol. To Freya it looked like a wall. Something designed to keep her out, to remind her she was still on the wrong side of everything.

"I need to see him." Her voice was flat. Not pleading, not yet.

"I understand," the doctor said, lowering his gaze. "But there are exposure protocols. He's in post-isolation until..."

"I need to see him." The second time cracked. Sharper. Almost torn from her throat. "I need to see that he's gone."

He hesitated. Hands slipped into his coat pockets, shoulders turning in a small defensive angle.

"He's still in post-isolation. We should..."

"I don't care."

Her feet carried her before he could finish. She crossed the corridor with more force than her body felt capable of. The pressurised door gave resistance, then relented with a hiss, as though she had broken some seal not meant to be broken.

Inside, the room waited.

The bed sat in the centre, drawn beneath harsh light. A sheet stretched across it in careful precision. The shape beneath it was unmistakable.

She stopped just inside the threshold.

The body's outline was intact: broad shoulders beneath linen, long legs aligned neatly along the mattress. Stillness wrapped every edge. It was not the ordinary stillness of rest, but the absolute absence of breath, of twitch, of possibility.

Someone had prepared him. Tubes removed. Lines tidied. A strip of medical tape still clung to his arm, curling at one edge like bark peeling from a birch. His hands had been folded across his chest, fingers aligned in unnatural repose.

The air smelled faintly of saline and latex, threaded with a scorched tang that clung to her nostrils like burnt hair. Machines had been wheeled out, leaving behind square indentations in the flooring. Plastic blinds rattled faintly against the vent as the circulation kicked in.

She stepped closer.

Every instinct braced against what her eyes already knew. He was there. She pulled back the sheet and looked at his face.

The skin had taken on a greyish tone. His brow had lost the knot it always carried. Even in sleep, he used to scowl. Not now. All of the hair was gone. Brows, lashes, even the soft fuzz along his jaw. In the muscles absence, the bones showed more plainly. The high arc of his cheek, the thin line of his temple, the shape of a mouth that had forgotten how to tense.

A small scar lingered beneath his chin. Faint and pale against the greying skin. She'd forgotten it was there. He once claimed it was from a boat cleat, a fishing trip gone sideways. She never pressed him. Freya looked down at the curve of his collarbone. His skin had taken on a strange translucency.

"You look more like yourself now than you did this whole trip," she said. It wasn't a comforting thought.

She dragged the chair closer, the legs shrieking too loud across the tiles. The sound scraped through her bones, but she didn't stop. She lowered herself slowly, knees clicking as she folded down, spine stiff as though she might splinter if she bent too quickly.

Her hands stayed in her lap, fingers twisted into the thin cotton of her gown. She didn't dare reach for him. Touch felt impossible. Instead she fixed her gaze on his chest, waiting for movement. Some shallow lift of rib, a twitch of breath. A flutter that might betray stubbornness. Johan had never been good at following instructions. He had fought doctors, bills, her, the world. Surely he wouldn't leave on command either. Surely he would resist even this.

But no breath rose. No twitch disturbed the linen. The stillness stretched on and on, absolute.

Time blurred. Ten minutes. Twenty. Her body stiffened, locked into waiting. She leaned forward eventually, elbows braced against her knees, chin sinking into her fists.

"You tried," she whispered. Her lips barely moved. "I know that now."

Her voice startled her, thin and hoarse in the filtered air. She swallowed hard, throat raw, and noticed for the first time that her hand trembled against her gown.

The half-hour allotted to her passed without her counting it. It dissolved into the hush of vents and the faint tick of her own pulse in her ears. When she rose at last, the motion was graceless. The chair scraped back, jolting her spine. Her legs carried her but only just. Her lungs lagged behind, dragging air into her chest as if reluctant to keep going.

He looked almost peaceful. That was the cruelty of it. Peaceful, as if ease had finally chosen him.

She wanted to rage at him. To strike his arm until it bruised. To hiss through her teeth, *you don't get to leave now.* Not after the fights, the break-up, the tent pitched on warm soil, the mushrooms Lena had begged to pick, the fleeting smile when marshmallows caught fire. Not after all of it. Not after she had begun to believe he might still come back, not as this husk under linen, but as the man she once thought she knew.

The words pressed inside her chest but refused to leave her mouth. The room smothered them. Its silence was too complete, too suffocating for anger. Her grief had to shrink itself into the shape the space allowed.

She stood one moment longer, her breath shallow, her throat closing around words unsaid. Then she turned. The door released with its soft exhale, the filtered air cool against her damp skin.

Lena's room pressed in with its own kind of silence. A mechanical quiet, full of low hums and hidden currents. Freya eased into the same chair as before, just beyond the transparent curtain. The air here always seemed warmer than in the corridor, as though it had been breathed already, passed by before reaching her skin. Each inhalation tasted faintly recycled, carrying an antiseptic taste, threaded with plastic and something sweeter that lingered beneath.

The vents whispered steadily overhead. A pressurised drone, soft and constant, as though the walls themselves were breathing. Lena slept curled sideways, one arm tucked protectively across her chest, the other stretched loose into the sheet. The drip lines traced gentle arcs from her skin to the stand beside her, tubes pale against the glow of monitors. Her lips twitched in small movements, murmurs half-born. Once, a fragile sound rose high in her throat, quivered like a bird against glass, and vanished almost instantly.

Freya's own breath slowed as she watched. Lena hadn't spoken since she'd come back in. Words felt heavy here, as though even a whisper might disturb something fragile. A tray of food sat cooling near the sink. Apple juice stayed waiting in its carton. A spoon still sealed in its sterile wrapper, waiting for a hand that had not reached for it.

The door broke the hush with a weighted hiss. Nurse Emelia entered, carrying something small between her fingers; a folded sheet of notepaper. The edges curled, softened by warmth, as though it had been held too long in a child's palm.

"She asked for paper earlier," Emelia said, her voice almost a whisper as not to wake the child. "Said she had something she needed to remember before it changed."

Freya turned, reached out instinctively without rising from her chair. The nurse placed the page into her hand, careful, as though passing something breakable.

"She didn't say anything else."

Emelia lingered for half a breath, then stepped back through the seal, the door shutting steady. Freya lowered her gaze. The note felt alive in her hand, faintly warm, as if it had been resting close to skin. She unfolded it slowly, palms smoothing along the creases. Hospital stock. Thick crayon scrawled across it in hurried strokes.

The page opened into a scene that shouldn't have belonged to a child. A cabin, or what remained of one. Roof-line sagging, timbers broken like ribs. The door hung at an angle, barely clinging to its hinges, grey smoke rose in a bent line, curling sideways as though even air had tilted wrong. Trees crowded the edges, jagged black strokes packed too close together, pressing in on the ruin.

In the centre stood a girl. The shape suggested Lena, yet the proportions betrayed it. Limbs drawn too long, face stretched wide, the smile uncoloured and fixed like a cut across paper. It was not a child's grin. It was something sharper, emptied of joy.

Beside her loomed another figure. Taller. Its body roughed in with bark-like texture, crude crayon strokes gouged into the paper until the fibres feathered. Arms hung rigid at its sides, fingers spindled too thin, branching into too many points. Where a face should have been, only a split, a wound slashed across timber. A mouth carved into nothing.

Freya's hand shook before she realised it. A weight filled her chest, dread thickening like sap. It wasn't only the drawing. It was the way the shading bled too dark, the way both figures leaned as though pulled by something unseen.

As if the paper itself still held the heat of what had already happened.

She folded it back along the creases, careful not to tear the softened edges, and placed it on her lap as though it might burn through her gown if she held it longer. Her breath had gone shallow, a cold film clinging to her skin.

Across the room, movement.

Lena turned beneath her blanket, slow and deliberate. Not the half-conscious twitch of a nap, but intention. Her small hand brushed the edge of the fabric, stilled, then dropped again. Eyelids opened with effort, lashes parting as though each one weighed her down. Freya straightened in her chair. She hadn't realised how far she had started to slouch, her body drawn in as if by the paper itself.

Lena blinked once. Her gaze roamed the ceiling, then slid downward until it caught the outline seated beyond the plastic curtain. Their eyes found each other. A breath seemed to pass between them, trapped in the hum of recycled air.

Lena's voice came thin, fragile but certain. "Is pappa gone now?"

Freya's throat closed before sound could form. Her lips parted, but nothing left them.

Lena turned slightly toward the window where late light pooled in fading gold. Her next words carried a weight far too large for her frame. "I saw the tree woman take pappa in my dream."

For a moment, neither of them moved. Then Lena pushed her hand against the mattress, testing it. Her arm shook, but she managed to sit upright. It was the first time she'd sat up in days. Her breath caught once in her throat.

She swallowed and winced, but didn't lie back down.

Freya rose partway from her chair, unsure whether to call for someone but Lena waved her off with a slight, shaky flick of her fingers. Like brushing dust.

The door opened behind them. A nurse stepped in, clipboard in hand, half-focused.

"You're up," she said gently, then approached the bedside. "That's good."

Lena didn't answer right away. She looked again at the window. Her voice, when it came, was light. "Is it okay to open it? I want to hear the river."

The nurse hesitated. "There's no river here, sweetheart."

Lena kept her gaze on the glass. "Not that one."

The nurse gave Freya a brief glance. Puzzled, but not concerned, then tapped something on the chart and stepped out. Freya remained still. She didn't ask what Lena meant. Outside, the wind blew a single tree across the garden wall. It swayed gently. The sky continued on, steel-blue and distant. Freya let the silence hold them a little longer.

Then, Lena looked softly to her mother "Tomorrow," she continued in a whisper "We'll go see it Tomorrow."

Omen

Grey cloud pressed low across the small window. Beyond the glass a birch shivered, branches twisting in a wind sealed away from the ward. The sun existed somewhere above it, blurred out by a lid of weather, its light reduced to a pale smear that never reached the room. Seasons didn't matter here. Day and night folded into each other, a summer that gave no rest.

Inside, the glow came from elsewhere. Screens blinked in steady rhythm, throwing pale green across the walls. Fluorescents hummed above, their flat glare sinking into every surface. Enough light to read by. Enough to track the slow descent of liquid through tubes, an IV bag thinning, a blood bag turning from full to empty.

Freya sat in the observation chair just outside the barrier curtain, legs folded tight beneath her. The clear plastic hung from a ceiling rail in rigid folds, sealing her away from her daughter with a clean sterility that still felt cruel. No contact allowed. No warmth. Just sight and sound, filtered and muffled.

Lena barely moved. Her limbs lay at strange, slack angles on top of the blanket, bruised at every joint from failed cannulas. One IV line fed through the bend of her arm, another disappeared beneath the thick dressing they had replaced overnight. Her skin looked thinner than it had yesterday. Not just pale but almost translucent, the blue of her veins webbing faintly beneath like cracked glass. Patches of her forearm had begun to darken, mottled black where the flesh was breaking down. A slow, intense rot creeping outward from the needle sites. Lesions bloomed across her elbows and wrists like bruises that refused to heal, edges cracked and angry. A faint sourness clung to the air when the blanket moved, the odour of skin that had started to die. More grey. More absent. Her mouth had dried slightly open, lips split at the corners, parted as though the act of closing them had become too costly.

The hum had returned during the night. Freya wasn't sure when. She had half-dreamed it at first, the sound creeping through the edges of sleep like static releasing in her bones. It wasn't from the machines. Nor from the room. Or even from Lena. It didn't rise and fall with the monitors. It didn't match the fragile pulse line. But when Freya whispered, even from this side of the curtain, the hum always seemed to lift. A response. A call. She told herself it was feedback from the IV compressor. Or the air-handling system overhead. Or perhaps a memory carried all the way from the clearing.

The nurse came in just past seven, the squeak of rubber soles softened against the polished lino. A clipboard balanced against her hip and a disposable cup of black coffee trembled faintly in her hand. She nodded politely without breaking stride.

"She had a rough hour around five," the nurse said, not asking permission to check the vitals. "Fever spiked again. Thirty-nine point eight."

Freya blinked, throat tight. "Is she septic? A doctor was muttering yesterday."

The nurse gave the kind of pause that professionals use when they don't want to lie. A careful reply was being formed to balance the truth and manage an emotional parent.

"Likely," she said. "Gut wall's probably compromised. She's been neutropenic since transfer. We're watching her closely."

Freya's hand twitched slightly under the edge of her dressing. The skin beneath her bandage was itching again, worse than yesterday. Most likely due to sweat. A breakfast tray followed on a rattling cart seconds later. Strong coffee, plain toast, and small cups of orange juice sealed with cling film. It was placed near Freya's elbow. She didn't bother to eat.

Lena hummed softly beneath the beeping of machines. The tone came and went. Sometimes just from breath, sometimes chest-sung.

"She does that when you talk to her," the nurse said absently. "The humming."

Freya looked up.

"She started again last night," the nurse added. "Maybe a trauma response."

Freya said nothing. Plastic dug into her thighs, the observation chair designed for durability rather than mercy. She moved once, twice, hunting for a position her back would accept, attempting to get comfortable but to no avail. The seat was cold, the kind that leached heat from skin until her muscles clenched in protest. Her shoulders ached from leaning forward, yet she bent closer anyway, just as Lena's eyes eased open. The lids moved as though glued with fever, a slow reveal of dulled irises that had once gleamed brighter than midsummer sun.

"Morning, älskling," Freya murmured, her lips almost brushing the clear barrier. "It's Saturday. We've been here almost a week."

The monitor answered before Lena could. A cuff inflated with a hiss around her daughter's thin arm, tightening until the small limb seemed swallowed by rubber. The machine clenched, paused, released.

Numbers lit up in jaundiced green:

BP 78/44, HR 126, SpO$_2$ 96%, Temp 39.7°C.

Every flicker felt like a judgement. Another bag of fluids hung ready beside the saline, half-dripped already. Plastic crinkled with each shift of liquid, a sound that made Freya's stomach twist. A nurse muttered something under her breath about escalation, pen scratching against paper as though the word belonged only on a chart.

Freya kept her hand flat against her lap. She wanted to reach through, to touch, but the curtain between them refused. She held still, though the itching beneath her dressing had begun to burn. Sweat seeped through bandage, damp and sour, staining yellow at her wrist. She imagined peeling it back, nails catching the tape, just to see what lay beneath. Maybe pus. Maybe raw pink skin. Maybe something worse.

A nurse's shadow crossed her peripheral. "Is that leaking?" The woman asked softly, nodding toward the spreading stain.

Freya flexed her hand once, then forced stillness. "It's fine."

The nurse lingered, as if waiting for honesty, before retreating.

Silence folded back around them. Freya and Lena, mother and daughter, each side of a plastic veil. Beyond it, Lena lay rigid, chest rising in shallow jerks, cannulas tugging faintly with every breath. The oxygen mask waited, coiled tubing like a snake at the bed's side. Not needed yet. Not yet.

Freya swallowed down words that wanted release. She hadn't spoken much since morning rounds. She wasn't sure why anymore. Silence sometimes felt like a shield; as if words might cut the air open and let despair pour through. Other times it felt like cowardice, a refusal to name the things devouring them. She looked down, then up, then anywhere but her daughter's eyes. Her gaze caught on the folds of the curtain, how the transparent plastic bent light until Lena's silhouette warped, ribs stretching, limbs twitching in ways her real body did not.

The hum was back.

It threaded through the machines, too low to belong to them. A breath felt across the skin of her neck, like someone leaning close from behind. She turned her head quickly. Only the drip machine ticked in rhythm. A nurse had once said it was "likely just the vents," but vents didn't make bone shiver.

Almost too faint to trust, Lena turned her face toward Freya. Lips cracked, parted. "Can we go see the river now?"

Freya froze. Her tongue pressed against the roof of her mouth, useless. She glanced sideways to the window, half-obscured by a forest of medical tubing and metal stands. Beyond them the sky sagged in pewter greys, but somewhere behind those clouds lingered a shy strip of blue. Rivers still ran out there. Real ones. Clear water with reeds that leaned toward current, with shelves shallow enough for a child to splash across. Lena had once darted barefoot along those shallows, hair plastered to her cheeks, her rabbit toy forgotten at the bank. That memory clung sharper than the room.

They'd been camping by a river once. Late spring; where there were ticks in the grass. The sun was still low enough that you could see your breath late morning. Lena had been five. Still all questions. They'd borrowed gear from a friend and driven out to camp near a river. The river was fast, but not deep. You heard it before you saw it; a sharp rush over stone. Johan had set up the tent too close, claiming the sound would help them sleep. Freya had moved it further back herself in the end.

Lena had waded in up to her thighs before either of them noticed. Freya remembered the shriek: high-pitched and sharp. She'd run, heart already halfway to collapse, only to find Lena standing in the shallows, pointing downward at her foot.

"Something grabbed me," she cried. "It's hiding."

Freya had pulled her out and checked her for cuts. Nothing was there. Just cold skin and the faint drag of river weed around her ankle. She'd said it gently: just reeds. Just plants. But Lena had insisted they weren't.

"They were waiting," she'd whispered later, wrapped in a towel. "They wanted me to go under."

That night, Lena spiked a fever. Nothing serious, just the usual childhood flame. Some flushed cheeks, restless limbs, a stomach too unsettled for food. Johan had grumbled about marshmallows going to waste. Freya had curled beside her in the tent, trying to whisper her down into sleep.

"What happens if I get lost on the other side?" Lena had asked.

Freya had blinked. "Of what?"

Lena didn't reply right away. She just stared at the nylon ceiling, eyes glassy, one hand curled around her mother's sleeve. Freya had invented something soft and shapeless; a story to help Lena sleep. A river that ran between worlds. A limbo in between. Something between life and death. A river you couldn't cross unless someone who loved you sang from the other side. You'd hear them, and the sound would make the path appear. It had worked. Lena had fallen asleep quickly.

Freya had half-forgotten the story. It wasn't written down. It wasn't told again. Just something thrown together one midnight, between temperature checks and the noise of the water. It had never been meant to come back. Now, from a hospital bed behind a curtain of plastic, her daughter had asked for the river again. Now here they were. Freya looked at her daughter's face. Slack-jawed and heated with infection. The hum beneath the bed felt steady again, barely noticeable unless you knew to listen for it. She did.

Lena's mouth moved once more. No sound this time. Just breath shaped into syllables that never came. She pressed one finger against the cold vinyl.

Freya hadn't meant to fall asleep. The chair had given in beneath her at some point. Her head pressed to the partition rail where the plastic curtain met the wall. Her neck ached from the angle. Her arm had gone numb. Through the sheet, Lena's monitors blinked a quiet, steady rhythm. Freya had missed an hour, maybe more. A nurse's footsteps moved past in soft rubber-soled waves. She sat up slowly, yet her tired body was slow to follow commands. The fabric at her wrist clung damp against her skin. She tugged it back. There was blood. Not fresh, but sticky in places where it had soaked through the bandage and dried.

She turned her hand over. Thin arcs of dried blood curled at the base of her palm, brittle as autumn leaves. The itch returned harsher this time, crawling under the skin as if something lived there. Each pulse of irritation clawed upward until her jaw clenched.

Lena had drifted off at some point. Her small shoulders faced the window. She breathed in shallow whispers, lips parted, chest rising unevenly. Sleep had claimed her, though not gently. Freya sat for several minutes watching the fragile rhythm. A thought pressed in, *stay*, but her body tugged toward retreat. She rose quietly, careful not to disturb, and slipped from the observation chair.

Her own room waited cooler. Antiseptic clung to the air from a recent cleaning, sharp enough to sting the nose. She sat on the bed's edge, unwrapping the top layer of bandage from her hand. The tape tugged, pulling a few strands of hair from her wrist. Beneath, skin wept fresh along a crescent wound that had almost healed days earlier. Now it glistened pink, raw again where her nails had raked open soft tissue in some unconscious frenzy of sleep. Three scratches crossed her palm in diagonal lines, angry and bright. Blood had dried beneath her nails in brown flecks.

Minutes blurred before the door clicked softly. A figure entered with the hush of someone used to moving through sickrooms. She stood taller than most, her shadow stretching across the floor before her. Pale scrubs rustled faintly as she crossed the space. Freya noticed the evenness of her breathing first, a steady calm that felt rehearsed.

The nurse's gaze dropped to Freya's hand. No sigh, no sharpness. Only the faint narrowing of eyes as she set a tray down. She started to unwrap the soaked bandage away from Freya's hands.

Fresh dressings laid out in a careful row on the tray. The motions felt almost ritualistic, an order she had performed so often it had become muscle memory.

"You were healing," she said, tone gentle, a question wrapped in observation. "This wasn't like this earlier?"

Freya shook her head. Words caught on the dryness in her throat.

"Did you wake scratching, or..."

"I don't remember." Her voice cracked, closer to apology than answer.

The nurse nodded once, accepting. She crouched and finished unwinding both bandages in spirals. Cold antiseptic wiped across the skin. Freya flinched as the sharp pain shot up her arm.

"You aren't in charge of recovery," the nurse murmured. Her eyes stayed on the wounds. "None of us are. The body decides. It always does."

Freya stared at her palms, free from bandages for just a few seconds. The graft had pulled taut. Ridges of new skin puckered and shiny. Moisture leaked where her nails had torn through in sleep. Cuts became raw again after days of fragile healing. Pink tissue shone slick against air, edges trembling as if they might split further. The itch had returned with more urgency, crawling beneath the skin like ants trapped under.

The door stayed half open. A strip of corridor light fell across the floor. Freya didn't lie down at once. She sat with hands resting on her knees, staring at bruises on her shins. Colours she hadn't noticed forming. Yellow deepening into purple. A faint tremor in her knee. She pressed it still, then it started again.

At last she laid down on the bed. Its sheets beneath smelled faintly of fresh laundry. Not the kind of comforting scents from home, just... Washed. Sterile. Her eyes fixed on the ceiling tiles. She tried not to feel the itch beneath the bandage. Tried not to think of heat rising from her palms as if the clearing had followed her here.

Sleep came subsequently. A blink that lasted too long. She had tried to fight it but her body gave in. When she awoke, corridor lights glowed duller. Footsteps were fewer. The quiet had become prevalent. Silence settled in the gap before evening staff assumed control. An empty silence. Nurses stations empty. Corridors empty. An evening handover in full swing.

An evening nurse eventually appeared in the doorway with a clipboard under her arm. "Do you want to see Lena before the curtain's sealed?" Freya swung her legs to the floor. Steps soft on cold linoleum.

Inside Lena's room the air pressed close. Heavy as always. Machines ticked in rhythm, quieter than before. No alarms. Just the slow count of fluids seeping into limbs that barely held pressure.

Lena's skin had taken on uneven bruises. Purples fading to saffron. Colours pulled out of place beneath the surface. The line at her wrist had failed again. Fluid trickled down her arm, clear tinged with red. Red that curled into clear, It caught in the crease of her gown before it reached the sheet. Someone had wiped once, but the skin was already sloughing where the cannula pressed. Tape refused to hold.

A junior nurse was crouched awkwardly beside the bed, face pinched behind her surgical mask. She had a tray of equipment laid out neatly. Yet her hands shook slightly as she worked; just tension held in the shoulders from a long shift.

"She's lost another site," the nurse mumbled to herself without looking up."

Freya stood on the other side of the barrier. Her hands tucked under her arms to avoid touching anything. Lena's fever hadn't broken. Her skin was pale across the shoulders. The new IV went in too shallow and folded before any fluids could run.

"Sorry, sorry," the nurse murmured, already withdrawing the line. "Her veins are... They're not holding."

Lena flinched as she let out a sharp breath. Freya stepped forward in a quiet panic. Close enough to see where the old tape had torn a layer of skin from the crook of her arm. Tiny red points blossomed from where needles had been attempted. The nurse kept her voice low, but the stress was there. She was still trying to find a vein that hadn't collapsed. One of Lena's feet had been propped up with a pillow. Freya could see the nurses hands pressing gently against the skin there, testing something; a pressure response perhaps.

She wiped the area and tried again. Freya flinched with the movement, but Lena didn't. Lena laid still, her fingers curled soft against the blanket.

"She's not on anything for pain?" Freya asked. The words felt slow in her mouth. The nurse hesitated. Not looking up from her work.

"She was," she said finally. "But the line didn't hold. We're trying something else."

Her elbow clipped the edge of the tray as she turned. A sealed swab fell to the floor with a soft plastic snap. The swab was picked up carefully and without complaint. Freya looked at Lena's face again. Her lips had cracked further. Her mouth seemed dry. She hadn't opened her eyes. Her breathing had changed, as if breath had become a decision, not a reflex.

The nurse held a fresh line in place, both hands steady as she taped it down. Fluid hesitated in the tube, drop by drop too slow.

"She might not hold this one either," she murmured, voice lowered as though softness might anchor the vein.

The hum returned. Not loud. Barely a vibration. Freya could not place it among the machines. Not the pump. Not the monitor. It sat beneath all that, threaded deep into her chest, a remembered drone her bones still carried from the clearing. No one else reacted.

The nurse leaned in, two fingers pressed below Lena's collarbone, watching for the faintest lift. Freya's throat locked. She could not stand to watch another vein fail. Clear liquid trickling out where it should flow in. Her daughter's body giving way inch by inch. She stepped back before she was told to.

Corridor air met her with a cooler breath. Fluorescents dulled to a late hue, casting the floor in pale blue. Freya rubbed her arms, shivering though heat still clung to her. She moved past the nurses station where new staff sat, pens scratching, eyes averted. A printer clicked to life, spitting paper no one read.

She carried on.

A vending machine stood in an empty stairwell. It clunked awake with a grinding hum, gears churning deep inside the cabinet. A paper cup dropped into place, crooked on its stand. Liquid poured in bursts, more steam than substance. A bitter smell curling into the corridor. Freya leaned on the wall while it filled, bandaged hands trembling as she lifted the burning paper cup out. Heat pressed through the cardboard sleeve but reached her only faintly, dulled by the layers of dressing. She sipped too soon.

Her tongue was scalded. She coughed once into the empty stairwell. The flavour was nothing. Just stale water and burnt grounds. Yet, she forced another swallow as though going through the motions might fool her body into steadiness. The warmth sat false in her stomach, heavy, a comfort she did not deserve.

She leaned back against the painted brick wall. Her cup balanced in her palms. She tried not to picture fluid sliding down her daughter's arm. She tried not to hear the slow peel of tape from raw skin. Guilt struck sharper than the coffee's boiling sting. What kind of mother left the room rather than watch? Yet here she was, cradling a drink she couldn't taste.

The thought pressed in, ugly and persistent. That she was weaker than the child behind glass. Lena bore the needles, the failed lines, the fever that burned through marrow. Freya couldn't even stay in the room. She told herself she was gathering strength, but her hands shook too much to pass for strength. She told herself she would be no use falling apart in front of Lena, but even that excuse rang thin.

Every swallow scraped her throat. She thought of Johan for the first time since his passing. How he used to drink such strong coffee, then spill it everywhere. He would always leave stains on his tops. He would have stayed, she thought. He would have forced himself to watch every needle go in. And then she hated him for it, because he was gone, and she was left here, tasting nothing, too frightened to stand by her daughter's bed. A voice broke the silence.

"Come on,"

She was startled. One of the night nurses had come looking for her, a clipboard tucked under her arm. Her expression held neither pity nor reproach, only calm insistence.

"We need to check your dressings."

Freya followed the nurse back to her room. She set the cup down. The nurse peeled back one edge of bandage carefully, enough to glimpse swelling skin beneath. Pink, stretched, shining faintly with damp. Just like the mornings. Not much seemed to have changed. It would blister again by morning, just as it's done today.

"Have you eaten today?" The nurse asked.

Freya shook her head.

"I'll have them send something down from the ward kitchen."

"Don't," Freya replied unphazed.

The nurse didn't press her to answer. She sat in the empty chair instead, pen moving once or twice across the clipboard. Then she paused.

"They've just moved Lena."

Freya's chest locked.

"She isn't far," the nurse continued, her voice lower, carefully worded. "Still on this floor. Room two nineteen. She's showing signs of systemic deterioration. Access points keep collapsing. Her immune profile has flat-lined. Any new exposure risks accelerating internal compromise."

The words fell one by one, heavy as stones.

"She isn't contagious," Freya said. It came out flat, more statement than question.

"No. We're protecting what's left of her defences. It isn't about us anymore. It's about keeping her from anything we might carry."

Freya swallowed, throat tight enough to ache.

"Has anyone told her?"

The nurse shook her head. "I don't think she's fully aware." She gathered the tray, balanced it against her hip, and slipped from the room without another word.

Freya pushed herself upright, arms heavy at her sides. Her legs felt stiff as she stepped into the corridor. Each pace dragged. Shoes stuck against the freshly mopped lino. The passage stretched ahead. No more than twenty steps. Yet each step felt further, carrying her slower than she intended. Ceiling strips glowed a dull blue, their tired light pooling shadows into the corners. Time stretched thin, each movement delayed, until the end of the corridor arrived all at once.

Room two nineteen waited just off the passage. A sealed door, seams braced with thick vinyl, edges pressed flush into the frame. A laminated sheet clung above the handle, bold black letters warning of isolation protocols, corners curled and soft with repeated handling. The sign's edges curled from repeated handling, corners lifting slightly in the draught that spilled from a vent overhead. Filtered flow kept the atmosphere controlled. A faint draught constantly brushing her skin. She stopped close to the room and leaned nearer. A narrow strip of glass had been cut into the door, barely wide enough to see through. The lower edge of the panel clouded with condensation where warmer air pressed against the cooler corridor. Freya set her temple near the glass, breath misting until her own outline merged with what waited beyond.

Inside, two nurses moved in silence. Plastic gowns crinkled at each bend of elbow, each turn of the body. Masks and visors hid their faces, the light glancing on curved surfaces, leaving only gloved hands to reveal intent. Fingers creaked as they pinched clamps, tugged tape, adjusted tubing. Their rhythm slowed, deliberate, the careful movements of people schooled not to disturb. One crouched by a cabinet, checked the seal, smoothed a palm over the strip before moving away. The other folded a towel into neat quarters, set it down, then dropped it into a yellow bin. Each action appeared almost ritual, a choreography built from repetition. They passed close to the bed but never touched the figure resting there, orbiting with the distance of attendants in a chamber that did not allow intimacy.

Freya pressed closer to the panel.

Lena lay turned partly toward the wall. Eyes half-open, lashes still, skin dull with fever. The hospital gown slipped low, baring the line of a shoulder and the ragged edge of a dressing stained yellow where fluid had seeped through. Straps had lost their grip, curling from the skin. Her arms showed thinner than they had that morning, bones rising sharp beneath the surface, angles that had once been soft.

Freya placed her hand against the glass, palm flat, skin cooling against the pane. A voice broke the silence behind her. Quiet, but firm.

Freya turned. An older man stood in the corridor. Broad in his protective gown, mask sealed across his face, visor catching the corridor light. Gloved hands rested against a clipboard he didn't look at. She recognised him from the night before. The same calm tone, though lined deeper now.

"Her blood counts have dropped further," he said. "She's bleeding micro across multiple sites. She doesn't have the platelets left to clot. We're also unable to get any new cannulas in."

Freya almost didn't hear the doctor. Her eyes were focused through the glass. Inside, a nurse adjusted the oxygen mask. The strap had rubbed raw along Lena's cheek, leaving a patch of angry skin. Hands moved carefully, barely pressing, tape lifted and replaced with the lightest touch.

Machines murmured steady until one broke rhythm. A pulse oximeter gave a shrill warning, then another tone joined it, higher, urgent. Numbers slid lower across the screen.

Freya's gaze locked on the glass. Lena's chest faltered, rising less each time, as though her body had forgotten how.

At her shoulder the doctor pulled his mask tighter, voice already clipped. "Counts have collapsed. Platelets are gone. No access left." He turned, pushed through the sealed entry, gown flaring as he moved inside.

The crash cart rattled forward, drawers opening in fast succession. Wrappings split, plastic dropped to the floor. One nurse leaned hard into compressions, the bed thudding with each push.

"Line! Get a line in!" "Right arm's gone! Calloused out!" "Veins are gone!" "No hold. Blown."

Alarms merged, a layered scream. Tubes juddered, pumps clicked dry. Freya flattened her palm to the glass, breath fogging the panel until the scene blurred. Through the haze she caught Lena's eyes flickered. One lid lagged, then rolled back.

The monitor shrieked. One endless tone, piercing through glass.

"Start compressions," the doctor ordered.

Gloved hands bore down, the bed jolting with each thrust. An oxygen mask sealed tight, straps digging into raw skin.

Plasma hung, fluid running dark through a tube that found nowhere to go.

Freya slammed her palm flat against the glass. Skin squealed against the cold surface, leaving a smear that spread with each breath. Her chest heaved. Breath came ragged, striking the panel until Lena's outline warped and vanished in fog. She opened her mouth to scream but nothing carried. She knew all she could do was watch. Powerless.

"Defibrillator in!" A nurse called. A cart rattled forward, paddles pulled free, gel smeared quick across plastic.

"Charge to one fifty."

A rising whine filled the room.

"Clear!"

Lena's body jolted. Limbs lifted once, then fell back heavy against the sheets. The monitor held its tone. A single red line. No rhythm.

"Again! Charge two hundred."

The paddles pressed down. A higher pitch filled the air.

"Clear!"

Another jolt ripped through her. The bed rattled. Her small frame lifted then dropped. The line on the monitor barely flickered. A beep. Then a long beep, flat-lined once more.

"Cycle compressions." "Still no output." "Charging again! Two fifty!"

The defibrillator built to a higher whine. Nurses' eyes fixed on the clock, hands moving with frantic precision.

"Clear!"

Another shock tore through Lena. Limbs jerked yet again. They fell limp. All eyes were on the monitor. A single red line. A long tone. No return. The silence inside was deafening. Nurses bowed their heads, sweaty hands clasped. The doctor raised his arm to see his watch. Sombre, he called;

"Time of death, twenty-three twenty-six."

Wither

A month had passed, though not in any way that felt like time had followed rules. Days blurred into medication, monitored meals, and the thin comfort of nurses who spoke with kindness but never stayed long. Now the bandages were thinner, the skin beneath less raw. Discharge had come, though it felt more like exile.

Outpatients today felt more crowded than she had imagined. A wide, open hall stretched ahead, rows of plastic chairs bolted in grids, nearly all occupied. Children with damp coughs, men with bandaged wrists, an elderly woman leaning sideways into her daughter's arm. Wet coats from a rainy day slowly dried, dripping onto linoleum already stained from years of use. Vinyl covers on chairs split along seams. Cushioning poked through in pale tufts where countless bodies had passed and waited. The air was heavy with disinfectant, soured by a trace of citrus from a plug-in dispenser that had long given up the fight. Conversations droned, broken only by the sudden burst of a ringtone or the scrape of chair legs against the floor. Above it all, the mounted screen blinked names in red dots.

She sat with her coat zipped tight despite the overheated room. Her breathing stayed shallow, counting seconds between chimes of other appointments. Other people leafed through magazines or scrolled their phones. Not Freya. She stared down at her palms still covered in bandages.

A nurse's voice broke across the waiting area. "Åström?"

Freya startled, expecting a beep; not a voice. She stood slowly, clutching her wrists together and followed the nurse into a room.

The side room felt colder than the waiting room. Partition walls painted the colour of old milk. A single window looked out onto another wing of the hospital, but the blinds were half-drawn. Machines gathered along one wall: a height measure, scales with their steel plate dulled from shoes, a trolley stacked with bandages and saline pods, and a camera on a fixed stand ready for charting scars. A thin computer monitor glowed green in the corner, numbers waiting for a body to define them.

Freya sat on a narrow bed covered in disposable paper that crinkled as she moved. The air carried that faint metallic tang of steriliser, undercut with the sharper note of latex gloves just pulled from a box.

The nurse unwound her bandages. Scissors slowly sliding through the last tape. Pale ridges were uncovered where grafts had taken, rawer islands where the body still debated. Coral pink around her thumb base, faint sheen of sweat. A smell, salt and faintly acrid, rose in the space between them.

"Any pins and needles?" The nurse asked.

"Sometimes at night."

"Tingling where exactly?"

Freya tapped the base of her thumb with her knuckle.

"Good. Nerve response present. Strength next. Squeeze when I say."

A rubber bulb was pressed into her palm. She closed fingers slowly. A pressure gauge twitched as she squeezed. Numbers climbing into a range that must have carried meaning for someone understood how to read them.

"Again," the nurse prompted.

She squeezed. Numbers rose and held. A third time. The bulb grinned back with its seam.

Photographs next. A camera on a stand, marks on a sheet to show where hands ought to lie. Blue paper beneath to balance skin tone. The nurse apologised for the flash; Freya nodded and looked up towards the ceiling tiles.

"You'll want to keep lotion up for two more months," the nurse said quietly. "Avoid hot water. Avoid the sun."

"Not hard," Freya said. "The sun avoids us."

They both smiled briefly.

The nurse wrote on a tablet, stylus tapping lightly. When she finished, she smiled briefly and gestured toward the door to the waiting room. Freya nodded and stepped into the corridor. The noise of the outpatient hall seemed harsher now. Every cough and scrape of chair legs dragged through her nerves. She chose a seat at the far edge beneath the clock.

Her hands rested in her lap. She flexed her fingers once. Scar tissue tugged, stiff and reluctant, like cloth stitched too tightly. A dull ache pulsed in time with her heart. Her left leg had begun to bounce. She hadn't noticed at first, not until the rhythm of it matched the tapping of someone's foot across the room. She stilled it quickly, flattening her heel to the floor.

When will they stop hurting?

The thought came quietly, uninvited. She looked down at her hands. It wasn't just pain that worried her.

What if this is it? What if healing means learning to live with what hasn't healed?

The room around her moved as if underwater. Voices muffled by distance. A child sneezed somewhere near the lifts. Someone else unwrapped a sandwich with a crinkle that scraped against her nerves. She rubbed her thumbs together, then stopped when the skin protested.

The mounted screen above reception blinked once. A soft beep followed, sharper than anything that had come before. Her name appeared in dotted red text.

The consultation room was brighter than the others. Bigger too. Two chairs, a sink, a desk, and the illusion of privacy. On the wall, a poster detailed skin graft after-care in four overly optimistic panels. Freya sat where she was told.

She didn't recognise the doctor waiting at the desk. He was already seated when she entered, a white coat folded neatly at the cuffs, tablet resting in one hand. Late fifties, perhaps. Clean-shaven, slight paunch, the kind of man who carried himself like he'd once worked in a busier hospital and now appreciated slower mornings.

He looked up as she stepped in. "Freya Åström?"

She nodded as she took a seat in front of the desk.

"I'll be quick," he said, already reaching for gloves. "Your chart's looking good. Hands healing well. Grafts are holding. Some contracture at the base of the left thumb, but nothing worrying."

He peeled a fresh bandage with steady fingers, pausing only to make a quiet sound in his throat as he continued. "Pink is good. Pale edges too. That shine will dull over time. A bit of tightness is expected."

Freya nodded once to acknowledge. She stared past him, eyes fixed on a poster. A cartoon arm waved back.

"No signs of infection," he added. "And no further treatment needed here. You'll be discharged to district care. Home nurse every couple of weeks at home, just to monitor healing and change dressings. After that, it's patience."

He began wrapping fresh bandages against her skin. Weaving around the palms and through the creases between her fingers.

"You're not due back in hospital unless something changes. If there's redness, swelling, bleeding that isn't from overuse..."

"I'll call," she interrupted, eyes fixed on a mark on the floor near the leg of his desk.

The doctor looked up, surprised by the interruption. But only nodded. "Good."

He stood and handed her a small envelope of paperwork. She took it without checking the contents and prepared to leave.

The ride through the city centre blurred past store-fronts and bus shelters. She watched it in fragments, catching herself in the glass now and then. Central Station felt overwhelming after the hush of the hospital. Motion and metal. Voices from every direction.

People rushing around. Healthy people rolling suitcases and carrying coffee. The tannoy mumbled platform numbers in Swedish and English as trains rushed in and out, keeping to their strict schedules.

Freya stepped off the escalator and paused beside the long row of ticket machines. Screens glowed with timed departures. Her train hadn't arrived yet, but she wasn't in a rush.

She took the lift down to the long-distance platforms. Signs for SJ Intercity hung overhead on dirt ridden signs. The platform was open to the sky. Wind funnelled in from the tracks. A scattering of other passengers stood in loose groups. Some with rucksacks, others with takeaway coffee and quiet phones.

Freya chose a bench beneath the departure board and waited. Her train wasn't due for another ten minutes. She hadn't flown since the air ambulance brought her south. Not that she'd tried. The thought of being carried into a metal tube again, sealed in with forced air and other people's breath, turned her stomach. Even now, the ghost-memory of that flight clung to her ribs. The medical straps, the quiet of emergency altitude, the humming beneath everything.

A train arrived, breaking her thoughts. A large hunk of silver and red metal lined the track. Scratches appeared on windows. People stood at the doors ready to disembark. The time - 12:12pm. She boarded. The train pulled in with the heavy sigh of steel and brakes lifting. Her seat faced backwards, revealing the city she had started to leave. They rolled out through Stockholm's edges in long stretches of fencing and concrete. Flats with peeling balconies gave way to business parks. The first stop, Uppsala. The carriage filled a little more before continuing its journey north.

The city gave way to vast forests. The occasional stop at a village along the way as people came and left the carriage. Somewhere along the route she stared out towards the trees. Just past the horizon she knew Forsmark's power station stood along the Baltic sea; not that she'd see it.

At Gävle, they paused for long enough to hear the overhead speaker repeat itself. The man beside her left, replaced by a woman who fell asleep almost immediately with her hood pulled tight. Hours ticked past as the train crawled north. Past Ljusdal. Past Ånge. Rain had begun, covering the windows with droplets that moved past the scratched window.

Mountains began to show in the distance. The colour of them bled into the horizon. Finally, she had made her journey.

When she reached Östersund, the platform lights had already come on. The time on her phone read 18:23. Freya stepped down onto the concrete with aching knees and no sense of arrival.

The city felt thinner than she remembered. Fewer people. Fewer cars. She walked. Past cafés and empty benches. Past the square where summer once spilled beer across the pavement from festivals that drove into the night, always light by twilight sky. The hotel was just beyond. She walked into the lobby. A radio playing low behind the desk was the only sound. A receptionist barely looked up as Freya entered. Just asked for her name, then handed over the key-card with a nod.

Room 413. Narrow. Clean. A single bed with a folded blanket. White walls, one chair, a desk too small to use. She left her coat on the hook and sat. She took a deep breath. A single tear slid down her cheek without warning. It left a thin trail to her jaw, cold against her skin. She let it fall.

The remote lay on the desk. She picked it up and switched on the television for a distraction. The screen lit the room with flickering blue.

A news channel filled the space. A male presenter in a slate suit was reading something from the auto-cue, but his voice barely registered. She stood and walked to the kettle. She reached for a teabag without choosing it. Whatever bag had been provided. She poured boiling water out and gave the cup a stir.

The volume was low, almost a whisper behind her. The newsreader spoke something about a foreign national on trial after being arrested on Øresund bridge. A grainy photo. A man escorted between two uniforms, face turned just enough to hide. The anchor continued in a flat tone. Freya caught none of the details.

She brought the mug back to the bed and sat back on the edge. The news kept talking. Eventually she muted it. Set an alarm. Switched the television off. Then lay down on top of the covers, still fully dressed.

She hadn't realised how tired she had been from the journey until she awoke in the morning. The tea had gone cold by her bedside. The wind had picked up overnight. She changed in silence, zipped the coat to her neck, and stepped out into the air.

Östersund was colder than she remembered. Autumn had settled in early that year. The wind curled through the chapel grounds like it had been waiting for her return. Gusts moved through the birch trees, drawing dry sounds from their thinning leaves. One leaf fell. Then another.

The chapel stood low and square at the edge of the cemetery. Stone walls mottled with age. Frost clung to the corners of its windows despite the hour. Inside, the air held the scent of wax and damp wood, sharpened faintly by the tang of soil.

Two coffins waited at the front of the hall.

Simple wood. Pale, unfinished. The grain ran in vertical lines, as if they had already begun returning to the ground. Both were closed. No flowers. No photographs. Just the shapes, side by side, under the chapel's high beam. They were smaller than she'd expected. Even Johan's.

Freya stood near the rear, just beneath the curve of the old stone arch. Her coat zipped tight to the neck. There weren't many people. A handful of extended family. One of Johan's brothers. An old mutual friend Freya recognised, there more from obligation than memory. They murmured among themselves, faces turned toward the floor. A few glanced in her direction. None approached.

The priest's voice drifted over the pews, soft and rhythm-less. Words were spoken. A psalm recited. The names read aloud. Johan first. Then Lena. Freya's hands remained in her pockets. Her fingers pressed into the lining until her nails found skin.

The child's coffin had been placed slightly forward. Smaller. Less weight to bear. On top of it rested a single drawing, weathered at the edges. Freya recognised the lines but hadn't looked at it closely.

The priest stepped back. Silence took his place. Someone sniffed behind her. A jacket rustled. A crow called once from the birch outside. The man seated near the aisle adjusted his collar.

Freya watched it all like it was happening through a pane of old glass. Like she was visiting a stranger's service, ticking off an obligation. The words washed over her and ran out of meaning. When the doors opened and people rose, she followed.

Outside, the wind had gathered force. The graves stood open just beyond the chapel wall, in the ground dark from rain. Mounds of soil sat beneath plastic tarps. A pair of cemetery workers waited nearby, their expressions carefully neutral.

The coffins were carried slowly. No speeches now. Just the creak of the frame, the scuff of boots on frostbitten grass. The child was lowered first. Then Johan's. The ropes slipped through the pulleys with a steady, scraping rhythm. Afterwards, people lingered for a few moments, then began to drift away in pairs. Freya remained.

Most nodded with a solemn smile as they passed Freya. A few stopped to offer their condolences and muted words, questions asked more out of politeness than care. She answered them softly, but nothing real came out.

Johan's brother lingered behind the others. He looked older than she remembered. Heavier in the face. His hair had started to shine grey since the last family gathering. He approached without a word at first, then reached into his inside pocket.

"They said this was safe," he murmured. "The hospital sent it back. No readings worth worrying over. Thought you'd want it. There's some nice bits about Lena."

He held out the journal. Brown leather, worn at the corners, softened by use. Johan's. The same one he had used throughout their trip. Freya took it gently. Her fingers brushed the grain of it.

"Thanks," she said, and slipped it into her coat pocket without bothering to look at the pages. The weight of it settled there, small but solid. He nodded, gave her shoulder a squeeze, then turned to follow the rest of the group.

She waited until the path was clear. Then turned back toward the headstones. Lena. Johan. Names etched newly into stone. Soil still lay unsettled around. She hadn't cried during the service. Hadn't cried when the coffins were lowered, when the ropes sang in their pulleys, or when the priest fumbled the blessing.

But now, standing in the cold with nothing left to respond to, her body decided it was safe enough to feel. The tears didn't come hard. Just slow. Warm at first, then ice cold as they rolled down her cheeks. She wiped at her face with her sleeve and looked away from the graves. Her train would leave in the morning. Back to Stockholm.

***

A few days later, she was back in Stockholm. The new flat smelled like plaster. White walls, white ceiling, white light. It had been advertised as bright and modern, but felt more like the inside of a waiting room. Somewhere colourless that people passed through on their way to something else.

A row of unopened boxes lined the hallway wall. The labels, written in her own hand, had already begun to fade: books, winter clothes, toiletries, spares. One was marked simply 'L'. It remained untouched.

The bedroom had no curtains yet. Light spilled in through the bare glass and coated the bed in grey. The duvet was still wrapped in plastic, thrown upon a bare base. Freya hadn't removed it yet. She slept on top, sometimes in her coat, but mostly not at all.

The balcony overlooked a patch of pines that clung to the rear edge of a park. Their trunks were thin. Ornamental. Planted for symmetry in a city's dull attempt at replicating nature. The kind of trees that were meant to behave.

She stood at the window, her breath leaving pale marks on the glass. She hadn't opened the door to the balcony yet. Something about stepping outside didn't seem necessary. Behind her, the door buzzed once. Then again. Eventually, she turned. With a sigh, she walked barefoot to the entry. A nurse stepped inside. Late twenties. Blonde, practical, smelling faintly of soap and winter cream.

"Hi, Freya. Just here to check on the dressings."

Freya nodded once and led the nurse through to the living space: an open-plan stretch where the kitchen faded into a bare, box-shaped lounge. The counter-tops were clean but empty, save for a kettle and an unopened roll of bin liners. Cabinets in flat white caught the light from the window, but nothing reflected. The fridge hummed softly beneath a duct that hadn't been painted properly.

In the centre of the room stood a single sofa. Unfurnished. No throw, no cushion. It faced nothing in particular yet. Just the blank wall where a television might go, one day. The nurse slipped off her shoes at the threshold and followed.

Freya sat and held out her hands, though they began to tremble almost immediately. The bandages were loose today, edges darkened from contact. The nurse unwound them gently. Layer by layer. The skin beneath was puckered and red, healing in uneven ridges that ran from thumb to wrist. Pale islands of scar tissue had begun to settle along the base of the fingers. A faint crust of yellow pus clung to the innermost bandage, with oxidised edges tinged brown.

"Still sensitive?"

Freya gave a slow nod.

The nurse opened a small pot of cream and dipped her fingers in. She worked the ointment across the scarring with a firm, steady rhythm.

"You're healing well," she said calmly. "They'll want to start reducing the visits soon."

Freya didn't respond. Her gaze had drifted past the nurse, out toward the balcony window. A faint smudge of light crept across the glass. She couldn't tell whether it was fog, or the city's reflection dulling against the pane.

The nurse repacked her bag, typed a note into her phone, then paused at the doorway.

"If you need the number again, it's on the fridge. You can call anytime. Talking about it helps."

Freya nodded a final time. The nurse gave a small smile and slipped her shoes back on without another word. A moment later, the door clicked shut behind her. The flat was silent again.

She stood barefoot in the doorway, one hand resting lightly against the frame. The laminate flooring beneath her feet had grown slick with condensation where the cold from the glass met the warmth of the room.

Beyond the window, the Scandinavian summer had finally surrendered. After weeks of brightness that refused to end, the sky had started to darken. Her eyes drifted to the kitchen.

A small note was pinned to the fridge with a red magnet. The one the nurse had mentioned. *'EMERGENCY NUMBER'*, scribbled in neat block capitals, beneath a ten-digit number. The ink was already smudging.

Beside the fridge, on the edge of the counter, sat Johan's leather journal. Freya stepped toward it, then picked it up carefully.

She didn't open at the beginning. She went to the back first. To the last few pages before the blank ones began. Notes and scribbles from the camp filled the pages. Notes of sobriety. Thoughts and feelings. Of her, of Lena, of himself.

She turned a few pages back, to the days before they'd left. The writing there was slower. Straighter. A title underlined twice, as though he'd once planned to copy it over somewhere nicer.

A poem.

I keep my hands still.

Soap instead of whisky.

It feels strange,

to be proud of nothing more

than clean fingers.

Tomorrow, the tent, the trees.

Her laughter, maybe.

A fire snapping open like a promise.

I wonder if she'll call me Papa

without flinching.

Her mother smiles now.

Not like before.

Not like we never broke it.

But enough.

I dream of burnt marshmallows,

her sticky fingers pressing mine.

The sound of frogs in twilight.

How ordinary salvation can be.

Happiness will come,

I feel it.

But maybe we can let it sit there,

another log on the fire.

Älskling.

Älskling.

Älskling.

I practised saying it

so it wouldn't sound borrowed.

It belongs to you.

Like I wish I still did.

Freya ran her fingers down the page. Her thumb paused against the last line. For a second she considered reading it out loud, just to hear his words in the air again. After a moment, she closed the journal and held it loosely in both hands. Then placed it down and stepped out onto the balcony.

Above her, the dark had come completely. Not the soft blue of summer dusk. Not the amber-drenched illusion of a late Scandinavian summer evening. This was black: clear and absolute. The kind that swallowed rooftops. Hid trees. Erased the outlines of the world.

There were no stars. No aurora. Just the dim orange bloom of the city pressing upward into the sky, turning the dark the colour of rust.

She let out a faint sigh.

The world, once again, had descended into darkness.

Acknowledgements

A huge thank you to Shana Roark for writing Johan's Poem. Discover their Instagram and TikTok for custom poems! @supergirlreject

A big thanks to my grandmother who read the entire first draft and gave her full review: *"Yeah, it's good."*

And a big thank you to yourself for reading! Check out other books and updates from Instagram: @danieldlsmith

This story draws on the dangers of orphan sources: abandoned radioactive materials left without control. Such events are extremely rare. Modern nuclear power, in comparison, is one of the safest and cleanest forms of energy we have. It's maintained through rigorous scientific oversight and safety design.

To learn more about nuclear energy, visit:

World Nuclear Association — www.world-nuclear.org

International Atomic Energy Agency — www.iaea.org

Phrase Translation Guide

Hey, thanks for reading! You're probably on this page now because you've either:

Finished the book and kept reading (congratulations, but you can stop now. Find a new book; I've heard *Detective Dion* is phenomenal)

You've been confused by a word (you're in the right place, well done on reading the contents)

You got bored and flicked to the end to see if anyone dies (no spoilers, read it or get the audiobook)

This is a little guide for English speakers who don't know IKEA is pronounced "ee-kee-a" - to help with some pronunciation, Swedish place names, and the little phrases that pop up through the book. To any Swedes reading this: *Dra åt skogen.*

Letters:

Ä - Similar to 'ai'. Pronounced like the 'ai' in 'hair' or 'air'

Å - Similar to 'aw' (it's a cute sound. awww). Pronounced like 'raw' or 'law'

Ö - We don't have a good sound for this... it's almost like you want to throw up. It's almost like the 'u' in 'fur' and the 'i' in 'bird'... imagine that together. Perhaps imagine a french person about to throw up, as in 'bleu'

My apologies for the Swedes who heard me pronounce ö as 'oo' in 'look' and wondered why a said I've been to 'Oyster Sand' and not *throws-up*stersund.

Words you came across, and some weird phases you read:

Älskling – Sweetheart / darling / beloved

Toppen – Great / fantastic / "It's top!"

Lagom – Just right. Not too much, not too little. Sweden in a word.

Hugaligen! – Oh dear! Good grief! Often heard near burnt sausages.

Dra åt skogen – Literally: *Go to the forest.* Use it when "sod off" feels too aggressive.

Ingen ko på isen – No cow on the ice. Meaning: No worries, no danger... yet.

More Svenska for Brits!

Although not used in the book, here's some more phrases that I found very helpful on my travels to write this novel! Hope they help you too!

Where is the pub? = Var är puben?

One local beer please! = En lokal öl, tack

Thanks (very much) = Tack så mycket!

I'm not drunk, you are! = Jag är inte full - du är det!

Why are you throwing me out, it's daylight? = Varför kastar du ut mig? Det är ju ljust ute!

What? It's 2am?! = Va? Klockan är två på natten?!

I'm hungover. Can I have some water? = *Jag är bakis. Kan jag få lite vatten?*

This isn't water, it's Absolut Vodka! = *Det här är inte vatten – det är Absolut Vodka!*

About The Author

DDL Smith is a novelist based in London. With a background in scriptwriting and short films, he honed a love for dialogue that cuts sharp since his young teens.

His work circles the shadows where **mystery, technology, and folklore collide**. The *Detective Dion* series twists classic noir through the lens of the modern world, while his upcoming horror novel *Decay* ventures into the myth-soaked forests of Sweden. You can find information on releases at **www.ddlsmith.com**

More books by DDL Smith

Check out the Detective Dion series. Now at brilliant local bookstores in the UK. You can find out where these are stocked, or order online at ddlsmith.com

Detective Dion: The Silent Blade

In a city where opulence masks treachery, Detective Dion Knight is called to the scene of a high-society murder. Lydia Harper, a glamorous socialite, lies dead in her penthouse, surrounded by a puzzle of shattered glass and a bloodless knife. As Dion and his ambitious partner, Officer Stevens, delve into Lydia's life, they uncover a web of deceit involving estranged husbands, secret lovers, and cutthroat business rivals. Each twist deepens the mystery, challenging Dion to untangle the lies and uncover the killer before they strike again.

Detective Dion: Tech Titans

When the sudden death of a prominent tech CEO sends shockwaves through the city, seasoned detective Dion Knight is partnered with Theodore Stevens. What begins as a high-profile investigation quickly unravels into something far more sinister; an elaborate web of sabotage and murder buried beneath the tech elite.